Praise for the Davis Way Crime Caper Series

"Seriously funny, wickedly entertaining. Davis gets me every time."
— Janet Evanovich

"Archer navigates a satisfyingly complex plot and injects plenty of humor as she goes....a winning hand for fans of Janet Evanovich."
— *Library Journal*

"Davis's smarts, her mad computer skills, and a plucky crew of fellow hostages drive a story full of humor and action, interspersed with moments of surprising emotional depth."
— *Publishers Weekly*

"Archer's bright and silly humor makes this a pleasure to read. Fans of Janet Evanovich's Stephanie Plum will absolutely adore Davis Way and her many mishaps."
— *RT Book Reviews*

"Funny & wonderful & human. It gets the Stephanie Plum seal of approval."
— Janet Evanovich

"As impressive as the amount of sheer fun and humor involved are the details concerning casino security, counterfeiting, and cons. The author never fails to entertain with the amount of laughs, action, and intrigue she loads into this immensely fun series."
— *Kings River Life Magazine*

"Slot tournament season at the Bellissimo Resort and Casino in Biloxi, Miss., provides the backdrop for Archer's enjoyable sequel to *Double Whammy*...Credible characters and plenty of Gulf Coast local color help make this a winner."
— *Publishers Weekly*

"Hilarious, action-packed, with a touch of home-sweet-home and a ton of glitz and glam. I'm booking my next vacation at the Bellissimo!"

– Susan M. Boyer,
USA Today Bestselling Author of *Lowcountry Bordello*

"Fast-paced, snarky action set in a compelling, southern glitz-and-glamour locale...Utterly un-put-down-able."

– Molly Harper,
Author of the Award-Winning Nice Girls Series

"There is so much humor and relentless action that readers will be propelled through to the explosive finale."

– *Kings River Life Magazine*

"A smart, snappy writer who hits your funny bone!"

– Janet Evanovich

"*Double Trouble* was an awesome story and it is the best book in this engagingly entertaining series."

– *Dru's Book Musings*

"Filled with humor and fresh, endearing characters. It's that rarest of books: a beautifully written page-turner. It's a winner!"

– Michael Lee West,
Author of *Gone With a Handsomer Man*

"It reads fast, gives you lots of sunny moments and if you are a part of the current social media movement, this will appeal to you even more. I know #ItDoesForMe."

– *Mystery Sequels*

DOUBLE WIDE

DOUBLE WIDE

A DAVIS WAY CRIME CAPER

Gretchen Archer

DOUBLE WIDE
A Davis Way Crime Caper

First Edition | June 2021

Gretchen Archer
www.gretchenarcher.com

Copyright © 2021 by Gretchen Archer
Cover design by The Creative Wrap
Author photograph by Garrett Nudd

This is a work of fiction. Any references to historical events, real people, or real locales are used fictitiously. Other names, characters, places, and incidents are the product of the author's imagination, and any resemblance to actual events or locales or persons, living or dead, is entirely coincidental.

Paperback ISBN-13: 978-1-7372456-2-9
Kindle ISBN-13: 978-17372456-3-6

Printed in the United States of America

Biloxi Police Ask for Help Locating Missing Women

BY NELSON MILLER
GULF COAST HERALD SENIOR STAFF REPORTER
Saturday, May 09, 3:11 p.m.

Biloxi Police have released the name of one of three women believed to have been abducted earlier today from Golden Oaks Golf Club, the eighteen-hole par-72 championship course owned and operated by the Bellissimo Resort and Casino. Authorities spoke to Clifton Estrada, Golden Oaks Club Manager, who positively identified one of the women as forty-five-year-old Bianca Casimiro Sanders, wife of Bellissimo owner Richard Sanders. "There isn't a doubt in my mind it was Bianca Sanders," Estrada said. "It's not like there's two of her."

The women who disappeared with Mrs. Sanders have yet to be identified. One is thought to be Mrs. Sanders's personal assistant. Witnesses describe her as tall, possibly six feet, slender, Black, wearing white jeans, a pale green t-shirt, flip-flops, large square sunglasses, and a pink ball cap spelling out the word "BRIDESMAID" in rhinestones above the bill. It is unclear who the third woman is or how she's connected.

Odis Beasley, groundskeeper at Golden Oaks and the only witness to have seen the three women together, described the third woman as in her late twenties or early thirties with long silver hair wearing a red golf dress with a PGA Tour logo on the sleeve. "She was loud," Mr. Beasley said. "I could hear her in the RV park from way out on the tenth fairway."

The third woman is thought to be a caddie for one of the five wild card players participating in the PGA Tour Qualifying Tournament after earning a spot in the Bellissimo's Hole in One Blackjack Championship. Please contact the authorities, or me, with any information regarding the abduction or whereabouts of the women. Biloxi Police Department's Public Relations Officer, Holly Griffin, issued the following statement: "At this time, we have no idea what happened."

Day One
Sometime in the Afternoon

Dear Bradley,

It's Saturday. As best I can tell, between four and five o'clock. I spent the afternoon stuffed in the basement of a motorhome with Fantasy and a golf caddie named Mango. Here's what happened.

Fantasy and I were on our way to New Orleans for Baylor and July's wedding via Golden Oaks because I had to present the trophy at the PGA tournament awards luncheon. Two seconds after we pulled up to the staff gate, a golf alert flashed across my phone from Bellissimo Security. I'm sure it flashed across Fantasy's too, but she was already on the phone with one of her sons who wanted to wear his Jordan Jumpmans instead of his suede oxfords to the wedding. He claimed the suede oxfords didn't fit. They squeezed his toes. Fantasy said they weren't squeezing his toes last Sunday at Mass and he could wear them one more time.

While all this was going on, I clicked the golf alert to read it. Not answer it. Just read it. Nothing terribly alarming on the surface. Someone called Bellissimo Security to report a woman running through the Golden Oaks trailer park screaming. (You know where the golfers and fans park their motorhomes? Behind the thirteenth hole? With the little lake in the middle? And all the parking spaces have built-in tiki huts with gas grills?) (I always thought it was cute that the golfers and their groupies traveled from golf course to golf course in their homes.) (I've since changed my mind.) (Where was I?) The alert said all of Golden Oaks' security staff was on the eighteenth hole, where one of the golfers had pitched a fit, spectators had been injured, and the screaming woman in the trailer park would have to keep screaming, because as soon as they finished up on the eighteenth hole, their presence was required at the awards luncheon. The alert went on to ask if anyone remotely associated with Bellissimo Security was close enough to Golden Oaks to check on the screaming woman. Beside me, Fantasy said, "If you show up tonight with Jumpmans on your feet, not only will you sit in the lobby while the rest of us go to the wedding, which I know you couldn't care less about, but you'll sit in the lobby for the reception too. You get me? Dinner out of a vending machine while the rest of us eat prime rib and wedding cake. This is Fantasy Erb. I'm Bianca Sanders's driver. I'm at Golden Oaks. What's the problem in the RV park?"

She'd switched over to the security call.

And told the dispatcher she'd check it out.

I said, "Why'd you do that?" (We were almost on wedding vacation. We were supposed to be in New Orleans at two for hair and makeup. I was five short hours from seeing you and the girls. Why take a screaming woman call? Neither I nor Fantasy even play golf.) She said, "Because they're serving egg salad and pimento cheese sandwiches at the luncheon."

That was a little disappointing.

Last year it was tenderloin sliders and lobster rolls.

We drove around the property to the RV park and found exactly what security said we would, a screaming woman running up and down the trailer park roads. We spotted her long silver hair flying behind her first. She wasn't injured that we could see, she didn't appear to have a weapon of any sort, and no one was chasing her. Fantasy beeped her horn. The silver-haired woman stopped and spun around—thick black eyebrows in stark contrast to her silver hair; think Lady Gaga—took one look at us, then shot between two motorhomes. I said, "Fantasy, let's turn this over to Golden Oaks. I don't see that this girl's in any immediate danger. It looks like she's just blowing off golf steam." She said, "Since when do you like egg salad?"

We eased down the next road between two rows of motorhomes and there she was again, the girl with the silver hair, beating on the door of the ugliest motorhome around. It was a rectangular metal box on wheels. It had no discernable color, it was filthy, the front windshield was cracked to the point of spiderwebbed, and one headlight was smashed. The outdoor furniture under the motorhome awning was an old folding lawn chair. The kind with basketweave strips of itchy plastic. The chair was surrounded by crushed Bud Light cans. At least fifty. I said, "Fantasy, whatever this is, we don't have time for it." She said, "We're already here." She rolled down her window and said, "Hey," to the silver-haired girl. "What's the problem?"

The problem, a man, opened the motorhome door.

The silver-haired girl whispered something in his ear, then pointed.

At us.

"Let's get out of here, Fantasy."

"Wait a minute," she said. "Something's going on."

"Nothing is going on."

"They're talking about us, Davis." She stuck her neck out the window. "Everything okay here?"

Everything was not okay there, because instead of answering, the man flipped the silver-haired woman around and put a gun to her head. A Beretta Nano 9mm pistol. The crazy golfer man—green pants, pink shirt, Golden Oaks visor—I'm sure you have him in custody by now—leaned past the silver-haired girl to yell at us. "Who are you?"

Fantasy yelled back, "What do you care? Let the girl go."

He pulled the gun from the silver-haired girl's head long enough to wave it in my direction. "Who is she?"

"None of your business," Fantasy told him. "Let the girl go."

He yelled, "Toss your phones."

Fantasy yelled back, "No."

He tightened his grip on the silver-haired girl. "Toss your phones."

"Or what?" Fantasy said.

"Or I'll kill her."

The girl with silver hair squealed.

We tossed our phones.

I said, "See?"

We should have gone the egg salad route.

Then he said, "Toss your keys."

She turned to me. "What do we do here, Davis?"

"I guess we toss the keys."

"What's it going to hurt?" She reached for the key fob in the console between us. "We can at least get to the clubhouse without the keys." Because Fantasy's car, like every other car in the world built after WWII, had an auto start/stop button. The car was still running. I say it all the time, criminals need to wise up.

Fantasy tossed the keys.

The crazy golfer said, "Now get out of the car."

I had no intention of getting out of the car. For one, I was wearing six-inch heels. I leaned all the way over to reach the open window. "No. We're not getting out of the car. Let the girl go."

Fantasy was busy batting the skirt of my dress out of her face. "I can't breathe. Could you lean out your own window?"

The crazy golfer said, "Get out."

Fantasy said, "Your elbow is in my liver."

I said, "Not on your life, buddy."

The crazy golfer said, "How about on yours?" then fired off a round straight through his own motorhome awning. It got our attention quickly. We hit the deck.

After a minute, I peeked.

The crazy golfer still had a gun to the silver-haired woman's head in the door of the motorhome. He tipped up the barrel and fired a second shot through his own motorhome awning—WHERE WAS GOLDEN OAKS SECURITY? BY THEN THEY WERE EATING EGG SALAD WAS WHERE THEY WERE—and we only had two choices: get out or peel out, at which point, we couldn't run off and leave the silver-haired girl.

We should have run off and left the silver-haired girl.

Two minutes later, we were stuffed and padlocked in the motorhome basement. Obviously, at gunpoint. And we already knew the gun was loaded because the crazy golfer had fired off rounds that NO ONE EATING EGG SALAD COULD HEAR. First, he moved Fantasy's car. To who knows where. I'm sure you've found it by now. Ten really long minutes later, when we were just beginning to realize there might not be an easy way out of the motorhome basement, the crazy golfer returned. He banged around unhooking this and that, then climbed into the cab and took off. With us stuffed in the basement.

Who knew motorhomes had basements?

I didn't.

Did you?

The basement was on the exterior, like the trunk of a car, but on the side. I assumed for storage. Golf clubs, maybe. Or outdoor furniture. Or hostages. We were padlocked in the basement, the three of us, barely above the road and not far from the gas tank. It's a wonder we lived through the fumes. It's a wonder we lived at all. That the basement door didn't fly open and spill us into traffic feels like nothing short of a miracle.

Right off the bat, we asked the silver-haired girl (Mango) what the crazy golfer was mad about. She said golf. Actually, she said, "Did you know golf is one of two sports that's been played on the moon?" We took that to mean he was mad about golf. You can't imagine how hard it is to dig information out of her. As best I can tell, she's his caddie, and earlier today on the eighteenth hole the crazy golfer was last on the leaderboard, about to fall off, and needed a double eagle. With a double eagle, he could still win $49,020. As he was teeing off, she told him his odds of a double eagle were one in six million while his odds of a hole in one were one in twelve thousand. She advised him to go for the hole in one. An argument ensued. I can see where that might happen, because they say golf is 90% mental and the other 10% is also mental, and while that's almost all I know about golf, I do know a little about odds, and a lot about common sense. And common sense would dictate that two chances to get the ball in the hole were better than one. Apparently, the crazy golfer agreed with me, because she wound up in the motorhome basement with us.

"And you're his caddie?" I asked.

"I'm his analyst," she said.

"His golf analyst?"

She said, "I'm his strategic intelligence research analyst."

"Who moonlights as a golf caddie?" Fantasy asked.

Bradley, have you ever heard of a strategic intelligence research analyst who moonlights as a golf caddie? With long silver hair?

Me neither.

We asked how she met him. She said, "Did you know *Craigslist* is one of the top twenty websites in the US and generates a billion dollars a year in revenue?" We asked if she had any idea where he was taking us. She said, "Did you know the only place in the world without any life form are the ponds of the Dallol Geothermal Field in Ethiopia?" Fantasy said, "Are you telling us you met him on *Craigslist* and we're on our way to Ethiopia?" We asked if she knew why we were locked in the basement. Why was he mad at us? How'd we get roped in? She said, "Did you know the word kidnap was originally kidnab? Kid as in child? Nab as in grab?"

She was telling us we'd been kidnabbed.

She went on to tell us what we'd really been was adultnabbed. She'd contacted Merriam-Webster several times about the word confusion, which meant, of course, that Mango the Silver-Haired Analytical Research Caddie was in on it. Or at least knew about the crazy golfer's plans to adultnab us beforehand. What I don't know is if he originally intended to adultnab her too, or if he was really that mad at her about the hole-in-one business, because there we were, the three of us, stuffed in the basement of a motorhome.

Bradley, Fantasy and I have been adultnabbed.

And we have a silver-haired analytical research caddie with us.

The whole time this conversation took place, I was busy kicking out the metal grid of an air vent about the size of an envelope near my foot. AM I ON NATIONAL NEWS? "WOMAN'S FOOT WAVING FROM RATTY MOTORHOME FLYING DOWN THE ROAD."

We drove for more than an hour stopping three times. I'm guesstimating how long we were on the road, because neither Fantasy nor I were wearing a watch, our cell phones were in the Golden Oaks trailer park, and it was hard to tell in the dark of the motorhome basement if time was standing still or moving at the speed of light. Fantasy asked the research caddie if she knew what time it was. She asked Fantasy if she knew all the clocks in the movie *Pulp Fiction* were set to 4:20.

The first and third stops were short—coffee breaks?—and we didn't have time to make a move. Although, given all the time in the world, we couldn't bust through the basement ceiling to get into the motorhome and overtake him while he was driving, and the basement door was padlocked from the outside, so there was no escaping and making a run for it when we stopped. We did exactly what you'd expect at all three stops, which was scream our lungs out. (I yelled, "Help!" and "We've been abducted!" and "We're locked in the basement!") (Fantasy yelled several versions of, "Somebody get us the hell out of here!") (Mango yelled, "Did you know claustrophobia is an anxiety disorder affecting up to ten percent of the world's population?") All to no avail. From where Fantasy was wedged, she had a sliver of vision through the open vent, like peeking under a closed door. She could see tires, rushing pavement, flashes of guardrail, and at the long stop, she saw what she thought were gas pumps. (They were. Two seconds after she said it we could hear and smell the gas hitting the tank a thin sheet of fiberglass away, and two seconds after that we were choking to death and our eyes were burning.) (Mango said, "Did you know that extended exposure to gasoline fumes can cause extreme fatigue and lead to loss of consciousness?") Twenty or thirty minutes of gasoline fumes and another short stop later, the crazy golfer finally killed the motorhome engine.

But we were still moving.

On water.

It was so disorienting.

We traveled by barge or ferry or on the back of a killer whale for about two hours. Wherever we are, it's roughly an hour from Biloxi by land and possibly two by water, but there was no gauging speed or distance from inside a motorhome basement on the back of a killer whale. We could be a mile from land; we could be a hundred miles from land. It all depends on how fast whales swim.

When we realized we were on water, and on the off chance we were on a ferry with other vehicles, more specifically the drivers of those other vehicles, we beat on the basement walls and screamed for help with everything we had.

Nothing.

We kept it up anyway.

After an hour, maybe more, we had to take a break. We were hoarse, exhausted, and deaf from screaming in each other's ears. We were sore from banging and kicking the basement walls, half the time accidentally banging and kicking each other. We decided a better play might be to stop altogether and make him think he'd killed us, because what good were dead hostages? Our plan was to take him out when he opened the basement door to check on us. We agreed to be still and quiet. What we didn't agree to was nodding off. The combination of the dark, the sudden still and quiet, and the gas fumes getting to us, plus the lull and rhythm of the water after expending so much energy for so long flipped our off switches. After fifteen minutes of peace and quiet, Fantasy said it first. "I'm going to close my eyes for half a minute. Wake me if anything happens." Then me. "I'm going to close my eyes for a whole minute. Wake me if anything happens." Then Mango. "Did you know giraffes only sleep two hours a day?" The next thing we knew, the whale we were riding beached itself.

We'd stopped moving.

We'd docked, or parked, or landed.

That woke us up.

The motorhome engine sputtered to life, the crazy golfer ground it into reverse, we bumped backwards fifty or sixty yards—again, hard to estimate from inside the basement—then he killed the engine again. It was so quiet we could hear waves slapping shore. Then we heard him drop from the driver's seat to dry ground and slam the driver door.

Bradley, he whistled.

As in not-a-care-in-the-world whistled.

We listened to him whistle his way around the front end of the motorhome, then closer, and closer, and closer, the whole time whispering to each other. "What is going on? Where are we? Please get your knee out of my ear." When the whistling got so close he couldn't have been more than a foot away, I opened my mouth to negotiate our release just as he fired four successive shots at what turned out to be the padlock on the doublewide basement door. By the time we realized we were still alive and spilled out onto packed sand in a body pile, ears still ringing, hearts still pounding, trying to decide if we'd been shot or not, we scrambled to get our bearings, find somewhere to take cover, and locate him. When we did, he was already on the water at the helm of the dilapidated work barge we'd obviously ridden in on, the greasy rusted kind of barge with tools and a small crane. The bumpers all the way around were old tires.

We ran to the water's edge, yelling and screaming things like, "Are you out of your mind? Get back here! You can't leave us here!"

He left us here. And we don't know where here is.

Standing on the beach watching the crazy golfer get smaller and smaller on the water, trying to figure out where we were and why we were there, we silently turned to Mango. She was between us, so I guess you could say we turned on her.

"What?" She stumbled back in the sand. "This isn't my fault." Her eyes darted between us. "I didn't do this."

"Do what, Mango?" I asked. "Adultnab us?"

"Did you know the largest ransom ever paid was a billion dollars?"

Fantasy said, "We're flattered, Mango. But I can assure you, we aren't worth a billion dollars."

"Is this about the Bellissimo, Mango? Does he—" I stabbed a finger in the direction of the ratty barge "—think the casino will pay a billion dollars for us?"

"Your husband will."

"My husband doesn't have a billion dollars."

"Did you know he's worth thirty billion?"

"Who, he, Mango?" I asked.

"Richard Sanders."

Her first straight answer.

I said, "Bad news. Richard Sanders isn't my husband."

"Yes, he is."

Fantasy's head dropped. "Oh, dear Lord." She crossed herself.

"Mango." I grabbed her by the forearms and shook her. I could barely hear myself above the waves slamming the beach. I could barely see for their spray. "Does your crazy golfer think I'm Bianca Sanders? Married to Richard Sanders, owner of the Bellissimo?"

She took a small step back.

"My name is Davis Way Cole," I said. "I'm Bianca Sanders's celebrity double." I pointed at the water on which there was a barge so far away by then we could barely see it. "Call your crazy golfer boss and tell him he's adultnabbed the wrong woman."

In a very small voice, she said, "Did you know one in five people would rather leave home without their clothes than without their phone?"

I was catching on. Mango was saying she didn't have a phone.

And it wouldn't have done us any good if she'd had one, because we were in the middle of nowhere. Bradley, this was all a setup, and the crazy golfer thinks he has Bianca.

But he has me.

MEMORANDUM

To: Bellissimo Security
From: Judson Reeves, Bellissimo Valet
Date: Saturday, May 9, 3:45 p.m.
Subject: Help

Hello, Security. My name is Judson Reeves. I'm the weekend valet supervisor. We have a problem. People are driving up to the resort entrance in golf carts. They're circling the fountain, beeping their golf cart horns, and throwing golf clubs into the fountain pool. Groundskeeping came to fish out the golf clubs, but after one of them was hit by a flying nine iron they left. Other golf cart people who are not in the fountain parade are parking under the porte cochère then getting out of their golf carts to tie huge yellow ribbons around the magnolia trees in the courtyard. They have confetti cannons and are shooting yellow confetti and streamers way up into the magnolia trees. Horticulture came and asked them to stop, but after one of them took a close-range confetti cannon shot to the face, they left too. All together there are at least two hundred golf carts at the entrance with more waiting on Beach Boulevard to get in. They're blocking all four valet lanes, the fire lane, and the limo lane. There's no room for incoming guest cars. The police can't come because they're busy at Golden Oaks. Could we get some help?

Mississippi Governor Vernon R. Wilson
Office of the Governor
Saturday, 09 May, 4:48 p.m.

GOVERNOR WILSON ORGANIZES SEARCH EFFORTS

Jackson, MS – Governor Wilson announced the immediate dispatch of State Emergency Services to Golden Oaks Golf Club in Biloxi moments after authorizing an official Kidnapping and Missing Persons Investigation regarding the suspected abduction of Biloxi's beloved Bianca Casimiro Sanders. Authorities believe Mrs. Sanders to be the victim of foul play. Mississippi Bureau of Investigation's State Crime Information team is on the scene in Biloxi. K9 ALERT Search and Rescue dogs have been dispatched and are en route from all corners of the state. Contact 911 with any information.

Later on Day One

Or Somewhere Between Day One and Two
I Can't Sleep
WHO COULD?

Dear Bradley,

It's the middle of the night. Maybe it isn't quite the middle of the night, but it's pitch-black where I am, so it feels like the middle of the night. It's probably more like eight o'clock. I wouldn't know. Just like I don't know where I am. I haven't seen you or our daughters since Thursday morning, and I can't help but believe your mother is largely to blame. When all is said and done and our bodies are found, or not, I want you to have a long talk with her. Your mother's birthday is in May. The PGA qualifier at Golden Oaks is also in May. Most Mays, in fact every May of our married lives, her birthday and the golf tournament have fallen at least three weeks apart on the calendar. One is near the beginning of the month, the other near the end. How is it that since Bexley and Quinn were born, which is to say for several Mays in a row now, she's managed to schedule her birthday celebration on the same weekend as the golf tournament? I'll tell you how. Intentionally. She wants you and our daughters all to herself without me in her way. I think she calls the Bellissimo, asks when the golf tournament is, then calls and tells you exactly when and where she wants to celebrate, always the weekend of the tournament and always in Tumbleweed, Texas, because she wants her nosy neighbors and her Bunco buddies to see how big the girls are. She knows I can't come. She knows I have to be Bianca and present the trophy at the golf tournament luncheon. All her, "Oh,

Davis can't come? She has to work? Oh, Bradley, darling, that just breaks my heart."

Bradley, darling, it does not break her heart.

She plans it this way.

Now look.

Just remember that every year I invite her to spend her birthday with us at the Bellissimo. Who wouldn't want to spend their birthday with their twin granddaughters at a five-star resort? I'll tell you who, YOUR MOTHER. And all her, "You live in a casino. I'm Baptist." That's ridiculous. No one lives in a casino. We live in a beautiful home twenty-eight floors above a casino and sin doesn't float that high. Her, "What if someone sees me?" doesn't make sense either. For someone from her tiny church two hundred miles away to see her at a casino in Mississippi, they'd have to <u>be</u> at a casino in Mississippi. Wouldn't the sightings cancel each other out? And then there's her line I appreciate the very least, "It's a shame your wife chooses to work." Bradley, number one, Bex and Quinn are in preschool now. What am I supposed to do while they're in school? Watch Housewives? Take up tennis? Needlepoint? Number two, I've been in one form or another of criminal apprehension my entire adult life. I didn't choose this path so much as it chose me. You didn't go to law school thinking you'd be a gaming attorney who would one day run a billion-dollar casino any more than I went to police academy thinking one day I'd be a <u>part-time</u> casino spy and Bianca's celebrity double. Do you understand what I'm saying, Bradley? Your mother doesn't hold it against you that your career path led to gaming while she totally holds it against me. That it means nothing to her that I work no more than twenty hours a week, except once or twice a year when we hit a really big case and I work two hundred hours a week, breaks MY heart.

It's been the longest, most frustrating, most baffling day of my life. Tomorrow, I have every intention of figuring out where I am so I can figure out how to get home. That is, of course, if you don't show up first. I'm assuming by now there's been a ransom demand for Bianca, you've met it, and are on your way. I love and miss you,

Bradley. I love and miss our daughters. One way or the other, I'll see you tomorrow. Because if you don't show up with the sun, I'll start swimming home. I'd leave now if I knew which way to swim. And if it weren't so dark out, except for the stars, of which there are an absolute blue million. And that I probably shouldn't brave the ocean at night because of sharks. And undertow. I'm going to sleep now with one ear open listening for rescue helicopters and one eye open watching for searchlights on the beach. Tell the girls I love them and they will get to wear their flower girl dresses. Just as soon as I find my way home. I love you.

MEMORANDUM

To: Special Events Catering
From: Marian Trevor, Curator, The Bianca Sanders Gallery
Date: Saturday, May 9, 8:45 p.m.
Subject: **NEED FOOD & BAR**

Hi, Catering. My name is Marian Trevor and I'm the person who babysits the portraits, sculptures, and Bianca Sanders fashion displays in the gallery on the mezzanine. Last week I logged twenty visitors. No one was here for more than ten minutes. Right now I have two thousand visitors and they won't leave. I don't know if it's Mrs. Sanders's birthday or if it's true that she's been kidnapped, but I do know her devoted fans are pouring into the gallery. My gift shop has been wiped clean of Bianca snow globes, magnets, and Special Issue Louis Vuitton Bianca keychains. (At four hundred dollars a pop.) The people inside the gallery have set up vigil. They are chanting, lighting candles (not allowed), and many are crying. I had one man crying so loud I had to call security. Please send food and liquor. I don't care what food you send. Cheez-Its will be fine. Mostly I want the liquor so the crowd will get sloshed and head to the casino. I don't know what's up with all these people, but I need help redirecting them.

From: MotherOfBradley@aol.com
To: BCole@Bellissimo.com
Date: May 09, 8:51:31 p.m.
Subject: Our Darling Girls
Sent from the Internet

Beloved product of my womb, why aren't you answering your telephone? I've called numerous times. I need to discuss two items with you. I'm forced to resort to electronic mail to reach you. I would imagine you are too busy with your wife to answer your mother's repeated telephone calls. What if this were an emergency, Bradster?

I'll start with repeating what I shared with you through my tears as you were, once again, leaving home earlier today. Darling son, I live for the short time you and our precious twins visit. That I can share the magnificence of my blooming buttercups, hyacinth, ranunculus, daffodils, and the truest symbol of Texas, my glorious bluebonnets, with you and our girls is my greatest joy in life. And that I was able to take several Polaroid pictures of you in front of my prize-winning gladiolus before they met their demise is nothing short of a miracle. I will treasure the photographs forever. I do hope Bexley and Quinn enjoy the gladiolus bouquets they picked for their mother from the flowerbeds that grace my front porch. I will now consider gladiolus their favorite as they picked every single bloom! I turned my head but for a brief moment to say good morning to Joyce White, and in that short time, in which Joyce and I discussed no more than the pleasant weather, my gladiolus were ripped straight from the ground! As soon as my grief at our parting subsided, I had Kevin Dodger—you remember Susan Dodger's son, Kevin?—harvest the few remaining corms to be replanted in the fall. My bridge club, all gifted gardeners, will be here tomorrow after worship service to help me determine what flowering non-perennial grown by a total stranger Walmart "gardener," probably under harsh greenhouse lights, to plant in the interim given that it's too late to seed anything that could possibly bloom before July, and I simply can't bear the thought of naked flowerbeds for that length of time, which is all to say I'm sorry your wife couldn't join us to celebrate my birthday and I do hope she enjoys my prize-winning gladiolus.

On to the two items I'd like to discuss.

Bradley, darling, the Jubilee corn I sent you home with from Maynard Turbin's bountiful crop is chock-full of vitamins and rich in antioxidants, both of which, as we discussed, you urgently need. Not to mention corn is a wonderful source of fiber. As I also mentioned, if your wife is unable to prepare the corn properly, I am always available to guide her. All she need do is call. If she's too busy with her job, remember, Bradley, the three steps we went over: shuck, boil, cover. Add the shucked corn <u>with all silk removed</u> to sparingly salted water that has come to a full rolling boil, cover the corn, <u>turn off the heat</u>, and set an egg timer for two and a half minutes.

The second thing I'd like to discuss is my newly decorated dining room wall. Bexley and Quinn are so artistically creative! They surely get it from their mother! The next time I see your mother-in-law, Mrs. Way, I will certainly ask her if she allowed your wife to take Estée Lauder Pure Color lipsticks to walls when she was younger and if the results were as glorious in her home as they are in mine! And the sentiment! So cherished! I certainly love them (more than life itself) too! I trust that you will continue and supervise **The Correct Spelling and Pronunciation of Grandmother** assignment I gave them. They seem to be enjoying it so very much! Don't forget, Bradley, language skills are acquired through repetition, a wonderful learning tool. As words are practiced by rote repetition, they are committed to memory. The twins will only learn to spell <u>and say</u> Grandmother correctly if they write it one hundred times a day <u>for ten full days</u>, then follow up with the exercise once a week until we are all together again. Which I sincerely hope is soon.

I must sign off for now, because I can see our favorite town criers, the Johnstons, Deborah and Phil, on their way up the walk with what could only be scandalous speculative gossip straight from the cable news channel they are so fond of. They appear to be unusually disturbed. And for some reason, the Carters, Betty and Roger, are on their heels. Followed by the McMurtrys! Gwendolyn and Bob! This must be about the loss of my gladiolus. The whole town has heard!

You are my pride and joy.

Love,

Forever,

Mother

Biloxi Police Identify Second Missing Woman

BY NELSON MILLER
GULF COAST HERALD SENIOR STAFF REPORTER
Saturday, May 09, 11:54 p.m.

The second woman believed to have been abducted this morning from Golden Oaks Golf Course in Biloxi has been identified. Security footage shows thirty-seven-year-old Fantasy Erb, a Bellissimo Resort and Casino undercover security operative for an unconfirmed number of years, scanning through the Golden Oaks employee entrance gate in a white Volvo XC90. Beside her, forty-five-year-old Bianca Casimiro Sanders. Bypassing the Clubhouse, Mrs. Erb's presumed destination, she drove instead to the RV park behind the thirteenth hole reserved for visiting spectator and golfer tour busses. Police spoke to Mrs. Erb's husband who said he hadn't talked to his wife since earlier that morning. She had left to run a work errand on her way to the wedding of coworkers in New Orleans that he and the couple's three sons were also planning to attend. He wasn't specifically aware of her plans to stop by the golf course on her way to the wedding venue but said that wasn't unusual. Her security responsibilities at the Bellissimo often required her presence at any and all Bellissimo properties and she seldom ran her schedule by him. When asked if he feared for his wife's safety in light of the suspicious circumstances, Reginald Erb said, "I fear for the safety of the fool who took my wife. He has no idea what he's done. Or who he took." Having been missing for more than eight hours at the time of this post, Biloxi police, fearing the three women could be far from where they were last seen at Golden Oaks, have established a national tip line. Call 1-877-FINDHER with any information regarding the whereabouts of forty-five-year-old Bianca Casimiro Sanders, thirty-seven-year-old Fantasy Erb, and the as-yet-unidentified female golf caddie believed to be with them. Police are also seeking information from anyone who witnessed an older model Fleetwood Storm 28MS Class A Motorhome previously parked near where Mrs. Erb's Volvo was last seen at Golden Oaks. Security footage shows no license plate or vehicle registration tag. Images retrieved from Mississippi Department of Transportation of the motorhome headed east on I-10 at the D'Iberville exchange are obscured and inconclusive, so authorities can't identify the driver of the motorhome. Mrs. Erb's Volvo has not been located.

Almost Day Two

Dear Bradley,

I'm trying to sleep at the front of the motorhome, Fantasy is somewhat successfully sleeping in the middle, and Mango is sleeping the sleep of the dead in the back. And as it turns out, it's a doublewide motorhome. The interior is twenty feet long, maybe twenty-two, and on the road it's maybe eight feet wide. After it's parked, the walls, complete with furniture and appliances, push out. Mango calls the walls sliders. Let's put it this way, what you see on the road is only half of a motorhome. It doubles when you park it.

The first thing we did was toss this place looking for—I don't know what we were looking for.

We didn't find much.

Two cans of Bud Light, eighteen boxes of mac and cheese, the Kraft blue-box kind that Bex and Quinn love, golf junk, and a drawer full of takeout menus. So far, I've written to you on takeout menus from Shaggy's, Sal and Mookie's, and Woody's Roadside, all close to home. So the crazy golfer either lives in Biloxi or he's been in Biloxi long enough to hit up every restaurant in town for takeout menus.

That's what we found.

Front to back, there's the cab, where the doublewide is driven, a small dinette with a bench seat behind it, a smaller kitchenette across from the dinette, an even smaller bathette past the kitchenette, then the bedroom. I didn't get a good look at the bedroom, but let's assume it's miniature too. That's where Mango is sleeping. In the bedroomette. We gave her the bedroomette knowing two of us would be trying to sleep almost on top of each other in the living quarters, and since neither me nor Fantasy wanted to sleep that close to a total stranger analytical research caddie who has silver hair and speaks trivia, and who we were mad at anyway, we said, "You take the bedroom, Mango," and we got no argument from her. She waltzed right in. Then slid the pocket door closed. Then locked it. One of those round plastic locks that you turn one click, which is to say, if we wanted in, we wouldn't have any trouble getting in. Instead of goodnight, she said, "Did you know that snoring is the primary cause of sleep disruption for ninety million adults?" There's a reason she shared that little tidbit with us, Bradley. And it's one of the reasons I'm still awake. MANGO SNORES LIKE A 747 WITH ASTHMA. SHE IS SHAKING THE DOUBLEWIDE WALLS.

"What is up with her?" I asked Fantasy.

"She's nuts," Fantasy said.

"She may be more than nuts."

"What do you mean?"

"I mean she's not upset."

She's not, Bradley. So far, Mango's taking everything in stride, like being adultnabbed and dumped on a deserted island in the middle of the ocean is something that happens to her every other day. Like this is a program she's familiar with. She's definitely familiar with the doublewide, she's familiar with our abductor, and she comes across as being familiar with us. She barely blinked an eye when I told her I wasn't Bianca. As if she already knew. I think there's more to Mango's role in our adultnabbing than she's letting on. Which is not to say she isn't trying. Like when she catches herself not participating enough in Fantasy's and my outrage, she jumps in with insincere indignation. "Did you know that fifty-five percent of kidnabbings are perpetrated by a biological parent?" Which has nothing to do with anything and I'm not buying it. This I know: the anger in her voice doesn't make it to her eyes. Which are navy blue, by the way. And being adultnabbed isn't bothering her enough to keep her awake either. She's in the only doublewide bed with her head on the only doublewide pillow absolutely sawing logs. Although it isn't much of a bed. And I wouldn't get anywhere near that pillow. From what I could see when I stuck my head in the bedroomette door for two seconds when we got here, her bed is a full-sized mattress on a wooden platform. The headboard is against a doublewide wall, there's an inch or two of clearance around the other three sides, the bedspread looks like it's made of cardboard and has never been laundered, and that's about it except for four tiny filthy windows with dirty dishrags for drapes. Fantasy's bed, a foot away from mine, is actually the dinette table. It lowers to just below the bench seat, which doubles as the doublewide's sofa, and the bench seat cushion flips up and out to cover the lowered table to make it a bed. I'm trying to sleep in what might be considered the bunk. It's actually the headliner above the driver and passenger seats that unsnaps, drops down, then catches on hooks to create a hard, flat, plastic surface half the width and length of a twin-sized bed with no more than eighteen inches of clearance. That's where I am. On a claustrophobic slab of plastic above the doublewide cockpit with my nose brushing the doublewide roof. I'm wide awake, wearing a smelly polyester golf shirt from Sunshine Family Golf Center in Grand Cayman that hits me mid-thigh, and I want to go home. One more thing, because I can't stop thinking about it in the dead of night while TRYING TO SLEEP ON A PLASTIC KIDDIE BED, I want you to know I really hope Baylor and July went through with the wedding. I hope, when everyone realized we weren't there and weren't coming, that they pulled the preacher aside and got it over with. "I do," and "I do too," and the preacher signed whatever it is the preacher signs, and I hope this for two reasons. One, it's ridiculous that July has spent years of her life planning weddings that have been interrupted every time by Baylor's job, first a hurricane, then a snowstorm, and most recently, killer tomatoes, only to have a fourth wedding postponed because Baylor's partners have been adultnabbed, which means he needs to concentrate on finding us instead of honeymooning. And two, because five weddings are ridiculous. Don't get me wrong; I love July. She's like family to us. She's been the best nanny for Bex and Quinn we could ever hope for. The girls don't remember when they didn't love July and she didn't love them back. And Baylor? He's like family too, because Fantasy and I have practically raised him. He's good at his job and he's an integral part of our team. BUT, Bradley, caring for them aside, does part of you, like part of me, think Baylor and July should take a hint? Read the writing on the wall? Maybe they shouldn't plan another wedding? What couple is forced to postpone their wedding four times without facing facts? Is Karma trying to tell them to stop setting wedding dates because every time they do THE WHOLE WIDE WORLD FALLS APART?

Our love story will
still be told...

DEAR FAMILY AND FRIENDS,

DUE TO UNFORSEEN CIRCUMSTANCES, WE'VE MADE THE DIFFICULT DECISION TO POSTPONE OUR WEDDING. AGAIN. BUT YOU KNOW WHAT THEY SAY, FIFTH TIME'S THE CHARM. WE HOPE YOU WILL JOIN US WHEN WE RESCHEDULE. WE WILL BE IN TOUCH WHEN WE HAVE NEW PLANS. WE LOOK FORWARD TO CELEBRATING WITH YOU SOON.

BAYLOR & JULY

MEMORANDUM

To: Mercedes Anderson, Bellissimo Director of Human Resources
From: Catherine McKenzie, Bellissimo Director of Communications
Date: Saturday, May 9, 11:50 p.m.
Subject: Resignation(s)

As of ten minutes ago, Bellissimo employees had taken to social media more than fifty-five thousand times speculating, lamenting, celebrating, and losing their minds over Bianca's abduction. Am I right when I say we have close to five thousand employees? That's roughly eleven tweets, posts, and Tik-Toks each. My team and I were able to control the narrative for the first fifteen minutes, or, I should say, until it became political when our own employees of one political affiliation began accusing coworkers with opposing political views of being behind the kidnapping.

What is wrong with people?

Within half an hour it was so bad with our employees slinging political mud at each other over our social media channels that our corporate accounts across all platforms were SUSPENDED. WhatsApp has already banned us for life. I blasted out an urgent text message to all employees reminding them that posting anything political and/or regarding Bianca Sanders would result in disciplinary action and/or termination, then went on to express my extreme disappointment at our own employees daring to politicize such an unpolitical and tragic event, and how did they react? They doubled down. Housekeeping's elaborate rendition of "Ding-Dong! The Witch is Dead" is impressive. Have you seen it? Surely you have as it's been shared more than six thousand times. Someone named Shannon in Player Services, obviously an animal rights activist and self-proclaimed proud rescuer of more than forty dogs, sixty cats, and four pot-bellied pigs—who lives with all these animals in an apartment at Bellissimo Employee Towers, by the way—posted an impassioned plea on behalf of Bianca's Yorkshire Terriers, Gianna and Ghita. In the eleven-minute video, viewed more than seventeen thousand times, she bawls her eyes out and begs her fellow animal lovers to adopt the orphaned Sanders dogs she claims she doesn't have room for. (I'll say. Aren't the Employee Tower units one-bedroom studios?) Most of her cats were crying along with her in the video. With our social media accounts suspended, where would you imagine the thousands of pet adoption applications landed? On my desk. Along with dog cookies, toys, and ridiculous dog clothing. But the worst? The very worst? The casseroles. Whose bright idea was it to direct the single women of all ages, shapes, and sizes from near and far toting sympathy casseroles for Richard Sanders to my office? It's unreal. And you should see these women. I've parked them and their casseroles in the press room. Go take a look. Most are half naked. Many look underage. All want to be the next Mrs. Sanders. Several fights have broken out, one involving two very heavy and blazing hot Pyrex casserole dishes that sent an innocent casserole woman bystander to Biloxi Memorial with a head injury and third-degree cauliflower burns. This is ridiculous. I'm done. I quit. Take this job and shove it. Neither I nor my team will be in tomorrow. Or any other day. Good luck, Bellissimo.

One More Thing

Dear Bradley,

I can't sleep until I say one more thing about Baylor: keep him off my computers. He has his own. It isn't my fault his computer is as slow as Christmas. I tell him all the time to delete the Warcraft and Minecraft and Stupidcraft from his hard drive and he won't do it. Surely by now he's managed to pull up Golden Oaks security footage ON HIS OWN COMPUTER. You have the name, make, model, license plate, and registration of the doublewide, which means you know who's behind all this, he's in custody, and you're on your way to rescue me. I'll pretend to sleep on this horrible bed until you get here, take me home, and I can sleep in our bed. Don't say anything to Bex and Quinn except that Mommy is proud of them for being good girls at their grandmother's (I hope) and that Mommy loves them. To say anything else will just scare them, and I'll be honest with you, Bradley, there's no reason for you or the girls to be scared. I'm scared enough for all five of us. I'm including Candy because dogs sense things. And I'm sure she's scared too. In her own furry way.

I love you.

Authorities Seek Witness in Golden Oaks Abduction

BY NELSON MILLER
GULF COAST HERALD SENIOR STAFF REPORTER
Sunday, May 10, 6:20 a.m.

Our formidable Biloxi Police Department says they're looking for a person of interest who may have witnessed the abduction of three women from Golden Oaks Golf Club yesterday.

A person of interest?

Ben "Finn" Finnegan, one of the five wild card participants in last week's PGA Tour Qualifying Tournament, who police say is wanted for questioning because they believe he can positively identify the third missing woman, has been described by multiple Golden Oaks witnesses as a male of unknown race, average height, average build, average weight, with no additional identifiers, such as hair color, eye color, facial hair, scars, or tattoos. No one even noticed what he was wearing. You read that right. The police are looking for an invisible man in hopes of identifying an unknown woman. And this man's name? Not his name. Ben "Finn" Finnegan is a treasure-hunting character played by Matthew McConaughey in the 2008 blockbuster rom-com *Fool's Gold*.

Come on, Biloxi. We can do better than that.

I've personally covered the casino beat for Gulf Coast Herald for two decades. I've interviewed hundreds of individuals who've witnessed a fellow diner double-dipping in the buffet line at one of our many casinos and describe the suspect down to the color and pattern of his socks. Someone has seen Ben "Finn" Finnegan. Someone knows Ben "Finn" Finnegan. It took me less than two minutes to find his golf stats, which led to a grainy image, which I ran through Biloxi PD's own arrest report archives and found multiple John Doe warrants with caught-on-camera likenesses that were dead ringers for Ben "Finn" Finnegan. What I learned about him after an additional five-minute social media image search in and around the Biloxi area? He's five feet ten inches tall. He looks to be in his mid- to late forties, although he could be much younger. He has shaggy brown unkempt hair, he has a beer gut, he appears to be loud, belligerent, and a sore loser. I broadened my search parameters and found the same man in and out of the Biloxi area going back years either golfing (for the most part, poorly), playing blackjack, or saddled up to a bar drinking Bud Light. And almost a full day later, between Golden Oaks, the Bellissimo, Biloxi PD, Mississippi Bureau of Investigation, search dogs, and the Governor of our great state, no one can find this man? Or provide any definitive information about him? Not even his real name? That means it's up to us, Readers.

We know he's a blackjack player because he won his spot in the PGA Qualifying Tournament at Golden Oaks at a Bellissimo blackjack tournament, unfortunately under the same alias. (Ben "Finn" Finnegan.) That and everything else about him says to me he's a frequent flyer at our casinos. Someone's seen him. If you don't want to tell the police what you know, what you've heard, or what you've seen, tell me. Because I don't believe for a minute that no one knows anything about him. Nor do I believe police suspect he witnessed the abduction of the three women. I believe they know good and well he perpetrated the abduction of the three women.

Who is trying to put a lid on this story?

Why aren't the authorities shouting what I just told you from the rooftops?

On the outside chance it was our friends at the Bellissimo who don't want information about the suspect made public yet, tread carefully. If you follow me, you already know the Bellissimo has an uncanny way of solving their own high-stakes problems—hello, Laverne and Shirley—and it only stands to reason they're working diligently behind the scenes to put an end to this latest perilous predicament they find themselves in. To be honest, Readers, I find it curious that the Bellissimo hasn't solved this case already, which makes me wonder if Thelma and Louise aren't on vacation, and if that's the case, hurry back, ladies. Unearth this mystery man and honor me with the exclusive. Because here we are, twenty hours later, and the invisible forces at the Bellissimo, along with local authorities, the Mississippi Bureau of Investigation, the Governor's team, and large packs of search dogs haven't produced Ben "Finn" Finnegan. What does that mean, Biloxi? It means they need our help.

Readers, if only for the sake of the women abducted, help me blow the lid off this story. Help me find Ben "Finn" Finnegan. Let's hold him accountable. Call or text me at 228-449-3038 or reach me by email at nmiller@coastherald.org. If for some reason you can't reach me, call Vince at the news desk at Gulf Coast Herald: 228-911-NEWS. If after all that we still haven't connected, call my mother. Lila Miller. She'll track me down. My mom, who many of you know was Biloxi's first female investigative news reporter for WLOX-TV, currently resides at Caring Star Senior Center. (Hi, Mom!) Call the switchboard and ask for my mother. If you can't reach her, ask for any member of Caring Star's mystery book club, We Know Whodunnit. Caring Star's number is 228-389-2777.

I believe this Ben "Finn" Finnegan has the three women. He tore out of Golden Oaks Golf Club in his motorhome yesterday destroying three holes on the front nine and sending a team of turf technicians to the hospital. Someone saw him. Someone knows him. Someone knew his plans. I need that someone to get in touch with me.

Day Two
Sunday
Hot Beer for Breakfast and *Fool's Gold*

Dear Bradley,

Have you heard from the adultnabber? Has a ransom request for Bianca been made? Have you heard from anyone on the road who might have seen us? Has Baylor run the doublewide through Prism, the software in our spy office that tracks vehicles by satellite, and pinpointed our location? I can't believe we're still here. I can't believe it's taking this long. I can't believe we haven't been rescued. What, Bradley, are you busy? Let me guess. After hearing I was missing, your mother, totally forgetting her casino phobia, showed up to help with Bex and Quinn and you're busy entertaining HER?

I apologize for all that.

I'm tired, I'm hungry, I'm wearing a nasty golf shirt, and I want to come home.

One last question. DOES BIANCA KNOW SHE'S BEEN ADULTNABBED? Saint-Tropez. The Sanderses are in a villa in Saint-Tropez. Someone needs to tell her she's been adultnabbed before she hears it on the news and believes it.

One last last question. DO MY PARENTS KNOW I'VE BEEN ADULTNABBED? I almost hope they don't. They'll be worried sick.

This morning, we spelled it out for Mango, and not over coffee, because there is no coffee. We sat Mango down across from us in the doublewide dining room and, after asking her politely to keep a lid on the trivia, we let her have it over a Bud Light split three ways.

Never have I ever had hot beer for breakfast.

Before this.

Never do I ever want hot beer for breakfast again.

I said, "Let's start with introductions, Mango."

She eyed the hot beer in her Waffle House cup.

"My name is Davis," I said. "I'm married with children. I'm a former police officer. Which means I know my way around interrogation, and make no mistake, you are being interrogated."

She downed her third of the hot beer.

"Currently," I went on, "and in addition to being Bianca Sanders's celebrity double, I work on a covert security team at the Bellissimo."

She checked her Waffle House coffee cup for more beer.

"This is Fantasy."

I pointed; Fantasy waved.

"She's my partner."

Fantasy waved again.

"She's also married with children. She was a prison guard for years. She could kill you with a paperclip."

Mango stared at Fantasy's Waffle House cup.

"There's a third member of our team," I said. "His name is Baylor. And you'd better believe he's looking for us."

Mango eyed my Waffle House cup.

"Baylor's a deadeye with firearms," I told her. "A sharpshooter. He could shoot a gnat off your nose from a mile away." Mango clapped a hand over her nose. "The three of us work for a man named No Hair." From above her hand, still on her nose, Mango raised two thick eyebrows. I would say thick black eyebrows, but like my Bianca Blonde from Saturday morning that was waning to Davis Red, Mango's ink-black brow gel was fading. "He has a real name," I explained. "It's Jeremy Covey. He was with the Mississippi Bureau of Investigation before the Bellissimo. He can find anyone, Mango. He has the resources to find your mailman's cousin's first-grade teacher in five minutes flat. He'll ultimately be the one who'll turn you and the crazy golfer over to the feds. So remember his name."

Mango's hand finally fell from her nose. "Did you know the best way to remember names is to attach a visual cue?"

I leaned in. "What's the visual cue you attach to the crazy golfer? What's his name?"

She said, "Did you know left-handed people have better memories?"

"Are you telling me you're left-handed, Mango, or are you telling me you've forgotten his name?" I didn't wait for her answer. "Either way, the fact remains, you are sitting across from two-thirds of a highly skilled security team for a billion-dollar casino. And we need information from you."

"Straight talk too," Fantasy said. "Not a word about soccer balls or zucchini."

Mango's eyes darted back and forth between me and Fantasy. They were less navy and more midnight blue just then. Almost black.

I asked, "What's the crazy golfer's name?"

She answered, "Did you know there are more than five million Roberts in the world?"

"That's his name?" I slapped the table. "Robert? Your boss's name, Mango. I want to know your boss's name."

"Which one?"

"You have more than one boss?"

"No!" Mango backed up. "I didn't say that!"

Fantasy said, "What's. His. Name?"

She said, "Finn."

"Finn what?" Fantasy asked.

"Finn Finnegan."

"No one is named Finn Finnegan," I said.

"He's named after a character in a movie," she said.

"What movie?" Fantasy asked.

"*Fool's Gold*."

Fantasy and I looked at each other. *Fool's Gold* wasn't an old enough movie for a grown man to be named after one of the characters. I asked Mango how old the crazy golfer was so I could make that point to her. She answered, "Did you know that by 2050 there will be two billion people older than sixty?" Fantasy leaned all the way in. "If you don't start talking, Mango, you're not going to see thirty."

Tempers were hot in the doublewide.

I tried a different route. "Do you have any way at all of contacting Finn, Mango? He needs to know I'm not Bianca. He's adultnabbed the wrong woman." Then Fantasy said, "And her innocent friend." That threw me. I turned to her. "My what friend? How are you innocent, Fantasy? You're the one who answered the golf call. If you hadn't, we'd be having chicory coffee and beignets for breakfast." Then Mango said, "Did you know voodoo was introduced to the world by New Orleans?" Fantasy said, "I'm going to voodoo you, Mango, if you don't stop with the trivia and start with some answers." She pointed at me. "Not Bianca Sanders. Not." Mango whispered, "Did you know mistaken identity is the most common defense used by criminal attorneys in murder trials?"

Fantasy all but crawled across the kitchenette table on all fours and got right in her face. "Did you know that five thousand people a year get away with murder? You start talking or I'll be number five thousand and one."

Mango ran screaming to the bedroomette and locked herself in.

While it was somewhat comforting to get a reaction out of her that felt genuine, it did nothing to help solve the mystery of Mango. Clearly, she deflects. Rather than answer a direct question, she gives us trivia that may or may not have a drop of an answer in it. Fantasy thinks she's a fountain of useless information who has nothing to do with anything and needs to be stuffed back in the doublewide basement. I, on the other hand, am not so sure. My jury is out on Mango. I don't know if Mango is a victim, an accomplice, or if she's the mastermind. (Fantasy laughed at that.) Don't forget, Bradley, the crazy golfer seemed genuinely confused as to who I was, and add to that the fact he was obviously, gun-to-her-head, not happy with Mango.

Why?

Another thing I keep turning over and over in my mind is the perfect timing of it all, specifically the Golden Oaks security call exactly when we pulled up to the gate that led us straight to Mango, and ultimately, the crazy golfer. Bradley, one or both of them knew we were coming. Which means one or both of them knew when we left the Bellissimo. Which means one or both of them were watching. Which means one or both of them knows I'M ME.

WHY ADULTNAB ME?

AND FANTASY?

One thing's for sure: Mango knows more than she's telling, and it looks like we're going to have to drag it out of her in fun facts and trivia. To drag anything out of anyone, we needed to eat.

Fantasy and I banged around the kitchenette looking for food other than mac and cheese to the soundtrack of Mango wailing in the bedroom, occasionally yelling at us. "Females are the victims 70% of the time in crimes perpetrated by intimate partners!" (So she's sleeping with the crazy golfer? Hard to believe, considering on a scale of one to ten, she's, generously, a 6, and he's, generously, a 0.) "Celebrities are at a higher risk of cyberstalking!" (So he's been cyberstalking Bianca? Or she's been cyberstalking Bianca? Or they've both been cyberstalking Bianca? Or maybe they've been cyberstalking me thinking they were cyberstalking Bianca?) "Property crimes are much more common than violent crimes!" (So this is about property? Surely not the property we're on.)

Fantasy yelled at the door, "Shut up, Mango. You're giving me a headache."

What was giving both of us a headache was hot beer instead of hot coffee for breakfast. Bradley, there is no coffeepot, and if there were a coffeepot it wouldn't do us any good because there's no coffee, or much else past the eighteen boxes of mac and cheese, which was apparently what sustained the crazy golfer when he'd had too many Bud Lights to navigate the doublewide through a fast-food drive-through. Other things in the kitchenette: the takeout menus I already told you about, golf pencils, which I'm flying through as I write you, one saucepan, two bowls, one saucer, four Waffle House coffee cups, three Waffle House coffee cup lids, one real spoon, five plastic spoons, and all manner of takeout accoutrements, like tiny packets of mustard and Sriracha.

Fantasy shook a box of mac and cheese. The macaroni rattled. "What are we supposed to do with this?"

"Cook it," I said.

"How?"

I reached for the faucet above the sink (a sink the size of a cereal bowl) and flipped it on. "Surely this is fresh water from a tank somewhere."

We looked around.

"How do you figure that?" Fantasy asked.

"Because we're not hooked up to water. It has to be coming from a tank somewhere inside the doublewide."

"How do we know it's safe to drink?"

From the bedroomette, Mango yelled, "Did you know you can survive without water for three days?"

We ignored her.

"We don't know it's safe to drink," I said, "but we can cook with it. Our choices are to cook the macaroni in the suspicious water or starve."

Mango yelled again, "Did you know that hunger strikes have proven you can live eight to twenty-one days without food?"

Fantasy and I looked at the door. Then we looked at each other in a "Really? We're stuck here with her?" way.

Fantasy turned back to the sink, flipped the faucet lever, dropped her head, and took a long drink. "It's bubbly," she said, "and it tastes like plastic."

So far, Fantasy hasn't died from the water. She said if she does die from the water, maybe Mango and I should boil it before we drink it.

Great plan.

We knew we had lights that we thought ran on the doublewide battery. Apparently, we have a generator too. Because when Fantasy said, "What now? Do we build a fire to cook the macaroni?" I said, "Let's try this first." I twisted one of the two knobs on the stovetop and the burner coils immediately turned red. And I doubted the doublewide engine battery could power a stovetop. So, more good news; we have a generator somewhere. We won't die of thirst or starve to death if you get here today.

We split the mac and cheese three ways and sat down at the dinette table to eat (it was so bland because we had no milk or butter to make it the way Bex and Quinn like it) and plan our next move when Mango yelled from the bedroom, "Did you know world hunger is on the rise?" Fantasy yelled back, "Then get out here and eat."

Misinformation Regarding Bianca Casimiro Sanders

NEWS PROVIDED FOR IMMEDIATE RELEASE BY
BELLISSIMO ENTERTAINMENT, INC
BILOXI/Sunday, May 10, 8:00 a.m./PRNewswire

In accordance with directives from legal counsel for Bellissimo Entertainment, Inc, it shall be noted that Bianca Casimiro Sanders, wife of Bellissimo Resort and Casino owner Richard Sanders, is not forty-five years of age as reported by Gulf Coast Herald's Nelson Miller. She is much younger.

P.S.

24 Hours In
Post Mac and Cheese

Dear Bradley,

Don't think I don't know what's going on in my absence. And I'm not talking about your mother. I know what you're doing. I'm assuming by now a ridiculous ransom demand has been made for Bianca and you're working around the clock to scrape together the money. You've emptied the Bellissimo vault, you've gone to every other Biloxi casino and asked them to empty their vaults, and, depending on how ludicrously high the ransom demand is, you've probably even hit up your old bosses at Grand Las Vegas. Meanwhile, No Hair's out for blood. He's probably walking the halls with an AK-47. He's calling in every favor from every MBI agent he ever worked with, he's paying off crackhead wino informants all over town for information about Crazy Golfer Finn, and his singular goal is ten minutes alone with him.

Neither way will work.

If you pay the ransom, you'll never see Crazy Golfer Finn again.

If No Hair kills him, you might never see me again.

So that leaves Baylor. Bradley, listen to me, and don't ever tell him I said this. Right now, Baylor is the only one of the three of you with his head on halfway straight. If he and July went through with the wedding or if they didn't, either way, he's the only one of you who can be objective. He's the only one with the ability to think this through. And that's what it's going to take. Listen to him. Nine things he says sound like they're straight out of the mouth of a juvenile delinquent—I don't know how July puts up with him—skip all that, because it's the tenth thing he says that will work. Give him some rope. Remember, he learned from the best. (Me and Fantasy.) And keep him off my computers, especially my laptop.

From: baylor@bellissimo.com
To: davis@bellissimo.com
Day: Sunday
Subject: Hey

Hey, Davis. It's me. Baylor. Remember that time we followed one of our new slot hosts to Foxwoods Casino at Biloxi Pointe because he was sending our players there? Remember that tool we hired who really worked for them and was passing out Foxwoods Executive Player Development business cards to our high rollers? He spotted us tailing him and trapped us in a Foxwoods elevator. That guy. I know you remember. Do you remember hacking into the elevator ATM (so dope, ATMs in elevators) and sending an email to No Hair telling him we were trapped in a Foxwoods elevator? Ten minutes later, No Hair shows up ready to burn the place to the ground. The only reason I'm bringing it up is because you're always telling me you'll kill me if I even breathe on your computers. I'm in our office, at your desk, breathing all over your computers ONLY because I'm trying to find you, and if there's any way you're stuck in an elevator and you've hacked an ATM and can check your email, I want you to know I'm using your computer before you come back and kill me for using your computer. Part of me thinks if you can read your email you'll write back. Which would be cool. Write me back. And don't start off chewing me out for using your computers. It'd be better if you'd start off telling me where you are. I wouldn't be on your computers at all if I wasn't looking for you and Fantasy. So is the whole world. You know who else I'm looking for? The woman. The woman you're with. Not Fantasy. The other woman. Something's up with her. She's like a game show expert. She knows stupid things. I found her under Research Jobs on *Craigslist* where she freelances finding stupid things for people like who their great-great-great-grandfather was and where his old truck is. That's how she hooked up with the golfer. Davis, I think he hired her to research something and it went sideways. But I'm the only one who thinks that. If you were here and seeing what I'm seeing about her (on your computer), you'd say she knows enough to be dangerous. So watch your back with her. I'm watching my back with No Hair, because he's about to kill somebody. He doesn't care who. And you need to know your husband is in BAD SHAPE. You'd better get out of whatever elevator you're in fast because he's not going to make it. But your kids are okay. Your mother's here. Maybe it's Brad's mother who's here. Somebody's mother is here taking care of your kids.

Last thing, we got a ransom demand on Bianca. A phone call from a burner phone. We have forty-eight hours to come up with fifty million dollars. But it's already been half that time. Are you even believing that? Fifty million dollars? Everybody's talking about it. We're not on the same page about paying the ransom here. Brad wants to pay it, every penny, I think he'd pay fifty billion to get you home, and No Hair doesn't. He wants to say we're going to pay it, nail the guy who shows up for the money, then right before he bleeds out, get him to tell where you are. I say give it some time because nobody's working harder to save you than you. I mean, I think there's a huge chance you'll save yourself before we can. Besides, we don't have fifty million dollars, and bummer, none of the insurance will cover that much money. Brad's plan is to scrape up the fifty million and No Hair's plan is to set a trap. I said don't do either of those. Because the guy's a dumbass for taking you and Fantasy. I said let's see how big of a dumbass he is. Offer a reward for Fantasy's car and see if he's stupid enough to show up for it. It's a big showdown between your husband and our boss every minute. I'm stuck in the middle. I see where both of them are coming from. I'll keep you posted. Not to worry you or anything, but July and I didn't get married. I'll see you and Fantasy soon.

Peace out.

Later on Day Two (Thousand)

Dear Bradley,

All day we waited for you to show up and save us, or at the very least we thought maybe the crazy adultnabbing golfer would return for us. None of that happened. While we waited, we tried to dig more information out of Mango and we explored. At her suggestion. ("Did you know The Golden Age of Exploration lasted three hundred years?") We weren't exactly dressed for it, something out there didn't smell quite right, but it wasn't like we had anything better to do. So we explored. Mango, enthusiastically. Fantasy and me? Not so much. And it could be you haven't found us yet because we might be nowhere.

We believe we're on a barrier island. A barrier island off the coast of what or where, we don't know. I assume we're in the Gulf, because we didn't travel long enough to be anywhere else, and everything looks somewhat familiar, which is to say the flora and the fauna of it all, but a barrier island off Louisiana, Mississippi, or Alabama, we don't know. We can't see land from anywhere. We don't think we're in a channel because we haven't seen anything on the water—no fishing charters, yachts, commercial barges, Carnival Fun Ships, or Coast Guard cutters.

Fantasy said, "We're definitely on a barrier island," then Mango said, "Did you know the largest barrier island in the world is Padre Island off the Texas coast?" Even though we'd already decided before we lured Mango out of the bedroom with mac and cheese that we'd try to ease information out of her rather than pull her fingernails out with pliers and demand it—we had no pliers—Fantasy stopped dead in her tracks. Mango ran into her. Fantasy whipped around and got in her face again. "Do you know where we are, Mango? Are we in Texas?"

Mango started blubbering about grasshoppers and windmills.

And the truth was, knowing where we were at that exact moment wouldn't help us survive where we were, so we went back to surviving.

We hiked the beach. And don't get the wrong idea. It isn't gentle turquoise water lapping white sand. The tide is brutal, the water loud and cold slapping coarse brown sand absolutely carpeted in shells, at least eight or ten inches deep, like walking on glass, and littered with dead fish. When the water isn't rolling, we can see huge schools of jellyfish and stingrays. Every fifty feet or so we have to dodge or climb black scaly rock formations. Nothing about this barrier island is pretty or anywhere near it. Girl Scout Fantasy has determined the island is a little more than a mile wide and could be up to ten miles long. We hiked a full seven miles of beach today, again according to Girl Scout Fantasy. It felt more like seventy miles there and back, because I'm wearing men's golf shoes with the sleeves of the dress I was wearing yesterday stuffed in the toes. After all that, we didn't find the end. Of the island. If we're still here tomorrow, we're going to try to hike the opposite beach and figure out where we are, which we dread. We dread it because, over Mango's protests, who for some reason absolutely didn't want to go that way, we ventured there this morning and found, first with our noses, a twenty-foot-long shark carcass in various stages of decomposition, depending on which end of the shark you were standing near (TERRIFYING and SMELLS JUST LIKE A TWENTY-FOOT-LONG DEAD SHARK SHOULD SMELL LIKE) (although the seagulls loved it), blocking our access to that beach. Bradley, it was so blown up we couldn't even see over it. To get to that beach, we'd have to climb over the dead shark.

HAVE YOU EVER?

We weren't that close, but I backed up anyway, covering my nose and mouth with the smelly golf shirt, I said, "How dead is that shark?"

Fantasy, backing up too, said, "Very."

Then I said, "I wonder how long it's been here."

Mango, who was at least ten feet behind us and turned the other way said, "Six weeks."

Fantasy and I shared a quick glance, waiting for Mango to realize she'd given us valuable information, that she was on this island six weeks ago. To get more out of her, keeping my voice conversational and steady, I said, "I wonder how it died."

Mango immediately answered. "Old age."

Fantasy was closest to her. She got in her face. "How do you know that?"

In her small voice, the one she used to weasel out of the compromising positions she kept putting herself in, she said, "Did you know you count a shark's age like you count a tree's? By the rings on its vertebrae?"

I jumped in. "How did you know this dead shark was here?"

She said, "I didn't."

"I think you did," I said. "This dead shark is why you tried to talk us out of coming this way today. You knew it was here because you've been here before."

Fantasy moved in. "Start talking, Mango."

Mango ran off screaming that if we wanted to go down that beach, have at it. But she wanted nothing to do with the dead shark. Then she yelled, "DID YOU KNOW THERE ARE MORE THAN THREE THOUSAND KEYBOARD SHORTCUTS?" Then, "DID YOU KNOW A DETOUR IS A ROUNDABOUT ROUTE TO AVOID SOMETHING?"

I took that to mean she wanted to find a way down the dead shark beach that didn't involve the dead shark.

She might be crazy, Bradley.

Why not fire up the doublewide and drive over the dead shark? The most disgusting roadkill situation you could ever imagine? For one, the dead shark is bigger than the doublewide, if you can even believe that. For two, the crazy golfer took the keys. Why don't we hotwire the doublewide? Because there's nowhere to go. We can't drive on water and we'd make it ten feet on this terrain. There are no roads. Or signs of human life. Or power. Or water. Or people. Birds, more birds, and even more birds, bugs, more bugs, and even more bugs, dead fish, more dead fish, and even more dead fish, all the way to the biggest dead fish you could ever imagine. But no Starbucks. No air conditioning. NO PHONES. We have a dead shark and we might have a mountain. And by mountain, I mean we can see elevation in the distance, almost in what could be the middle of the island, but we don't know what's up there or how to get to it. We've determined that this island was, at some point, ravaged by a storm, and what we're calling a mountain is most likely where everything landed. My feet look like they've been ravaged by men's golf shoes. And I want them to land at HOME, but instead, they landed back at the doublewide.

We filed in the door, blazing hot, and listen to this: Mango went straight to the refrigerator. She yanked open the door and almost climbed in. She waved the door, back and forth, fanning herself with cold refrigerator air. Fantasy and I stood there looking at her in disbelief.

"Mango," I said.

She'd flipped around, holding her silver hair off her neck with one hand, cooling her backside. She was practically sitting in the refrigerator. "What?" Wide-eyed. "Do you want a turn?"

"No," I said. "We've been over this already. We need to conserve whatever generator juice we have for cooking mac and cheese."

"Then we should turn off the refrigerator," she said.

"We tried that yesterday," Fantasy said. "Remember?" (After we found the refrigerator and took inventory—yellow mustard and olives so old they were furry—we looked for a plug. So we could unplug it. And conserve power.) (We couldn't find a plug.) (And the fridge was wedged in there so tight we couldn't even fit a golf club between the fridge and the walls to pull it out and get to the plug.) (Mango watched the whole unplug-the-refrigerator show without saying a word.) Then, a whole day later, she said, "Did you know in Pennsylvania it's illegal to sleep outdoors in a refrigerator?"

"Do you know how to unplug this refrigerator?" Fantasy asked.

"Do you know where the generator is?" I asked.

Mango, looking as innocent as the day was long, shrugged.

Fantasy and I stomped out the front door, both on another generator search and to get away from Mango for a minute. We nosed around the exterior of the doublewide long enough to calm down and find the generator in a basement compartment much like the one we were stuffed in yesterday, but this one in the back, behind the spare tire, and square, as opposed to rectangular. We tossed the tire, which was flat anyway, to find the generator and the propane tank fueling it. Trust me, Bradley, there's nowhere to refill the tank when it runs out. And it's not like we could see inside to know how much propane was in it. Back in the doublewide, because the bugs were eating us alive, and considering it looked like we would be spending a second night there, we found Mango where we'd left her. In the open refrigerator door. I gave her a nudge, closed the refrigerator door, and said, "We found the generator."

She said, "Did you know it's easier to find your car keys than the television remote?" I said, "If you know how to turn off the refrigerator, we'd really appreciate it." She said, "Did you know the average life of a new refrigerator is twelve years?" Fantasy said, "Your average life is going to be twelve more minutes if you don't tell us how to unplug this refrigerator."

Mango must have believed her. She held up a finger, pushed past us, crawled under my bed, which is to say between the driver and passenger seats up front, then clicked one of the four hundred black buttons on the dash.

See, Bradley? She knows this doublewide. In addition to being his girlfriend analytical research caddie and knowing there was a dead shark, did she live in the doublewide too? Does she have an extra pair of shoes back in that bedroom? Instead of asking her that, I tried to catch her completely off guard. "Mango, when is he coming back?" I swear to you, Bradley, she opened her mouth to accidentally answer me, then changed her mind. "Did you know boomerangs were invented by Aboriginal hunters to disable animals? They don't come back. They were never meant to come back." Fantasy said, "Are you saying he's not coming back?" She said, "Did you know that when people return home from vacation the thing they look forward to most is water pressure they're familiar with?"

This is no vacation.

This could be war. With Mango.

I said, "Mango, what's going on here? You knew about the shark and you know your way around the doublewide. What else do you know? It's time to come clean. Just tell us."

She ran off screaming.

I turned to Fantasy. "She knows where we are and why we're here."

She said, "Davis, she smelled the shark before we did, and she found the right button to turn off the refrigerator. Past that, she knows how many ladybugs it takes to change a lightbulb and that's it."

"As soon as she goes to sleep, we're going to turn this place upside down again to find what we missed yesterday."

Fantasy surveyed our fifty square feet. "What could we have possibly missed?"

"Something," I said, "and Mango's not talking."

"What secrets do you think she's keeping from us?"

"Like I said, where we are and why we're here."

"If she knows all that, Davis, why wouldn't she just tell us?"

"Because she wants us to figure it out on our own."

"Davis, she's busy trying to figure out how many pineapples it takes to reach the moon. But if you want to rip this place apart again, have at it. Maybe you'll find a television remote."

"Maybe I'll find something that leans toward the how and why of it all, and maybe that will lead us home."

"And maybe pigs really can fly."

While we wait for pigs to fly, we intend to conserve the generator propane. Nowhere nearly as hard as we're trying to conserve the water. (We still can't find the water tank. Mango swears she has no idea.) (She's probably lying.) Let's put it this way: we're trying to conserve everything until you rescue us.

No pressure, but it's really hard to believe you haven't found and tracked Fantasy's car, which would lead to the crazy golfer's doublewide parking space at Golden Oaks, which would lead to paperwork with his real name, which might lead to WHEREVER WE ARE.

I love you.

Bellissimo Resort and Casino Offering $1,000,000 for a Used Volvo

BY NELSON MILLER
GULF COAST HERALD SENIOR STAFF REPORTER
Sunday, May 10, 9:35 p.m.

The Bellissimo Resort and Casino is offering a cool million dollars for a used car, but not just any used car. They want Fantasy Erb's used car. And they're willing to pay $1,000,000 for it. Cash. Turn in the Volvo, collect your cash, no questions asked, then go buy yourself a Volvo dealership.

What a deal.

The Volvo they want was last seen at Golden Oaks Golf Club prior to the abduction of Bianca Casimiro Sanders, Fantasy Erb, and an unidentified female caddie. It's a 2016 XC90, white with beige interior, Mississippi vehicle registration plate number J7R-5711, VIN number YX7B88QR2J3847209, and was last seen tearing across the ninth hole at Golden Oaks six hours after the women's disappearance. Evidence indicates the Volvo was hidden in the woods behind the fourteenth hole sometime between when the women disappeared and when the Volvo tore up the course hours later. That's all the bad news. The worse news is the GPS tracking on the Volvo has been disabled. So don't bother logging on, hacking Volvo, then entering the data to look for the blinking dot. The million dollars will have to be earned the old-fashioned way, by actually finding the Volvo. Show up at the Bellissimo with it or news leading directly to its current location and $1,000,000 cash will be yours.

Happy Volvo hunting, Biloxi, and you'd better hurry, because the We Know Whodunnit book club at Caring Star Senior Center is on the prowl for it too. Good luck, Mom.

Day Two Still or Maybe Already Day Three
Which I'm Having A Hard Time Processing
(That We're Still Here)

Dear Bradley,

I'm writing to you by moonlight through a window the size of a postage stamp. There's a map light in my bunk that runs off the battery, or maybe the generator, but like I told you before, we don't want to waste generator fuel, which is secondary to THE MOSQUITOES. To flip on the map light might be to send a beacon to the one mosquito separated from his million mosquito friends who already know where we are. This barrier island is home to prehistoric, scary big, pelican-like wingspan mosquitoes. They found us as we were eating our mac and cheese dinner under the bullet-riddled awning of the doublewide (retractable) (Mango showed us how to crank it out) (for sure, she lived here with him) and now we're covered, head to toe, in mosquito bites. If we aren't rescued during the night, we plan to stay in the doublewide at dawn for as long as we can and be back inside before dusk to avoid them. (That's Plan B. Plan A is to be out of here before dawn breaks again.) I don't know which is worse, the mosquitoes or the suffocating heat and humidity inside the doublewide with no air and the windows closed, because there are no screens. And the reason I'm not trying to sleep through the sauna is because I can't fall asleep before I tell you what we found.

As soon as we heard Mango's first sound-barrier-breaking snore, we started tossing the doublewide from the cracked windshield to the (locked) bedroom door. We still don't know the crazy golfer's real name, and Mango claims she doesn't know it either, although somehow she knows everything else. (She told us, apropos of nothing, that otters have favorite rocks. They store them in little pouches in their arms.) Our second search, more thorough than our walk-through yesterday, still didn't turn up registration for the doublewide with his name on it, proof of insurance, or a Costco Membership card. What we found was Bianca. We found storage under the bench seat, a panel on the base that slid open. Fantasy had been sleeping on top of all manner of uselessness, including a broken toaster oven, a weather radio that didn't help a bit, because it had no batteries, more golf garbage, a filthy moldy blow-up mattress that looked like it might fit my bunk (no, thank you), a crumbling Rand McNally 1961 Road Atlas (like that would do us any good), and a dossier on Bianca inside a cheap metal lockbox. We had nothing to pick the lock with, so we smashed it off with a golf club, and inside found Bianca. Articles, feature stories, a hundred photographs (ninety-nine of them me, not her), newspaper clippings about the Bellissimo going all the way back to Bianca's father buying the land, the construction, and the ribbon cutting. Bradley, did you know it was a short sale? Did you know (I SOUND LIKE MANGO) Bianca's father, Salvatore, bought the land he built the Bellissimo on out of bankruptcy from a railroad company on the courthouse steps for pennies? (Well, millions of pennies, but considering it was ten miles of Gulf waterfront, he paid ludicrously less than it was worth.) In the middle of all that, we found a Gulf Coast Herald feature story about Bianca shyly suggesting she has a celebrity double by boldly applauding her for seemingly being two places at once. (The article ran in the Gulf Coast Herald about two months ago and included photos with time stamps of Bianca boarding a Bellissimo jet in Gulfport at noon, and me, posing as Bianca, attending a noon-oh-five ribbon cutting for the new children's wing at the art museum in downtown Biloxi. Remember? I showed it to you.) It was written by Nelson Miller. You know him. Casino Nelson. The guy always saying hi to his mother? The guy I tell you all the time we should hire because he's onto us but never outright exposes us? How many times have I told you he knows who Fantasy and I are and he suspects Bianca has a celebrity double? That man knows the Bellissimo has behind-the-curtain security, he's always alluding to it, he knows about our team (although he only posts the occasional picture of Baylor, never me or Fantasy, which is more proof he doesn't want to expose us), and I tell you all the time he writes to us between the lines. Is it even possible the crazy golfer, or more likely Mango, read between the lines too?

The crazy golfer doesn't seem that sharp to me, and maybe I'm saying that because the man is a PIG. You should see how he lives. Mango, on the other hand, seems that sharp in a very convoluted way. So where are we? Literally and figuratively NOWHERE. Except for this—all the intel on Bianca stopped six weeks ago.

Stay with me, Bradley.

Everything in the dossier came to an abrupt halt six weeks ago. All the Bianca intel just stopped. I can place the general dates of the photographs because most of them are really me. And I remember every one. And they're all more than six weeks old. Nothing in my (Bianca's) immediate past. What point am I trying to make? I think the crazy golfer, or way more likely Mango, put two and two together six weeks ago. I'm more convinced than ever that one or both of them knew exactly who they were adultnabbing.

It would help a lot to know the crazy golfer's real name. Maybe I'd recognize it. Maybe it would make me feel better. I've tried to pry it out of Mango ten different ways. I came right out and asked her during dinner as we were swatting mammoth mosquitoes. "Mango?" She looked up from her mac and cheese. Her eyes were a little buggy. And bloodshot. "What's Crazy Golfer Finn's real name?" She slapped her arm and took out ten gargantuan mosquitoes, then said, "Did you know John is the most popular name in the English language, and there are variants of it in seven other languages?"

She knows his name and she's not telling.

What does all this mean, Bradley? It means my arm is about to fall off from writing you, and it means that Mango may very well have stumbled across something big in her analytical research six weeks ago.

"Davis." (Fantasy whispered even though Mango had been snoring for more than an hour.) "Mango is as dumb as a fencepost. If she stumbled across anything big it was a big fencepost."

I said to her what I'm saying to you, "I think she found something so big that she cut Crazy Golfer Finn off six weeks ago." I shook the Bianca evidence. "She stopped feeding him information."

"Why would she do that?"

"So she could keep whatever it was she found to herself."

"What are you suggesting?"

"I'm suggesting Mango's the reason we're here. She needs us on this island, Fantasy."

"For WHAT?"

"I don't know yet."

But I'm working on it.

Hard.

It could have something to do with Mango's constant, "Let's go this way. Let's go that way." She's looking for something on this island, and rather than tell us what it is, she wants us to find it.

(Find WHAT?)

My goal is to live long enough to work it all the way out. If I'm right, Mango navigated us to this vicious barrier island for a reason. But what reason? None of this will matter when Bianca hears what happened to her dress. She'll hunt me down. And then we'll be rescued.

Authorities in Theodore, Alabama Search for Missing Biloxi Women

BY NELSON MILLER
GULF COAST HERALD SENIOR STAFF REPORTER
Monday, May 11, 6:14 a.m.

In what could be considered the first major lead in the search for three Biloxi women abducted from Golden Oaks Golf Course Saturday, local authorities responded to a call from Fay Gilliam, Pilot Travel Center manager on Theodore Dawes Road in Theodore, Alabama, southwest of Mobile, where the tulle skirt of an Oscar de la Renta® cocktail dress was found in the parking lot near an RV pump station behind the store. It is believed to be a portion of the same dress worn by Bianca Casimiro Sanders at the time of her disappearance. The thirty-inch skirt, without the bodice, is black tulle, embellished with sequins, and features a painted floral motif. The skirt is silk lined. The dress retails (intact) for $6,990. Ms. Gilliam is in negotiations with the Bellissimo Resort and Casino to keep the skirt. "Finders keepers, I say," said Ms. Gilliam. "What's anybody going to do with half a dress? It's ripped all to hell and back. I'm going to piece it back together and make it a princess costume for my granddaughter after the police get through with it and give it back to me 'cause I'm the one who found it."

Considerable search and rescue efforts for the missing Biloxi women are now being redirected to south Alabama. Mom, keep your seat. Remember the last time you and the We Know Whodunnits took a field trip to Alabama? The day you were supposed to be shopping at Springdale Mall? And you drank Frozen Mudslides at Applebee's all day instead?

Forty Hours

Dear Bradley,

I'm the only one awake. It's just before daylight if the sleeping birds are to be believed, and out the tiny window above my head for the second morning in a row I don't hear the buzz of helicopters and don't see spotlights searching for us along the beach. I think I slept. I'm pretty sure I slept at least two hours. And that's out of the two thousand hours we've been here.

Why haven't we been rescued?

Maybe it's only been forty hours or so, but an hour here is like a hundred normal hours, and what I'm so struck by this morning is how, in forty hours, everything I knew is gone. Everything has been taken away. You, our babies, my dog, my family, my home, my job, my world. Life, as I know it, feels over. Past thinking about you, about our daughters, our home, family, and friends, more and more, my mind goes to the little things. What I wouldn't give for a hot shower. What I wouldn't give for news. (Is the national news covering our disappearance?) What I wouldn't give for a cup of coffee. What I wouldn't give to sit on the floor of Bex and Quinn's playroom while they play grocery store. What I wouldn't give to GO to the grocery store. The freedom of pushing a grocery cart around the grocery store. Maybe my grocery store references are more about me being hungry than anything else. Do you have any idea how long it's been since I was truly hungry? Neither do I. I can identify with the idea of hunger and can conjure up the distant memory of being hungry, but looking back on the truly privileged life I've lived, I've never known real hunger.

Until now.

Two days of not being rescued has us at the point of conserving not only the power and water, but the mac and cheese too. Twice yesterday we split one box three ways. Today, who knows. One box three ways? Between us, no one really knows how to fish, and it's not like there are fishing rods and a *Fishing for Dummies* book in the doublewide. We won't wade out into the water to catch a fish with our saucepan—as if a fish is going to swim into a saucepan—because of the huge schools of jellyfish and stingrays in the water we're close to and the shark carcass blocking our access to the water we're not close to. At some point, I guess we'll have to get in the water, because exploring is messy work. And we're not going to use what fresh water we have to take showers in what the doublewide thinks is a shower stall, which is nothing but a showerhead the size of a lemon over a bathroom sink the size of an orange in a bathroom the size of a grapefruit that hasn't been cleaned in ten years. I'd rather take my chances bathing with the stingrays. If it gets to that.

All that to say we haven't been fishing.

Girl Scout Fantasy used golf clubs to build a crab trap on the beach before we went to bed last night. She says we're having wild crab mac and cheese tonight.

The few crabs we've seen look positively prehistoric.

No, thank you.

I'm not that hungry.

Yet.

I wonder if, in the end, I'll have to stuff the book I'm writing you on takeout menus into a bottle and send it out to sea. I'm putting that on my scavenger hunt list today, a bottle to stuff takeout menu love letters in.

I see the first traces of what will be daylight, Fantasy will surely wake up soon, and Mango must already be awake because the doublewide walls aren't shaking. Today's plan is to get closer to whatever it is we can see in the middle of the island, gather information from Mango on the way—what, exactly, did Crazy Golfer hire her to research?—and gather brush and wood on the way back for a bonfire. If you or the Coast Guard or Rescue at Sea or even the crazy golfer isn't waiting for us at the doublewide at the end of the day, we're building a fire on the beach tonight. A big fire. Big enough to burn all night. We want someone, anyone, YOU to see us.

Does Pine Apple know I'm missing yet? Are my parents okay? Are they frantic?

I love you.

Vulnerable Persons Alert Issued for Bianca Casimiro Sanders

BY NELSON MILLER
GULF COAST HERALD SENIOR STAFF REPORTER
Monday, May 11, 10:55 a.m.

In addition to the Missing Persons Alert already issued for Bianca Casimiro Sanders, wife of Bellissimo Resort and Casino owner Richard Sanders, last seen at Golden Oaks Golf Course in Biloxi almost forty-eight hours ago at the time of this post, the National Crime Information Center (NCIC) in conjunction with the FBI's Kidnapped and Missing Persons Division, and after reaching out to known associates of Mrs. Sanders, have determined her "psychologically unstable" and "mentally unable to protect herself or those with her." As a result, Mrs. Sanders is now deemed vulnerable by authorities, meaning, in simple terms, a danger to herself and others. The determination was concluded after authorities turned to social media outlets for help in locating Mrs. Sanders and the two women believed to be with her. Almost immediately the authorities were inundated with information regarding Mrs. Sanders's precarious mental stability. It should be noted that the medical professionals weighing in do not personally know Mrs. Sanders, rather they represent her former employees, associates, and shockingly, extended family members. Her current team of medical professionals most decidedly do not agree, describing Mrs. Sanders as "misunderstood," citing "jealousy" and "retribution" as factors in the "smear campaign" against Mrs. Sanders they are calling "fake news." Although with so many stepping forward to question Mrs. Sanders's mental health, the authorities are taking no chances and want the public to know the danger for Mrs. Sanders and those with her is greater than originally believed. With this development, fearing the worst, police and federal agents are begging for the public's help with information regarding her whereabouts. If you have information, it is imperative you contact authorities immediately.

"I could give you a million examples of how unequipped Bianca Sanders is to process her current situation," said Dr. Magdala Barrios, Clinical Psychologist at Biloxi Memorial and therapist of record to a long list of Mrs. Sanders's many former (unnamed) personal assistants. "Across the board, my patients suffer from severe post-traumatic stress disorder in addition to anxiety, depression, and ongoing anger-management issues after being in Mrs. Sanders's employ. We're talking about a woman (Bianca Sanders) who once chartered an international flight on a private luxury jet to dump a third-generation American manicurist of Asian descent in the middle of a Cambodian jungle as punishment over a fingernail filed too short. It could have been a thumbnail," Dr. Barrios said, "I'd have to check my records." When asked how she thought Bianca Sanders might be reacting to the life-threatening circumstances authorities believe her to be in, Dr. Barrios said, "There's no telling how she's handling it or what she'll do. My advice to the authorities is to identify the person or persons behind the kidnapping immediately and protect him, her, they, or it. Because Bianca Sanders could very well be capable of ripping that person or those persons to absolute shreds with her bare hands."

In stark contrast, authorities are also sorting through the wealth of information pouring in defending Mrs. Sanders, including that from a woman claiming to be her "very best girlfriend" who is now being sought for questioning by the authorities. Beatrice Crawford, female, sixty, from Pine Apple, Alabama, said moments ago in an interview on NBC's *Today Show*, "She's [Bianca Sanders] a little bit hoity-toity, I'll give you that, but underneath it all, she's a good old girl. Hell, I stayed in her home not long ago. Slept in her big white bed. How crazy is a person who lets her best girlfriend sleep in her big white bed? I'll tell you how crazy," Mrs. Crawford said, "not a bit crazy. Bianca might be a lot of things, like rude and way too skinny with a big stick up her [deleted], but she's not crazy. Now, don't ask my ex-ex-daughter-in-law, Davis, about her, because she'll tell you Bianca's crazy as [deleted]. Which isn't true. At the end of the day, Bianca's no different than me or you. Especially me. She wants the finest things in life. Just like me. And when you hang out with Bianca, you get the finest things in life too. When you eat at her place, she doesn't even have salt and pepper shakers. Her salt and pepper's in teensy little glass bowls with little baby silver spoons. Cutest thing I've ever seen. And the butter at her house is little pats shaped like shells. They look just like little ruffly seashells. First time I saw them I thought they were fancy rich people candy. Ate the whole bowl. Turns out they were butter. You stab them with a little silver flat fork. Maybe it's a little silver flat spoon. Whatever, Bianca's one of my best girlfriends in the world. And let me tell the [deleted expletive] lowlife who took her, I'm coming for you, buddy. Run and hide, [censored expletive]. You don't treat Bea Crawford's friends like that."

48 Hours

Dear Bradley,

As best I can tell, it's the forty-eight-hour mark. Please don't pay the ransom. We've been left here to die. And paying the ransom won't do anything but make whoever's behind this rich. If we're going to be saved, we're going to have to save ourselves. We're going to save ourselves by building a raft. You should see the blueprints Fantasy has going on Taco Bell napkins. Wish us luck. Ahoy, Matey.

I love you.

Biloxi Casinos to Temporarily Close

NEWS PROVIDED FOR IMMEDIATE RELEASE BY
BILOXI GAMING COMMISSION
BILOXI/Monday, May 11, 11:45 a.m./PRNewswire

At the behest of Bellissimo Resort and Casino's President and CEO Bradley Cole, in an effort to redirect cash on hand, staff, and resources to assist in the ongoing search and rescue efforts for Bellissimo's Bianca Casimiro Sanders and two other women who were abducted from Golden Oaks Golf Course on Saturday, Biloxi casinos will temporarily close. Casinos participating in Operation #FINDHER include Bellissimo Resort and Casino, Boomtown Casino, Foxwoods Casino, Golden Nugget Biloxi, Hard Rock Hotel and Casino, Harrah's Gulf Coast, IP Casino Resort Spa, Palace Casino Resort, and Treasure Bay Casino and Hotel. All heartily agreed to temporarily cease operations effective at midnight tomorrow, May 12, until the women are found and/or until further notice. Cash Cow Casino, located behind Walmart Neighborhood Market on Ellzey Drive, cast the single dissenting vote. Cash Cow General Manager, Vice President of Marketing, Slot Technician, and Holy Cow! Hot Cook Jimmy-John Jones said, "Ya'll bring your money and come on here. We don't even know that lady." In response, Biloxi Gaming Commissioner Lynne Jamison said, "Use your best judgment, Biloxi. Use your best judgment." During this temporary closure, reservations at all participating properties will be cancelled and guests will receive full refunds for any hotel deposits in addition to generous complimentary casino-play vouchers upon reopening.

Any casino guests in the area affected by the temporary closures and willing to help in the search and rescue efforts, please contact a casino host at any Biloxi casino. (With the exception of Cash Cow.)

Way Past 48 Hours

Dear Bradley,

It's sunset.

Which makes it fifty-two hours since we were abducted.

It feels like fifty-two years.

If you paid the ransom to the crazy golfer, he must not have disclosed our location. Because helicopters. You'd be in one by now.

If you didn't pay the ransom, I'm proud of you for having faith in me. Part of me is worried you did pay it and No Hair put a bullet between the crazy golfer's eyes before he could tell you where we were, but a bigger part of me thinks Baylor has figured it all out and will be here any minute.

I'll tell you about our day while I wait.

Instead of ripping the roof off the doublewide to use for our raft, which was a much better idea last night than it was this morning, we decided to use island supplies to build our raft. Which meant traversing the nasty island again. We were better at navigating the shell beach today, got farther faster, and while we didn't find a single thing that would help us build a raft, we found a bay. It's a horrible bay, we think it might have been a port a long time ago, and that would mean at some point there was something on this island. Evidence suggests that wherever we are wasn't always the ravaged wilderness it is now. And that evidence is the bay with the port.

We know which beach is the north side of the island and which is the south. East and west are easy because of the sun. Girl Scout Fantasy said so. I think she's good at this nature business because she has three sons, and by good, I mean better than me, and I'm a hundred times better at it than Mango, who is debilitatingly terrified of the dead shark, and the live fish, and everything else ocean, so that's where we are on the survival scale.

Fantasy's flip-flops died.

They no longer flip or flop.

She's barefoot now.

We have another pair of crazy golfer shoes, but they're woolly inside, like science experiment woolly, and an odd shade of green. Fantasy said no thanks. Where was I? North and south. It's this easy: the waves and wind and shells are hitting the south side of the island. So that's south. The more time we spend exploring, the more we can see that the constant battering from the ocean and storms have actually pushed this island to the north. Everything is leaning north, and I think it's to protect the landmass north of us—wish I knew which landmass that might be—and all that's to say at the end of this long day, I have an entirely new respect for barrier islands. Because this one has saved whatever is north of it many brutal beatings. This island stands guard for the mainland. Storms hit here first and soften the blow for it. Which makes me wonder why people build on barrier islands. Wouldn't the barrier islands provide better protection if they weren't developed? For instance, Alabama's Dauphin Island. Did you know (I SOUND LIKE MANGO AGAIN) Dauphin Island's nickname is Unluckiest Island in America? It's like a bowling alley. Every storm in the Gulf hits Dauphin first, like a wrecking ball, and knocks everything down. Then the residents rebuild and rebuild and rebuild. (Why wouldn't they? Our government pays them to rebuild.) Right here and right now it feels crazy to me. Dauphin needs to be like this barrier island. Left alone. So it can protect Alabama's coast. And I wish I hadn't gone down this borderline environmentalist road, Bradley, because now I want to go to Lighthouse Bakery on Dauphin Island so bad I can't breathe. I want a pot of coffee, two huge sandwiches, and three dozen glazed donuts. Or maybe it's just that I'm thinking of home. I might be thinking about Alabama because I'm worried about my family. Which is a much closer-to-my-heart subject than barrier islands. And that's not to say sandwiches aren't a close-to-my-heart subject. Right now, they really are.

Back to barrier islands, because thoughts of sandwiches aren't helping.

This barrier island has taken such a beating that there's not much left of it. But at least we know north from south, which tells us which way to swim home so we don't end up in Mexico. When we figured all this out, I stood still and faced north, because I knew that's where you and the girls were. Fantasy snapped me out of it. She said, "On the off chance you're right, Davis, and Mango has some secret agenda, I say we tie her up, take her into custody, then interrogate her."

"How are we supposed to do that?" I asked. "Flash our badges and cuff her? We don't have badges or handcuffs. For that matter, what are we going to tie her up with? Dish towels?"

"There are two of us and one of her."

That was true, but Mango didn't have her head on exactly straight. And I couldn't see where bullying information out of her would help our cause. She doesn't know how to answer a direct question. So why not dig the information out of her piecemeal? And what information did we want? I'll tell you, Bradley. We wanted to know if it was his or her intent to adultnab Bianca or me and Fantasy. We wanted to know if he or she knew that Bianca and I were, at times, one and the same. We wanted to know what his or her huge interest in the Bellissimo was, specifically regarding the land purchase and what the old railroad company had to do with it. But mostly, we want to know why we're here. This horrible island here. This wilderness. Was this just a dump site where no one would find us? (Mission, so far, accomplished.) Or—what I am believing more and more—is there something on this island past the dead fish, sandpipers, seagulls, pelicans, seaweed, marsh grass, and sand dunes that Mango knows about from her research, but can't find? And she thinks Fantasy and I can?

"Which one do we want more, Fantasy?" I asked. "Information out of Mango or off this island?"

Off the island was the runaway winner.

She agreed to back off Mango.

Mango kept up with us on the way out for Day Two of our island tour but dragged her feet so hard on the way back we had to keep turning around and waiting on her until we figured out she was finally far enough away from us that we could talk about her without her hearing and without us trying to whisper about her in the dark over her snores. And it wasn't bothering me a bit that Mango kept taking five, plopping down where she stood, because the trivia on the way out was overwhelming. We thought we saw bananas. (They weren't bananas.) Mango said, "Did you know bananas are curved because they grow toward the sun?" Which made me think about Frosted Flakes and Fantasy think about banana splits, because she said, "If we don't get off this island, I'm going to miss my brother-in-law's birthday party. And I'm in charge of the banana split bar." Mango said, "Did you know you are fourteen times more likely to die on your birthday than any other day of the year?" We were all but attacked by a huge colony of white herons who thought we were food. There were thousands of them, Bradley. They came out of nowhere, and there were so many of them flying at us so fast that for an instant they blocked the sun. We hit the beach (we hit the shells), covered our heads, and screamed. When they finally realized we weren't crayfish and flew away, while Fantasy and I were still trying to breathe, Mango said, "Did you know all seabirds have built in sunglasses to filter the glare from the water and sand?"

It was maddening.

Fantasy and I had a really good Mango talk when we finally got back to the doublewide. The plan was to start gathering wood in earnest for what we are now calling our rescue bonfire, which we decided would be a lot easier than building a raft for which we have absolutely no tools or materials, but Mango called in sick. She said she had a headache and needed a nap.

Fantasy and I watched her drag into the doublewide. As soon as she'd cleared and closed the door, I said, "She doesn't want to help with our rescue fire because she doesn't want to be rescued until her mission is accomplished."

"What mission is that, Davis?"

"I don't know yet."

"Please fill me in when you do."

"She has the bedroom, Fantasy."

She said, "So?"

I said, "What's she doing in that bedroom with the door locked?"

Fantasy said. "If you're right and she knew we were headed here, she might've stockpiled supplies. She's probably in there eating enchiladas and brushing her teeth and drinking wine is what she's doing." (All at the same time?) "We need in that bedroom, Davis. The minute she starts snoring, we're storming in and taking her down."

"So you believe me?" I asked.

"I don't believe you at all, but I want her enchiladas," she answered. "And I'm sick to death of Mango."

"I thought we agreed we'd go easy on her until we figure this out."

"We did not agree to go easy on Mango until we figured this out, Davis. You agreed to go easy on Mango. I agreed to take her ass down."

"Then let me get our plastic spoons, because they're the only weapons we have."

That made her a little testy.

"We don't need a weapon to ambush her, Davis. Then we restrain her. Then we eat her enchiladas. I don't think she'll be a bit of help figuring any of this out unless we want to figure out rubber bands." (Mango told us rubber bands last longer if you keep them cool and dry.) "Or roller coasters." (Mango told us riding Big Thunder Mountain at Disneyworld could dislodge kidney stones.) "Or lamps." (She told us no two lava lamps were the same.) (WHO CARES?) "Face it, Davis," Fantasy said. "She's the enemy."

"Fantasy." Somehow, we were nose-to-nose. Had we been wearing clothes with sleeves—we were barely wearing clothes at all—we'd have pushed them up. "She knows way more than she's telling. You know she knows his real name and she won't even tell us that.

We're on this island for a reason, Mango knows the reason, and we need to ease it out of her before we declare outright war."

Which sent Fantasy over the testy edge to outright cranky. (Not that I was in a good mood.) "We know the reason. Do you not remember what we found last night, Davis? Bianca. Intel on Bianca. Why are you trying to make this bigger than it is? Why are you looking for the reason behind the reason? The only reason we're here is Bianca. Ransom for kidnapping Bianca and nothing else."

She had a point. Her case was strong. But so was mine. While Fantasy believed we were dumped here for Bianca ransom money and only Bianca ransom money, I believe we were dumped here for a more specific reason. And two of the dumpees taking the third dumpee hostage wouldn't get us any closer to the reason.

"I'll agree not to kill her, Davis, if you'll agree we need in that bedroom."

"Believe me," I said. "I want in that bedroom too. She's hiding something in there."

"Enchiladas."

"Tomorrow, we'll tell her it's our turn for the bedroom. And not take no for an answer."

Fantasy said, "And drink her wine."

Somewhere in there, although I didn't notice when, we'd plopped down in the sand. Which was a mistake. You know when you're so bone tired but aren't finished yet and have to keep going or you'll lose momentum? We sat down and lost momentum. And that was when the mosquitos swarmed. Momentum or not, we had to stop. We did not build our rescue bonfire, but earlier we found what used to be a bay, and maybe a port, and that was our victory of the day. From what we could see, the bay was in front of the elevation in the middle of the island we already knew about, but we couldn't get to whatever it was from the south. Bradley, it's like the bay we found has been the Gulf's dustpan since the beginning of time and everything in the ocean that hasn't had anywhere else to go has been swept into it. We couldn't even identify half of what we could see from the beach. We think there's a tidal pool back there, a strong tidal pool, too strong for us to dare try to swim it, and even if we could, we'd hit a fifty-foot jungle wall we'd have no way to climb. Have you ever heard of a jungle wall on a barrier island? Neither have I. We're not here to find the jungle wall, because it's too out in the open. Bex and Quinn could find it. Whatever is past the jungle wall could very well be why we're here. Because I truly believe Mango had a heavy hand in our adultnabbing, if not single-handedly orchestrating it, because she wants us to find something she can't. The pot of gold at the end of Mango's rainbow. Or in this case, at the end of the uninhabited barrier island. Our new plan, formulated in the doublewide over mac and cheese with two packets of mild taco seasoning, which we split two ways, because Mango said she wasn't hungry and for us to have at it, and we were hungry enough to do just that, is to hike the north beach tomorrow—hello, huge dead shark— and if we can't talk Mango into it, fine, she can have the doublewide to herself for the day. Fantasy and I will head out early enough to get back in time to build our rescue bonfire after we find what is or was inside the bay from the other side of the island. That is if you don't show up on your white horse tonight. I love and miss you so much it hurts.

Gulf Coast Herald Says Farewell to One of Our Own

BY VINCE BRUNNER
GULF COAST HERALD ASSISTANT EDITOR IN CHIEF
Monday, May 11, 10:15 p.m.

Please join us in wishing former senior staff reporter Nelson Miller our very best as he leaves to pursue other interests. Continuing coverage of the abduction of Biloxi's own Bianca Casimiro Sanders along with two other women from Golden Oaks Golf Club on Saturday will be assumed by Gulf Coast Herald intern Tiffanee Jones. Tiffanee comes to us from Chris's Beauty College in Gautier, Mississippi, where her concentration was glamour and beauty blogging. Welcome, Tiffanee!

Day Whatever
Tuesday, I think

"Why don't we try this way?"

That was Mango, this morning, who insisted on going with us when we set out for the north (DEAD SHARK) beach after a delicious breakfast of mac and cheese drizzled with Arby's Horsey Sauce, which Mango, again, declined.

Maybe she does have enchiladas in the bedroom.

What she doesn't have, that one, is stamina. After snoring for ten straight hours to my three measly hours of restless sleep, she had no energy. The island was taking its toll on her. Not that the island wasn't taking its toll on me and Fantasy.

It was.

It is.

"You need to eat, Mango." Fantasy pushed her saucer of horsey mac and cheese closer. "You need to keep up your strength."

"Have you ever heard of the Sleeping Beauty Diet?" Mango pushed the saucer of mac and cheese back. "It was Elvis's diet. He took sleeping pills and slept for days to lose weight."

"Are you saying you skipped dinner last night and you're skipping breakfast this morning to lose weight?" Fantasy asked. "Or are you saying you have sleeping pills in the bedroom?"

I raised my hand. "I could use some ZzzQuil."

"You can't sleep because you're scribbling all night," Fantasy said.

"Are you writing a book?" Mango asked. "Did you know that Theodore Roosevelt read a book a day every day?"

I couldn't sit in the stifling doublewide and listen to fascinating facts about dead presidents all day. I stood. (And banged my head on the doublewide roof in the process.) "Let's go." I took our dishes to the sink, setting Mango's mac and cheese aside for later—waste not, want not—wiped down my bowl, Fantasy's saucer, and our spoons with a damp Kentucky Fried Chicken napkin, then peeked out the dish towel curtain above the kitchen sink to take the mosquito temperature outside. The sky was orange, which meant the sun was peeking above the waterline, and there were only three mosquitoes at the window, which meant there were only three thousand at the door. We could bat our way through three thousand. I carefully filled our Waffle House coffee cups with water, not spilling a drop, pressed on the lids, and passed them out. Fantasy passed out golf clubs. "Are you sure you don't want to eat, Mango?"

She was sure, and she was the last one out the door, dragging her feet, her golf club banging down the doublewide steps behind her.

We all took deep breaths of sea air that was cooler, and there was so much more of it, than inside the hothouse doublewide.

Fantasy set out for the north beach. "Let's go, ladies."

Mango didn't move. "Why are we going that way? I don't want to climb over the dead shark. Let's go the other way."

"We're going down the shark beach," Fantasy said over her shoulder. "We've been down the shell beach twice. We don't need to go down it again."

That was when Mango said, "Why don't we try this way?"

She didn't point to either the shark or shell beaches, she pointed at the sea oats behind the doublewide. At a deep thicket of sea oats taller than me that we already knew hid a marsh, probably home to the many mosquito families feasting on us. The shells on the south beach were hard to plow through, especially considering Fantasy's barefoot and my golf-shoe situations, the shark leftovers we didn't want to go anywhere near were disgusting, but a marsh? Who wants to slog through a marsh? Because SNAKES. Because ALLIGATORS. Just BECAUSE.

Bradley, after much debate, we slogged through the marsh, our eyes peeled for gator tracks in the mud or gator air bubbles in the stagnant water, and to our surprise, we caught a break. We found something somewhat firm underfoot along the edges—yay—and there were only twenty feet or so of mid-calf disgusting muck before we were on solid ground. Yay again. We were still in muck, but only up to our ankles. We slogged through another twenty feet or so, then fought through another thick patch of sea oats, and were rewarded with a garden. Bradley, on the other side of the sea oats, past the marsh, there were enormous white waterlilies, pink morning glories, blooming yellow camphorweed, pale green sea grapes, and deep green palmetto, all on a bed of lemongrass and mint, everything growing wild and free all over itself, like a lost and confused floral heaven in the middle of hell. Your mother would have loved it. Past the botanicals, there was a stretch of flatland, and past the flatland, WE FOUND A TRAIL.

Don't get the wrong idea. It wasn't a trail-trail, with arrows pointing this way or that way with water fountains and benches in the shade, but there was a somewhat clear path, almost a straight shot, to the middle of the island. To the mountain. To whatever was behind the jungle wall. It looked way less than half the distance by beach and didn't look nearly as treacherous as the shells or as rancid as the shark, so to us, it was a trail.

At that, I got mad at Mango again. "Did you know this was here?"

"This what?" Her silver hair that wasn't hanging in her face was matted to her head.

"This shortcut."

"Did you know that most shortcuts are actually—"

Fantasy whacked through the air with her golf club and landed it with a thud at Mango's feet. "Save it," she said. "We've had enough factoids from you to last a lifetime."

"You were the one who suggested we go this way, Mango," I said. "How did you know this way was here?"

"I didn't."

Oh, yes, she did.

Fantasy looked at me like, "Let's kill her now." I looked at her like, "Because she knew there was a path? Don't you get it, Fantasy? It's additional proof she knows exactly where we are. All the more reason to NOT kill her." She looked at me like, "Maybe you have half a point," then followed up with a look at Mango like, "I've about had it with you, Trivia Queen." What was Mango doing the whole time this silent conversation was taking place? Scratching mosquito bites.

After taking a minute to determine someone might have once had a home where we were standing, a home with a garden, and a garden with what might have been a wading pool then but was a smelly marsh now, we decided it was all that and more, the that being an island plantation, the more being the pathway to a destination, and the destination being whatever was in the middle of this island.

For the millionth time since we were stuffed into the basement of the doublewide, Bradley, I wondered where in the world we were and why we'd been dumped there.

We took a good look at the terrain from A to B and gave ourselves a snake pep talk which mostly boiled down to this: we had less visibility and more ground cover than on the beach, so look before you leap. Then Mango weighed in with useless information about snake eyes, snakes in the grass, and snake oil salesmen. She finished up with, "Did you know there's an island in Brazil that's home to four thousand poisonous snakes including pit vipers?"

Fantasy raised the business end of her golf club and lined it up with Mango's nose. "Is there anything you want to say that isn't snake trivia?"

She shook her head no.

"Then shut up."

We fought our way to the bay at the base of the mountain. It was no more than two miles via our alternate route, and on an incline. Almost like climbing steps. When we finally arrived, hot, sweaty, and out of breath, we weren't at the wide mouth of the bay where we'd been the day before, but farther up, near the round cove. We made it within a hundred feet of the jungle wall. We were so close we could have bounced seashells off it. The first ten of those hundred feet between us and the wall were wildly overgrown, with what, I didn't even know, thick ropey vines of some sort, three or four feet deep above still black water. (Talk about a snake sanctuary.) Then the tropical jungle floor dropped off sharply to give way to the other ninety feet, which was more of the rolling water we saw yesterday, but from a totally different perspective. Up close and personal, we saw it was indeed the tidal whirlpool we thought it was from the south beach. We could clearly see (and hear) the swirling center. It looked like it could swallow a car. We pushed through shoulder-high scratchy trees for a better look and were rewarded with midday sun. Straight in our faces and bouncing off the jungle wall.

The wall behind the jungle was gold.

Gold, Bradley.

Not twenty-four-carat gold, not gold bricks, not a solid sheet of pure gold, because it couldn't have been real gold. (Could it?) It was more Liberace, a heavily gold-adorned wall. More Mr. T, a way overdone gold wall. It looked, honestly, very Vegas. The wall underneath the overgrowth was either gold lamé, gold leaf, or it could have been a thin sheet of gold metal covering something more solid. I think we were looking at what used to be the entrance to a gold palace.

HAVE YOU EVER?

I said, "The wall is gold."

Fantasy squinted. "The wall is a jungle."

"Behind the jungle," I said.

Fantasy golf club hacked a foot closer to stand beside me, then leaning on her golf club and shielding her eyes from the sun, said, "Still a jungle."

"You can only see it from this angle." I tugged her sleeve, she ducked her head, and I took the last step I could before falling off a cliff into the tidal pool below. And that's when I saw what looked like a pattern in the gold. "It's carved," I said. "Or something. I can see a prism of some sort." I turned around. "Mango?" She stared straight through me. "What is this geometrical shape?"

Mango blinked. That was it. She just blinked.

I told Fantasy, "This gold wall isn't here accidentally. It was placed here. Brought here. Installed here."

"How?"

"I have no idea."

"I wonder what it's worth," Fantasy said. "I wonder why someone hasn't uninstalled it."

"Because this island is off the map? No one knows it's here?"

I kept speculating, hoping Mango would toss out some revealing trivia, while Fantasy tried to golf club hack the other way, through the vines again, probably disturbing the snakes in their sanctuary, who were the only thing between us and certain tidal whirlpool death. Do you see what I'm saying, Bradley? There was no moving forward from where we were. There was no way to the gold jungle wall, so there was no way to the other side of it. The victory of the morning would have to be the garden, the trail, and that we made it closer to the jungle wall, which turned out to be a gold jungle wall, and the gold jungle wall had a shape carved into it, but we couldn't reach whatever was behind it from where we were. We'd have to find another way. While Fantasy and I were looking for just that, another way, Mango was looking for somewhere, anywhere, to sit, and she was mumbling. Fantasy turned to look at her, a good twenty feet behind us.

"What's she saying?" I whispered. "She's probably babbling about polar bears," Fantasy whispered back. PAY ATTENTION TO THIS NEXT PART, BRADLEY. IT'S PROOF MANGO KNOWS EXACTLY WHERE WE ARE. "Mango?" She looked up. "We can't hear you. What are you saying?" She mumbled, "Drop down and crawl." Fantasy said, "You drop down and crawl with the snakes, Mango." But I dropped down and crawled, scooted, rather, on my belly, in a golf shirt, scratching what was left of the dried marsh muck off the front of my legs, to the edge. What did I see? What we thought might be a port yesterday was for sure a port today. The bay was the inlet to a destination, Bradley. A destination with a gold entrance. Many millions of years ago. On the other side of the whirlpool, past the gold jungle wall, and around the debris we were too far away from to see yesterday, along the east wall of the cove, was coral. Incredible coral. I said, "Fantasy, get over here."

She got over there.

Laid out flat on the ground at the edge of a deadly abyss, we could see water on the other side that was clear enough to make out vibrant, beautiful, every color in the rainbow coral. We stared at it long enough to see the coral had a distinct shape. It had formed around what might have once been a structure, a very large, currently underwater, but probably previously above water, structure. It looked like it once may have been a massive dock.

Why would this island need a massive dock?

Because massive ships.

Let's put two and two together, Bradley.

One. At some point, this might have been a beautiful island. (It isn't now.)

Two. It looks like massive ships once docked here at the foot of a massive wall of gold.

Three. How old are cruise lines? What luxury recreational water travel was before cruise lines? Single cruise ships? I think individual cruise ships go way back. If there's a QEII there had to have been a QEI, right? And who could forget Titanic? Or the Mayflower? Back in the day, were there any privately owned cruise lines? Like pre-Norwegian and Carnival and Royal Caribbean? Have any old privately owned defunct cruise lines ever owned their own island? WHAT I WOULDN'T GIVE FOR A LITTLE GOOGLE. I said, "This was once a destination."

Behind us, Mango said, "When are we going back?"

Fantasy said, "This absolutely was a destination."

I turned my head back to yell at Mango over the roar of the tidal pool below and the screeching birds above. "How do we get behind the gold wall, Mango?"

She said, "Did you know lockjaw is caused by tetanus poisoning?"

Bradley. This was Mango's way of telling us she didn't feel well.

I'm onto her.

"What's wrong, Mango?"

She said she had a headache.

Fantasy told her we all had headaches and advised her to suck it up. Then Mango whined about being hot. Fantasy told her we were all hot. Suck that up too.

Bradley, do you remember Halloween last year? When Bex and Quinn woke up with strep throat? I knew they were sick before I ever set foot in their room. (Well, big clue, they never slept late. Other big clue, they looked sick. From the door I watched them sleeping and knew they were sick.) (Now I'm worried about the girls being sick.) (Are the girls okay?)

Back to Mango, I think if I'd been able to see her better, I'd have known she was sick. Let's talk about why I couldn't see her better.

Things in the doublewide:

1. Mac and cheese
2. Three dirty blankets
3. One dirty pillow
4. Golf junk
5. A television that doesn't work
6. A microwave that doesn't work
7. A toaster oven that doesn't work
8. A weather radio with no batteries
9. A filthy moldy blow-up mattress
10. A bottle of Tabasco so old it's brown
11. Porn
12. One threadbare, stiff, and filthy towel, several threadbare, stiff, and filthy dish towels/curtains
13. Two bowls, one saucer, six spoons, four Waffle House coffee cups, one saucepan
14. Takeout napkins from Wendy's, Zaxby's, Dunkin Donuts, and every other fast-food restaurant on the face of the earth
15. Takeout menus from Pizza Hut, Subway, Winn-Dixie's deli, and every other fast-food restaurant on the face of the earth

16. Other stupid things that aren't helping

Here's what we DON'T have:
1. Any tools, just golf clubs
2. Any weapons
3. Coffee, or a coffeepot
4. Anything resembling a first aid kit, not a single aspirin, and certainly not a thermometer
5. A hairbrush

Bradley, all morning long Mango's silver hair had been falling in her dirty face and she hadn't bothered to push it back, plus I was looking for snakes and alligators and gold walls and docks the whole time, otherwise I might have been able to look at her and see she was sick like I can look at Bex and Quinn and see they're sick. She kept staring at us but not really seeing us. Fantasy and I crawled back from the edge and sat up. "What is it, Mango?" I asked. She answered in a whisper, "Did you know Hepatitis B is the most common infectious disease in the world?" then she dropped in her tracks.

Fantasy and I scrambled her way. We stood over her. Fantasy said, "She should have eaten."

We half dragged and half carried Mango back to the doublewide. And the only thing I have to say about that is we weren't eaten by an alligator and we didn't step on a water moccasin nest, but we did see pawprints. Tiny, busy pawprints and lots of them. "There must be racoons on this island, Fantasy."

She had the front half of Mango. "What makes you say that?"

"Because racoons have thumbs," I said. "The pawprints have thumbprints."

"Mango," Fantasy said, "wake up and tell us about racoons."

She didn't.

Bradley, we think Mango has Zika virus from a rogue mosquito bite.

Life is Snappie! Buy the Stomps, Gurl!

BY TIFFANEE JONES
GULF COAST HERALD INTERN REPORTER
Tuesday, May 12, 11:00 a.m.

YOYO, Eagle Eyeballs!!! Especially Deb-Deb Gibson and her adorbs daughter, Jilly-Jills!!! Deb-Deb and Cutie Patootie Jillio stopped at a house selling their stuff in the yard in Mon Louis, Alabama, and what did they find? Can anyone guesstimate? (Hinty-hint look up!!!) Yittle Jilly, whose hobbies are finger painting, playing dress-up, and *Sesame Street*, found a Stuart Weitzman ankle strap leather sand! Guess whose spunk shoe it was?! Just guess!!! BIANCA'S!!!! It's BaBa's size, it's totes her style, and she was wearing it when she vamoosed Saturday. Can you believe some daf was selling BaBa's foot thong in her yardination??? The PoPo in Mon Louis, and shout-out to Blue Boy Trevor Hamilton, who granted your gurl an awesome interview at Starbuckian, plus showed her his HEAT and said she could trigger it anytime she wanted, said finding the strappy kick means our very own BaBa was there!!!!! (At whenever, he said.) And by the bye-bye, BaBa's head is on straight. She'd be totes devo if she knew what that old fart wrote about her, but his bad and my good cause I snagged this shiny NEWSCHICK gig out of it.

The skinny: if you hang in Mon Louis, Alabama, keeps those peeps peeled for BaBa and for sure be on the low-low for her other dope shoo-shoo!!! And keep blowin' up the Old Fart's phone whose job I snagged with your FYIs, cause you're making this gurl's new newschick gig easy peasy!!!!!!!!!!! And shout-out to MY BOO BOY

José at headquarters for givin' this gurl some EDITORIALS 'cause I'm on the learnin' curves.

Back at the Doublewide Ranch
Noonish

Dear Bradley,

By the time we made it back to the doublewide, Mango was blazing hot, and not from the sun, but with fever. We dragged her to the beach, the shell beach, of course, because it was closest, and because dragging half-dead Mango to the all-the-way-dead shark wouldn't help, then into the water to cool her down, using our golf clubs to sweep around her in huge arcs just below the water's surface to keep stingrays and jellyfish at bay. I was barefoot in the water up to my knees, and it felt so good with the rest of the marsh mud melting away that I stopped worrying about the stingrays and jellyfish.

I took a single shift of golf club patrol while Fantasy ran to the doublewide for one of the smelly blankets we could use as a makeshift stretcher to haul Mango without having to manhandle her again, and she returned with one of the smelly blankets and half a bottle of Dial for Men Infinite Fresh Body Wash.

"Where'd you find this?" I cradled the Dial for Men like it was something I'd pulled out of my stocking on Christmas morning.

"Under the bathroom sink," she said. "I was looking for meds."

"Where under the bathroom sink? There no under the bathroom sink."

"The bathroom sink pops out," she said. "It lifts."

"What else was under the bathroom sink?" I asked. "Motrin for Mango? A satellite phone? A map of this island? Coffee?"

"Trojans," she said. "Ultra-ribbed. Size compact."

(Gross.)

(Size compact?)

We stripped Mango out of her red golf dress. (Red silk undies.) Out of her golf dress and with the marsh mud washing off, we could see she had a million mosquito bites, a few that looked infected. Swiping my golf club with one hand, I shampooed Mango's matted hair with the other (brown roots) while Fantasy, swiping her golf club with one hand, patted Dial for Men bubbles all over the rest of her with the other. We dragged her to the blanket to dry in the sun then took turns on golf club patrol while the other quickly lathered, rinsed, and repeated. Let me say this, all three of us were Dial for Men infinitely fresher. We carried Mango to the doublewide on the blanket like it was a hammock with me at one end and Fantasy at the other.

It was the first time either of us had really been in the bedroomette. We'd peeked the first day, and since then the door had been closed. All four dish towel curtains over the small square windows in the bedroom were billowing. Maybe not billowing, but definitely fluttering. Mango had been sleeping with the windows open, Bradley, and the mosquitos had eaten her alive.

We lobbed her onto the bed then closed the windows. "This is proof she has wine in here, Davis."

"How?"

"Because you'd have to be drunk to let the mosquitos feast on you all night."

I thought it said more about Mango's island mission than wine. In that there was something on this island she wanted so much she was at the point of carelessness to get it. Her ocean bath had rallied her, a little, and boy was she carelessly blabbering. The name of John Lennon's first girlfriend was Thelma Pickles. Snails can sleep up to three years. An octopus has three hearts, nine brains, and blue blood. X-ray machines don't detect diamonds. There are ten billion tons of gold in the world's oceans.

I took first shift on Mango medical patrol while Fantasy left to gather deadwood and brush for our rescue fire. The best wood was on the path we'd traveled earlier, but we decided it was a terrible idea for Fantasy to go through the marsh alone. Not to mention the wood probably wouldn't burn well after being dragged through the marsh. And we want wood that will burn, because tonight, no matter what, we're building a beach fire so big Fantasy said the man in the moon will see it. And rescue us. Not only do we desperately want off this island, now we desperately need off this island so we can get Mango to the nearest hospital.

She's sick.

Right before her lights went all the way out, she whispered, "Thank you."

I whispered back, "If you want to thank me, Mango, tell me his name."

She whispered, "The Conductor—"

(Was this about the railroad again?)

I whispered back, "His real name, Mango. His real name."

She whispered, "Cosmo—"

So, Bradley, Mango's sick and the crazy golfer's real name is Conductor Cosmo. Or maybe just Cosmo.

It's a start.

Who Doesn't Love a New Job?

BY NELSON MILLER
WEBMASTER @ BiloxiTruth.org
Former Staff Investigative Reporter with Gulf Coast Herald
Tuesday, May 12, 2:00 p.m.

First, I'd like to welcome my three followers—waving at you, Mom—and ask for your help locating the women abducted from Golden Oaks Golf Club on Saturday. In my efforts to do just that, which necessitated telling the story from start to finish without subjective assessment or giving false information completely out of context, I lost my job. To a fourteen-year-old beauty blogger named Tiffanee. (Not meant to be slanderous. I'm not sure how old the young lady is, but I am sure she has my job.)

How did this happen?

I'll tell you.

From the minute I learned the women were missing, I've felt there was something going on behind the scenes at the Bellissimo. The stakes were higher than just the abduction of Bianca Casimiro Sanders, which I had a hard time wrapping my head around, because I couldn't imagine the Bellissimo stakes going higher than the abduction of Mrs. Sanders. And when President and CEO Bradley Cole reached out to local competitor casinos for help, I knew I was right. This was about more than Bianca Casimiro Sanders. I took it upon myself to investigate what that more might be and almost immediately uncovered information I felt certain the Bellissimo needed. I went straight to the executive offices and joined a press pool of more than a hundred reporters who also desperately wanted a Bellissimo ear.

My editor was demanding a headline. I told him I was working on one, but not only did the information need to be vetted, the Bellissimo needed to hear it first. From me. My editor disagreed. He demanded the information. I refused to give it to him, citing source protection rights, and negotiated for more time. He agreed to give me until noon, but only if I'd run a Bianca-angled story in the interim to fill the dead space. And it had to be a bombshell. Why a bombshell, Readers? Because bombshells sell advertising. I declined, because I felt certain the story he suggested I write would jeopardize the safety of the missing women and told him as much. I reasoned that I was in the process of a much larger story, a huge story, a headliner, a picked-up-by-the-AP story, and couldn't stop to help Gulf Coast Herald sell advertising with yellow journalism.

In retaliation, my boss, Gulf Coast Herald's Editor in Chief Ty Towns, instructed Erica Beck in Lifestyles, who he's sleeping with, by the way, to work behind my back on the sensationalized and damaging hack job detrimentally targeting Bianca Casimiro Sanders. (Thanks a lot, Erica. And you could do better than Ty. Anyone could do better than Ty.) Gulf Coast Herald posted the fluff piece without verifying the information, with my byline, to an immediate 1.2 million views, then fired me by text message, supposedly because of the Bellissimo's outrage. Over a story I didn't write. Thanks a lot, Ty Towns, you total jerk. And on the off chance you bother to read this, let me say you have no idea how to run a newspaper, a job you shouldn't even have. Everyone knows Vince was next in line for EIC. And to you, Vince, how long are you going to be Gulf Coast Herald's resident doormat? How many more years of your life are you going to spend locked up in the basement digging through the property archives, playing with your junctions and whistles, answering the news tip line, and turning a blind eye to Ty's womanizing? Could you not have bothered to give me a heads-up? Have you wasted even a single brain cell wondering what I was doing as all this went down?

I was sitting on vital information outside of a Bellissimo conference room as I was being fired and replaced. In other words, I was doing MY JOB. Waiting patiently for the conference room door, or, better put, war room door, to open. And spill out either Jeremy Covey, Head of Bellissimo Security, or Bellissimo President and CEO Bradley Cole.

A word about Bradley Cole: he hasn't slept in days.

Jeremy Covey wandered in and out of the conference room all morning as I was losing my job, often admitting law enforcement types, tacticians, a Gulf geographical strategic systems team, and several hostage negotiators, knowing and acknowledging that I was impatiently waiting to talk to the Bellissimo team privately. Every time the door opened or closed, he'd look my way and say, "I'll get to you in a minute, Miller." Every time I would say, "It's imperative you do, Mr. Covey."

At exactly 11:19 a.m., Jeremy Covey burst through the conference room doors headed straight for the press pool, and what appeared to be straight for me. Was this him getting to me? It felt more like him getting at me. I wondered if I shouldn't step out of his way via an unscheduled flight out a third-story window, because his intent seemed to be to plow straight through me. I considered that it might be one of my neighbors Mr. Covey was intent on beheading. On my left, a reporter from *The Birmingham News*. On my right, a reporter from *World Casino News*. As Jeremy Covey continued to barrel our way, the other journalists and I glanced at each other, speculating as to which of us was about to be hanged and quartered.

It was me.

"MILLER!" Jeremy Covey's blood pressure appeared to be alarmingly high.

I stood. "Yes, sir."

"Did you just post an article about Bianca?"

"No, sir, I did not."

"Did you post anything about the Bellissimo?"

"No, sir." I'd like to interrupt myself to give you a visual, Readers. I am forty-two years old. I am five feet, nine inches tall. My shoe size is ten and a half. I weigh a hundred and sixty pounds. Jeremy Covey, on the other hand, is in his mid- to late fifties. He's eight-ball bald and stands six feet, ten inches tall. His shoe size is Shaquille O'Neal. His weight? I would guess three hundred and fifty pounds. The man is not to be lied to. By me or anyone else. "The last story I posted was at 6:14 this morning, Mr. Covey." I gave a nod to my laptop, waiting in the seat I'd reluctantly abandoned. "Please help yourself."

He contemplated my future for a long moment. As in should I be allowed one. Thankfully, he let me live. He ushered me into the sanctuary of the conference room, heard me out, and gave me exclusive permission to break the story I'd been sitting on.

So here you go, Readers. The following is what you need to know: COSMO BOOKER. That's his name.

Cosmo Booker.

On Saturday morning, Golden Oaks PGA Tour Qualifying Tournament competitor Cosmo Booker had a fit on the back nine. We're talking Happy Gilmore meltdowns on the sixteenth, seventeenth, and eighteenth holes. After missing his putt five times on the par 4 eighteenth hole, he turned on his caddie first, then attacked a collection of spectators behind her with a five iron in one hand and a putter in the other, sending several to the First Aid tent and two to the hospital, before barricading himself in his motorhome. All that went down, according to witnesses, at 11:34. A Bellissimo Security Alert was issued at 11:42 a.m. just as a woman believed to be Bianca Casimiro Sanders (more on that as the story develops) along with Bellissimo security operative Fantasy Erb arrived at Golden Oaks, there to present the trophy at the championship luncheon on their way to a wedding in New Orleans. The women responded to the call at Cosmo Booker's motorhome in the lot behind the thirteenth hole. They haven't been seen since.

Stay tuned. And if you have any information about Cosmo Booker, it would be in everyone's best interest for you not to call it in to Gulf Coast Herald. This isn't a case of sour grapes, Readers, rather my replacement's woefully inadequate grasp of English, which doesn't make for news you can trust. It is without animosity that I say Tiffanee Jones appears to be linguistically unstable. A Gen Zer who is only capable of communicating the news via incoherent slang. And no offense intended to you either, José, you're a great guy, a hard worker, but let someone else edit for my replacement. Stay out of it. And to you, Readers, I'm worried Gulf Coast Herald wants you looking somewhere else instead of at this story. It's as if they actually want to throw you off. As if they don't want you to know the truth. So contact me directly if you have information. You can reach me by email (nmiller@BiloxiTruth.com), by phone (228-449-3038), by knocking on my front door (Royal Oaks Townhomes on Big Ridge Road, just ask the guard to point you in the right direction), by carrier pigeon, smoke signal, or morse code.

I'm off to learn as much as I can about Cosmo Booker via Theodore, Alabama, where the skirt of Bianca Casimiro Sanders's dress was found, via Mon Louis, Alabama, where Bianca Casimiro Sanders's shoe was supposedly found, and via Pine Apple, Alabama, to talk to sixty-year-old Beatrice Crawford, who claims to be one of Bianca Casimiro Sanders's best friends.

If you can't reach me directly, please contact my mother (Hi, Mom!), Lila Miller @228-389-2777.

While I'm very sure of what the bosses at Gulf Coast Herald have up their sleeves (suppression of the truth), I'm not exactly sure what the Bellissimo bosses have up theirs, giving me so much rope with which to hang myself, and not wanting to jeopardize any part of their internal investigation, I'm not necessarily asking the public to approach or attempt to detain Cosmo Booker, who is most certainly armed and dangerous, so much as I'm asking you to provide any information about him I can pass along. Who is this man? Where's he from? Did you know him in high school? Is he your second cousin? Is he your ex? Were you ever locked up with him? What does he do other than play golf and drink Bud Light? Does he own property other than his motorhome? Any and all information might help the Bellissimo and the authorities find the missing women.

Afternoon at the Doublewide Resort

Dear Bradley,

I wish I knew more about Zika virus. Is it contagious? Can we catch it from Mango? How do you treat it? All I know about Zika virus is don't get it if you're pregnant. That's almost all I remember hearing, reading, or knowing about Zika. I hope Mango doesn't die. She's really sick. What are we going to do with her body if she dies?

From: baylor@bellissimo.com
To: davis@bellissimo.com
Day: Tuesday
Subject: Hey

Hey, Davis. It's me again. Baylor. And I'm on your computer again. I'm about to blaze a trail to you. I hope you don't mind if I take your laptop. Mine exploded, which I didn't tell you about when it happened because it was right before my wedding that didn't happen. The keyboard is okay, but the screen is one green line in the middle. Guess who's going with me. Reggie. Fantasy's husband Reggie. Your husband should be going but he is gray. I just left him, and when I said bye I said, "Dude, you're gray." I mean like his skin is gray. His hair has turned gray. He's had the same gray clothes on for two days. Can't really count on someone who's that gray for backup. But Fantasy's husband is pissed. Pissed is good backup.

Listen to this. Remember my excellent idea to offer a reward for Fantasy's car, because I thought the idiot who took you might show up with the car for the reward money? He did. He did and he didn't. He didn't bring the car, but he brought all your junk. Have you ever heard of that much dumbassery? He shows up with yours and Fantasy's bags and your luggage and your phones. Says he found it all on the side of the road and thinks he ought to get half of the reward money for finding your stuff. So much crap in Fantasy's bag. Why does she need to drag Diet Coke around in her bag? You can get Diet Coke anywhere. Ever heard of a wallet? When you and Fantasy get back I think you should ditch the bags for a week and just carry wallets. You'll never go back. And here's how we knew the moron who showed up with your wallets plus the million other things you and Fantasy drag around was the person who kidnapped you. He showed up ten minutes after the Gulf Coast Herald casino writer, you know him, Newspaper Nelson, told us who he was. We were trying to decide if we believed Newspaper Nelson or not when exactly who Newspaper Nelson said took you shows up with your junk. Then we believed Newspaper Nelson. He's a nice guy. Got fired. Bummer. But back to the jerk showing up with your junk, is that the most bonehead thing you've heard in a long time? My idea again, we let him have a thousand dollars and put a tracker on it. Guy comes in asking for half a million and was thrilled to get a thousand. Desperate dude. And now me and Reggie are leaving to follow him, because no doubt he's on his way to you. I asked your dad if he wanted to ride shotgun, and he said no. He said this is way more a local problem than it is a problem somewhere else. Whatever that means, because the rest of us think you're somewhere else. So I asked what that meant. Your dad thinks whoever is behind this has roots in Biloxi, and regardless of where you are now, you're going to end up in Biloxi and he's going to be here when you do. Your husband is staying because he's halfway through pumping up the fifty million and wants to hand it off in person. So he's set up camp in the Bellissimo lobby. I think he's even sleeping there. No Hair is staying because he says your husband needs backup, which I agree with, and I don't know when the last time you tried to pump up fifty million dollars was, Davis, but it's not that easy to do. It's on the news every minute and Bianca doesn't even know. She and Mr. S are on vacation, and when we tried to call them we found out they were on vacation from their vacation. They're on a private chartered sailboat somewhere like four oceans away. Must be a big sailboat because it has a big crew with chefs and waiters and someone who puts Bianca's makeup on her with them. Speaking of makeup, still watch out for the woman with you, because I think the airhead I'm following, Cosmo Dumbass, really does think he took Bianca, mostly because he never even looked in your bag, and there's your driver's license in your wallet—oh, and it's expired—but I think the girl knows she has you. So don't fall for any of her crap. She knows who you are.

Oh, hey, July moved out. She didn't really move out, but her mother showed up and moved her out. She said if I tried to stop her, she'd call security. I told her I was security. Then she said I was irresponsible and immature and that I ignored what was in my face. (She was what was in my face.) She says we need to step back and think about things. I was like, what do we need to step back and think about? You're July's mother. She said she meant me and July need to step back and think about things. About if we're in this for the long haul. I told her I had never once cheated on July and if that didn't prove I was in it for the long haul I didn't know what did. She said she was not impressed. I asked her if it was July's idea to move out. Because I couldn't see that happening. She said for me to mind my own business. Since when is July not my business? She's been my business since the day I met her. Then her mother told me to grow up. Which made me think of you and Fantasy always telling me to grow up. I'm six foot four. I weigh two-ten. How grown up do you people want me to be? I wish you and Fantasy were here to explain it to me. So I'll get back to finding you so you can explain it to me.

Peace out.

Have You Ever Heard of Pine Apple, Alabama? How About Green Pond, Alabama?

BY NELSON MILLER
WEBMASTER @ BiloxiTruth.org
Former Staff Investigative Reporter with Gulf Coast Herald
Tuesday, May 12, 4:17 p.m.

Welcome, new followers. All 117,000 of you.

I'm a little floored. So is my mom. Waving at you, Mom. I appreciate that so many of you who know me from twenty years of covering the casino beat for Gulf Coast Herald have enough faith in my work to support me as I strike out on my own. Welcome, and thank you, unsolicited donors and entities seeking advertising opportunities. Welcome, Associated Press. Welcome Bloomberg Media, News Corp, Tribune Publishing, U.S. News & World Report, Access Hollywood, E! News, and Las Vegas Review-Journal. I'll be in touch as soon as I'm able.

I'm reporting to you from Woodstock Library in Green Pond, Alabama.

More about that in a minute.

Following up on the hatchet job released by my former publisher under my byline that ultimately took my job, and after my meeting with Bradley Cole, Jeremy Covey, and the Bellissimo's Baylor, followed by my inaugural post on this website and with their blessing, I fired up my Suzuki GSX 750 and took off for Theodore, Alabama, where I did not speak to Fay Gilliam, manager of the Pilot Travel Center, who found what was believed to be the skirt of the dress Bianca Casimiro Sanders was wearing on the day of her disappearance. I wanted to know if she'd also found (or caught any whiff of) Cosmo Booker, the man I believe is most assuredly behind the abduction of the three women. After half an hour of banging on Ms. Gillam's door—we both knew she was home—I moved on. To Pine Apple, Alabama. To talk to the woman interviewed by the *Today Show*, Beatrice Crawford, who apparently knows Bianca Casimiro Sanders well enough to convince the producers at NBC. What did I find in Pine Apple, Alabama? Beatrice Crawford. And not much else.

Located in southcentral Alabama, Pine Apple is one hundred and thirty miles northeast of Mobile, fifty miles southwest of Montgomery, or better put, in the middle of nowhere. After an absolutely beautiful twenty-mile ride down two-lane US-82 through hundred-year-old oak trees and grand magnolias, I thought I'd landed in Mayberry. After five minutes, I changed my mind and worried that I'd found the Twilight Zone instead, although every time I closed my eyes and looked again, the sign still said Welcome to Pine Apple as opposed to You've Reached the Very End of the Earth. I parked in front of Town Hall, which also served as police headquarters, as the same man, Samuel Way, was both mayor and chief of police.

His office was locked down tight, as was everything else; Pine Apple was a ghost town. After fifteen minutes of walking the entirety of downtown three times, finding no signs of life, all four shops closed, no traffic whatsoever, I finally found a beating heart in the form of exactly who I was looking for: Beatrice Crawford. At a restaurant formerly called Mel's Diner. I say formerly because all signage clearly indicated in red spray paint that what once was Mel's was now Bea's. The obligatory bell chimed when I entered the all-but-deserted diner. The proprietor, Bea, who I recognized from her *Today Show* appearance, and the only person there, woke from her catnap at the soda fountain. The following is a transcript of our conversation retrieved from iCloud.

"Mrs. Crawford?"

"Mrs. Crawford is my dead mother-in-law. She fell out of a tree. She climbed up there trying to talk her cat down. Broke her own neck. My name is Bea. Don't call me missus. I look a little different from that picture on Silver Singles, but it's me. You here for a date? You don't look like a Silver."

"Do you mind if I record our conversation?"

"What did you say?"

"I'd like to record our conversation. My name is Nelson Miller. I'm an investigative reporter from Biloxi."

"So this is about Davis?"

"Davis?"

"Look around, boy. You see anybody? This whole town's gone looking for Davis. I'd be gone looking too but the alternator on my truck's busted and nobody would give me a ride."

"I'm sorry to hear that."

"You're sorry to hear about my alternator or that nobody'd give me a ride?"

"Both. Could you tell me about Davis?"

"Davis who?"

"The woman you said the whole town is looking for."

"Oh, that Davis. She must'a been playing golf with Bianca, because Bianca's missing too. You know Bianca?"

"Bianca Casimiro Sanders? I know of her."

"Yeah, Bianca gets around."

"Yes ma'am."

"What's that supposed to mean?"

"I was agreeing."

"Don't talk bad about Bianca to me. She's one of my best girlfriends. Don't you watch Al Rockers?"

"I didn't mean anything by it. I was more acknowledging than agreeing, ma'am."

"What's this ma'am business? First you call me missus then ma'am. Didn't you say you was a Silver looking for a date with me?"

"I didn't say that. I'm a reporter from Biloxi."

"So you don't want a date with me? What the hell do you want?"

"I'm a reporter. I'd like to talk to you."

"Oh, yeah. Davis. Cryin' shame."

"What is, ma'am?"

"If you know what's good for you, you'll stop with the ma'am."

"Bea."

(*Sorry, Mom. I know you raised me right.*)

"Have you found Davis?"

"Can we back up, Bea?"

"What's that supposed to mean, boy?"

"Who is Davis?"

"She's my daughter-in-law. She owns a casino."

"Excuse me?"

"Maybe she doesn't own it, but she runs it. Or maybe it's her husband who runs it."

"Would that be your son?"

"Eddie? What's he got to do with anything?"

"If Davis is your daughter-in-law, wouldn't that mean she's married to your son?"

"Are you trying to confuse me, boy?"

"No."

"You better not be."

"Bea, can we get back to Davis?"

"Your dime."

"Davis owns or runs a casino where?"

"I thought you said you was from Biloxi."

"I did."

"You never heard of the Bellissimo? And you don't know Davis?"

I didn't have the chance to say I did know Davis, certainly of her, anyway, because judging by Ms. Crawford's increasingly aggressive delivery and demeanor, I knew my time with her was nearing its bitter end. I quickly showed her a photo of Cosmo Booker and asked if she'd seen him. She paused only long enough to inquire as to his Silver Singles status, then, finding something about me, my line of questioning, or life in general threatening, without warning, Beatrice Crawford relieved me of my cell phone on which I'd been recording our conversation. I attempted to convince her I meant no harm, I was only trying to help, and somewhere in her response, which I won't print, it was confirmed that Davis Way Cole, wife of Bellissimo President and CEO Bradley Cole, is also missing.

Which explains the shape Bradley Cole is in.

This might be what we didn't know.

Readers, the entire town of Pine Apple, Alabama, with very few exceptions, has formed a search and rescue team and are in south Alabama following the clothing and shoe trail furtively looking for the missing women, including their own. Davis was born and raised in Pine Apple. She's the daughter of Mayor and Police Chief Samuel Way. Pine Apple's First Daughter, if you will.

What does that mean, Readers? It means we're looking for four women. In addition to Bianca Casimiro Sanders, Fantasy Erb, and the unidentified caddie, Davis Way Cole is also missing. If you have any information about Davis Way Cole, don't hesitate to contact the authorities. If you're reluctant to speak to the authorities, get in touch with me. You can reach me by email (nmiller@BiloxiTruth.com), by Pigwidgeon, by bat signal, or cell phone as soon as I get a new one. My old one is somewhere at the bottom of a large vat of gelatinous gravy in beautiful Pine Apple, Alabama. And losing my cell phone isn't the reason I'm reporting via a forty-year-old eight-bit Commodore 64 computer held together with Scotch tape and chewing gum from inside a study room at an obscure library in the middle of Nowhere, Alabama. That would be because when I walked out the door of formerly Mel's, currently Bea's Diner in Pine Apple, Cosmo Booker, the very man I was looking for, had also been looking for me.

He found me.

He was armed. And at the wheel of Fantasy Erb's million-dollar Volvo. Make that Fantasy Erb's one-million-and-one-dollar Volvo, factoring in the car's new one-dollar camouflage paint job. Had my phone not been swimming in gravy, I might've dialed 911, although I couldn't imagine anyone within a hundred miles in any direction would have responded. What did Mr. Booker want from me? Unaware of the fact that I was no longer reporting for Gulf Coast Herald (thanks a lot, Gulf Coast Herald), he'd tracked me to Pine Apple to request my help. Mr. Booker has a story to tell, wants me to tell it, and until I do for all the world to hear, says Mr. Booker, he will not reveal the location of the missing women. I convinced him the only way I could be of any assistance was to not just tell his story, but to prove it. And to prove his claims, I'd need access to birth and death records, in addition to historical property, deed, and title information. After much negotiation, we settled on obscure public libraries for my research, a solution that will both provide cover for him and give me access to computers, so I can keep the Bellissimo and the public at large informed. I convinced him public libraries would be a win-win solution: low traffic, helpful staff, no surveillance, and access to information and resources, which led to a long discussion about microfiche, something Mr. Booker had never heard of. I reasoned that while I attempted to validate his claims, he and his gun could sleep at my side. And one among many things Cosmo Booker desperately needed was sleep.

What does all this mean, Readers? By his own admission, I can confirm Cosmo Booker was responsible for the disappearance of three women from Golden Oaks Saturday, make that possibly four women with Davis Way Cole also missing, and add yours truly to the abducted list. According to him, we will all be released unharmed and forthwith, just as soon as I can prove that by birthright, he's a billionaire. He says he's not the down-on-his-luck, golfing, gambling, beer-guzzling bum everyone thinks he is; he's the rightful owner of not only an undisclosed and uninhabited island that he believes is flush with treasure, but also the rightful owner of the Bellissimo Resort and Casino.

Wish me luck.

I'll stay in touch as much as I can with my primary objective being that of gaining Mr. Booker's trust and convincing him to lead me to the missing women. Mom, don't worry, I've got this. You will hear from me as often as Cosmo Booker's fast-food consumption and sleep schedule allows. Would someone please retrieve my Suzuki from formerly Mel's, currently Bea's Diner in beautiful Pine Apple, Alabama? The key is in it.

From: MotherOfBradley@aol.com
To: BCole@Bellissimo.com
Date: May 12, 5:48:31
Subject: It Will All Be Okay
Sent from the Internet

Beloved son, fruit of my loins, know I am here for you.

I can only surmise you are too terribly busy with our twins to have not called me on the telephone to personally tell me of your wife's demise. I learned by reading that darling Nelson Miller's informative news article. (I would so like to meet his mother one day. Perhaps you might arrange that?) It was through Mr. Miller I learned of the loss of your wife. I am heartbroken for you. Deep down, Bradster, we knew this day might come due to the dangerous nature of her chosen profession combined with her reckless spirit, never truly believing any harm would ever befall her. Yet here we are. Know that I am holding up well. I am surrounded by my Prayer Circle and a display of delicious food lovingly prepared by devoted friends, neighbors, and the Civitan Club. I only wish you and the twins were here to help me consume it! Jeanie and Luke Howard drove all the way to Abilene for a Honey Baked Ham! (Of course, I will freeze a more-than-generous portion as I know you adore Honey Baked Ham.) I regret the banana pudding lovingly prepared by Betty Cate Campbell (your second-grade teacher) will not keep until we're together again, unless, my son, you find yourself in dire need of your mother's comforting arms. Know that they are wide open and impatiently waiting. I am here for you. Son, would you agree that it would be best to turn over the responsibilities of the details to professionals and come home until final arrangements are made? Please remind yourself often that the twins are young. Their memories of their mother will fade. I will leave the porch lights on for you and we'll get through this enormous loss together.

Love,

So much,

Mother

Zika Afternoon

Dear Bradley,

Mango isn't better. In fact, she's worse. She's covered in a head-to-toe rash and her eyes are red-rimmed and bloodshot. Honestly, she has a vampire look about her, and it happened so fast. I'd been in seven or eight times to check on her and every time she was the same—burning up with a fever and completely out of it—until the last time I checked on her and she'd taken a turn for the worse. I lifted the damp dish towel on her forehead to soak it in more of our dwindling water supply and saw the rash. I made her wake up, I made her drink water, I made her talk to me (covered wagons didn't have brakes until 1760), then she went right back out.

Where's Fantasy while I'm trying to keep Mango alive?

There's a golf club called a sand wedge, I'm sure you know it, and after much trial and error with other golf clubs, Fantasy is chopping wood with a sand wedge. The island is dotted with clumps of three-foot-tall skinny ugly dune trees with bare trunks, spindly limbs, and scratchy brown brush for leaves. Maybe I should call them dune bushes. Whatever they are, they're surely flammable. And Fantasy is digging up the smaller ones and chopping down the larger ones with a sand wedge, dragging them to the shark beach on the blanket we carried Mango on earlier, then lobbing them on this side of the shark remains.

I CAN'T BELIEVE IT'S COME TO THIS.

We're building the fire on the shark beach because we know it's closer to land. So you'll have a better chance of seeing it. We plan on burning the shark carcass while we're at it, because for one, we can't get past it to build the fire anywhere else on the north beach, for two, without the shark corpse, we'll be free to travel that beach, and for three, because Fantasy says it's more respectful to the shark to cremate his remains instead of letting the birds feast on him. I'm not sure if I agree with her reasoning at all, but I'm in no position to judge. When she finished wrestling her first load of wood, she stopped by the doublewide for a sip of water, to check on Mango, and to look for something to wear because she'd tied her t-shirt around her nose and mouth as a shark-remains-aroma mask. I reached in the bathette and passed her our only other dirty golf shirt from Devil's Creek Golf Club in the Caymans. Then I said, "Which way?"

"Which way what?"

"Should I go?"

"For what?"

"For wood," I said. "Where's the most wood on that side of the island?"

"Why?"

"Because it's my turn to chop wood."

She said, "No way. I'll chop. You stay on Mango duty. Do I look like Florence Nightingale?" She did not. She looked more like Nurse Ratchet just then. But it made me think of my grandmother.

Granny Dee.

At the first thought of my sweet grandmother, and what she must be going through, my knees buckled. She's surely worried for herself, for her son, for her granddaughter, and for her great-granddaughters. That's four generations of bloodline worry. Then my mind jumped back to what Fantasy said that made me think of Granny Dee in the first place—Florence Nightingale. I heard Granny Dee say it so many times growing up. About me. "Do not give that child prescription medicine that tastes like bubblegum. She'll develop a resistance to it, and when she really needs it, it won't work. All she has is a sore throat and all she needs is a mint gargle. Someone run out to my Nightingale (as in Florence) Garden and pull me some mint." Bradley, the Nightingale (as in Florence) section of Granny Dee's garden was her medicine cabinet. When I had chickenpox, it was chamomile baths. When I had a cough, it was hyssop syrup. And when I looked at her sideways, I had to eat a handful of elderberries. I knew exactly what my Granny Dee would do. She'd use something on hand to bring down Mango's fever, and we didn't have much on hand. But we had a garden on the other side of the marsh. A garden with lemongrass. GRANNY DEE STILL TREATS FEVERS WITH LEMONGRASS TEA. AND BUG BITES WITH CAMPHOR. AS IN CAMPHORWEED. (You know camphor. Remember Vicks VapoRub? It's made of camphor. That's what camphor smells like.) I'm off to gather lemongrass and camphorweed, Bradley. I'm going to make lemongrass tea for Mango's fever with what are surely our last drops of fresh water, and I'm going to make a camphorweed paste for her rash.

    I love you,

    Florence

Hell's Oldest Angel Trashes Casino!

BY TIFFANEE JONES
GULF COAST HERALD INTERN REPORTER
Tuesday, May 12, 6:00 p.m.

An old biddie named B took a roadie to Biloxi on a Suzuki donorcycle and Evel Knieveled through the lobby of the Bellissi! I'm like, for reals, Big Grandma? She did a parkie in my fave vino haunt, Stems! Where my gurls and I juice it up on Rosé All Day!!!! Gramazon said she was looking for her bestie, BaBa Casimiro Sanders, and her DIL, Davis. I was like, "Throwback Chick, get in line. There's a flash mob looking for BaBa! And woot-woot on your DIL's kewl name!" Twisted Old Sister is okie dokie artichokie, no boo-boos. The scooter she blew in on is trashed and Stems is totes smashed. (SOBBING!!!!!!!!) But none of that is the headline statuz. The hawg Aunt Sabertooth beat up belongs to the old fart who had my newschick gig before me! Now we're on the sniff patrol for him too! Reality check, Old Fart. You're not getting your newsgig job back. And winkie-winkie to you, Hot José, for all ur helpicizing.

Silver Alert Issued for Seven Residents of Caring Star Senior Center

Source: WLOX CBS Biloxi
Tuesday 12 May 6:30 PM EST
Biloxi, Mississippi

Biloxi Police have issued a Silver Alert for seven elderly women ranging in age from 76 to 88 last seen at Caring Star Senior Center on Maple Street one block north of Harrah's Gulf Coast.

Authorities said the women left the residential home in a Caring Star van driven by Caring Star Transportation Manager Antonio Rhodes earlier today to attend a memorial service for a friend at Rock and Brews Casino. When asked if memorial services were regularly held in the casino, Rock and Brews General Manager Robert Patrick said, "Never." Caring Star Transportation Manager Antonio Rhodes, eventually located at a bank of video poker machines adjacent to the Here We Go microbrew bar five hours after delivering his elderly wards to the casino, had this to say: "They was supposed to call me when they were done. They'll turn up. They always do. I know Beulah will because I got her hearing aids."

Anyone who has seen the elderly women is asked to call Caring Star, 911, or Biloxi Police.

Lemongrass Tea Smells So Good
Mango's Fever Hasn't Broken Yet
I KNOW WHERE WE ARE

Dear Bradley,

Boiling lemongrass is the best thing I've smelled since I climbed out of Fantasy's car with my hands in the air Saturday at Golden Oaks. The doublewide basement smelled like the inside of a diesel tank on the ride over, only outranked by the locker room smell of the doublewide itself, and for the most part the island smells terrible, especially when the dead-shark wind blows the wrong way. And while we're on the subject of smells, let me add I don't ever want to smell mac and cheese again. But boiled lemongrass? First, in spite of the heat, I leaned into the steam, giving myself a mini facial. After that, I strained the hot lemongrass water through Burger King napkins. (Um, didn't really work.) I poured the concoction into a Waffle House cup and let the lemongrass purée settle to the bottom. I took a sip. Just to make sure it wasn't too hot for Mango.

(Just to taste it.)

(It could use some sugar.)

(We have no sugar.)

It took an hour to get four, maybe five ounces in Mango, an ounce at a time. What'd I do between ounces? I smeared camphorweed paste on her. I guess I more patted than smeared. What'd I do after all that? I nosed around and found the water tank, her stash, and our location.

I know where we are.

I asked before I snooped. "Mango." I had the Waffle House cup to her lips tipping the last few drops in her mouth. "Do you mind if I look around?"

She told me a pregnant goldfish was called a twit.

I took that to mean she didn't mind.

Her bed is on a frame made of wood panels. What did I find behind the wood panels? The water tank. The water tank is what the mattress is sitting on. The wood panels are just for show.

I showed them.

I ripped them off.

Mango slept through it all.

The water tank is made of thick opaque plastic. It's the full width of the bed and almost the entire length. It's half full. And that's good news. Before I found the tank, I'd have guessed we had four drops of water left. As it turns out, we have four thousand drops left. If Mango would wake up, I'm sure she'd tell me what percentage of a stalk of celery is water. Or how many gallons of water it takes to wash a load of laundry. Or how much water the average person needs to find the Lost City of Atlantis. Or in our case, the lost Isle of Aurum.

That's where we are, Bradley. On the Isle of Aurum.

HAVE YOU EVER HEARD OF THE ISLE OF AURUM?

Neither have I.

There's a foot of dead space between the water tank and the wall right under Mango's head. I almost missed it. I couldn't see anything, so I stuck my arm all the way in (terrifying) and found Mango's stash. A quilted duffel bag was shoved all the way back and it was stuffed full. I pulled it out. In it, from top to bottom—

Clean clothes. (Two pairs of shorts, two golf skirts, one long-sleeved t-shirt, two short-sleeved golf shirts, one tank top, lots of lingerie, mostly red silk. I wish you could see my new outfit!)

Sperry Duck Boots! (On. My. Feet.) (Too big. I don't care.)

FootJoy Pro golf shoes. White leather. Soon to be on Fantasy's feet. (Too small, but we'll chop off the toes and they'll work.) (The toes of the shoes.) (Not Fantasy's toes.) (Good grief.)

Two books, one journal. *Lost Treasures of the South* by W.R. Oden, *Gulf Coast Tall Tales of Buried Treasures* by Bruce Rhy, and a journal, *Last Ferry to Paradise: The Destruction of Isle of Aurum* by Coraline Broussard. The bad news there is the journal was handwritten. In October of 1961. And at some point between then and now, it drowned. Page after page of water blobs, large chunks of pages too stuck together to separate, and the occasional page with a legible word—I've seen "Cornelius" several times—but not enough words to piece together to mean anything except this: we're on the Isle of Aurum. Exactly where the Isle of Aurum is, or was, I do not know, but remember the Rand McNally 1961 atlas? Maybe I'll know soon. What else did I find? VODKA. A HUGE BOTTLE OF VODKA. ALMOST FULL. What else? Under the vodka? ME. AND FANTASY.

A dossier, just like the one we found under Fantasy's bed on Bianca, but this file was about me and Fantasy.

Mango has known from the start exactly who we are. This was a setup from the word go, but now I'm wondering if the crazy golfer wasn't set up too.

By Mango.

Who might not live long enough to explain herself.

Partizzle Barge!

BY TIFFANEE JONES
GULF COAST HERALD STAFF REPORTER
Wednesday, May 13, 2:52 a.m.

Your NewzGurl is pulling an all-nighter. So my new BossLady, Shawnta Kimbell, who I call BossLady Shaw-Shaw, ringy-dinged my phone last night when I was having cuddle time with my pillow 'cause I'm zoinked from this newsgig. It musta been after Cinderella Hour, 'cause she sayz, "Morning, Glory! Time to wake and bake!" (This gurl's joshing you. 'Cause reefer ain't cool in Mississippi yet. And I don't ever hit weed before bacon.) For reals, she said I had to pull a graveyard. She sayz, "Tiffee, get up and go to Heron Bay."

I sayz, "Dudette, I'm on Z-patrol. I'll go when it's sunnytime."

She sayz, "You'll go now. They've found a barge hidden in the marsh in Heron Bay, Alabama—"

I sayz, "Whoa there, BossLady. DixieDoo again? Why do I have to go back to RamaBama? 'Cause once was 'nuff."

She sayz, "You go where the story takes you, Tiffee. And it's taking you to Alabama again."

I sayz, "Can Hot José go wiff?"

She sayz, "Tiffee, if you choose to climb the corporate ladder in that manner, I'd advise you not to start on the mailroom rung. No, José can't go. But why don't I ask Ty Towns if he'd like to accompany you?"

BossMan?

I wuz like, HELLZ TO THE YES!

Turnt out someone found BaBa Casimiro Sanders's OTHER Stuart Weitzman kick on a partizzle barge! Then I understoodimated. She was axing me to pick up BaBa's second kick and give it to cutie-patootie Jilly who found BaBa's first kick so doll-baby would have a pair. 'Cause what good is one Jimmy Choo Choo??? That wasn't what BossLady was axing. BossLady thinks BaBa pulled a Hansel and Gretel, but instead of Skittles, BaBa left a happy trail of her threads for your NewzGurl to follow.

Lady Shaw-Shaw sayz, "I want you on the scene before Nelson." (Old Fart who had my kewl job before me.) "I need four hundred words and a photograph of the barge." That's when I took off my shluffy mask to see what time it was. Holy flabbergast, it was already TGIHD. And this gurl loves HUMPING ALL DAY!

Gotta bounce and count these wordamajigs. Here's a groupie pic of me and my new Besties in Blue from Heron Bay and BossMan TyTy on the partizzle barge. Word word word word word word word = 400!

Fantasy Found a Fork

Mango's Still Sick Sick Sick

Dear Bradley,

The doublewide has a horn.

When I found the (vodka) dossier on us, I needed Fantasy. I couldn't run off and leave Mango and was busy wishing I had a bell to ring, or a megaphone to yell into, or a horn to honk, then smacked my own head.

We had a horn to honk.

If it worked.

It did. Either the doublewide horn works when the engine is off—maybe all horns do?—or the doublewide horn runs on battery or generator power. Whichever, I climbed under my bunk bed to the driver's seat and gave the horn three taps. It was the loudest thing I'd ever heard in my life. After the three taps, I gave it a long loud blast. I guess it's a good thing we didn't think about or discover the horn earlier. We'd have blasted it around the clock the first few hours, not yet knowing there was no one around to hear it, and our heads would have exploded.

I ran back to check on Mango to see if the horn woke her.

(It hadn't.)

I waited five minutes, or maybe it was just one minute, then laid on the horn again just as Fantasy flew in the doublewide door with a gold fork. It scared us both to absolute death. She waved the fork and yelled, "IS SHE DEAD?" Then, "WHERE DID YOU GET THOSE CLOTHES?" I yelled, "WHERE DID YOU GET THAT FORK?"

I told her Mango was still alive then pointed to the kitchenette table. On it sat Mango's library, the dossier on us, Mango's clean clothes, folded neatly, the golf shoes, and the vodka.

Guess which one she went for.

Just guess.

I had a sip.

Or twelve.

Fantasy (who smelled like a dead shark) (until she smelled like a dead shark shooting vodka) thumbed through photograph after photograph of us. Me and Fantasy. There are pictures of us working undercover all over the casino. In one photo, we were blackjack dealers. In another, we were slot attendants. In another, we were working the desk at Player's Club. There are pictures of us in street clothes stepping in and out of Bellissimo elevators. There are several time-stamped shots of Fantasy's car in the vendor lot. There are photographs of me and YOU. There are photos of me and you and BEX AND QUINN.

They were all taken in the past six weeks.

Mango has been following us for six weeks.

Which was exactly when the dossier on Bianca ended.

Six weeks ago.

IS THIS FREAKING YOU OUT?

It is me.

If you're not sitting, find a chair and sit down before you read the Gulf Coast Herald article I found with the photos. Read this, Bradley, read it, and see if you come up with the same conclusion I have. It was written by Casino Nelson. It's that big feature article from earlier this year about me and Fantasy taking down the German man who'd been on INTERPOL's Most Wanted List for forever. "Amazing work by two Bellissimo cocktail servers! Not only did the women, who this reporter thinks should trade passing out martinis at a southern casino for criminal investigative gigs at Homeland Security, miraculously spot Aelbehart Günter behind sunglasses and under a fedora on third base at a five-thousand-dollar-minimum blackjack table, they somehow convinced Günter to reveal the location of the twenty-six million in British pounds he walked off with seven years ago in Belfast. On Christmas Eve. Dressed as San Nicolás. These two cocktail servers, who this reporter can't find to save his life—poof, they're gone—remind me so much of the two female members of Bellissimo's housekeeping staff who found the hotel guest room armoire full of silver bricks last year. The same silver bricks that went missing the week before as they were being transshipped from Cozumel, Mexico, to the Federal Bank of Atlanta's New Orleans branch. Their good deeds for the day not yet done, the same mysterious housekeepers, who have since vanished, just like the cocktail servers, after discovering the silver worth twelve million dollars, just happened to stumble into the criminal mastermind behind the silver heist in a hotel stairwell—what amazing luck—then managed to retain him long enough to turn him over to the feds. Talk about cleaning house! Like I tell my mom all the time, international crime lords who think they can check into the Bellissimo, hide their ill-gotten gains in their luxury hotel rooms, and escape detection by blending in with the casino crowd, think again. Choose any other Biloxi casino. Because it would seem the Bellissimo has two women floating around who are the greatest duo since ham and cheese, since crimson and clover, since gin and tonic. I don't know if they're more Daphne and Velma or Cagney and Lacey, but this I do know—you rarely see Taco without Tuesday. These two women will sniff you and your treasure out, and you will be brought to justice. One of them reminds me so much of someone else at the Bellissimo, but I just can't put my finger on it."

MANGO KNOWS WHO WE ARE.

Are you ready for my working theory? Crazy Golfer Cosmo hired Mango to research either the land the Bellissimo was built on, this island, or both. I think Mango found way more than she was looking for (namely, me and Fantasy) at the Bellissimo, and way less than she was looking for on the island. (Namely, I don't know.) (Yet.) Bradley, I think Mango orchestrated mine and Fantasy's adultnabbing to kill two birds with one stone. Not only could she distract Cosmo with dreams of a ransom payout for Bianca, she'd have me and Fantasy to find WHATEVER IT IS ON THIS ISLAND SHE CAN'T.

What could be on this island worth more than Bianca?

Once we'd angrily established all this—it took several more vodka shots and considerable shock and awe that a crazy golfer and a trivia queen pulled this off on their own—we moved on to the books and the journal. Fantasy said Broussard was an old French name. No argument from me. Then she said—remember, she went to a prep school, and she's so good at crossword puzzles—AURUM IS LATIN FOR GOLD. Remember me telling you about Mango slinging gold-in-the-ocean trivia after her Zika bath? Remember the gold behind the jungle wall? Remember Fantasy walking in with a gold fork she found while she was chopping dune trees for our rescue fire? HAVE YOU EVER HEARD OF GOLD ON AN ISLAND?

Neither have we.

"Where—" Fantasy slugged back more vodka "—is this gold island? Where in the world are we?"

I said, "The atlas," because that was when I remembered the atlas that I'd remembered earlier. I guess you could say my brain was vodka fuzzy.

She said, "What atlas?"

(So was hers.)

I said, "The one you're sitting on."

She grabbed the vodka and jumped up so fast the gold fork and the two books clattered to the doublewide floor. We slid the kitchenette bench door open, dragged out the atlas from under the moldy blow-up mattress, then spread it out on the kitchenette table. We started west, with Texas. No Isle of Aurum in 1961. Then Louisiana. No Isle of Aurum. Then Mississippi, then Alabama, where we hit paydirt. We found Isle of Aurum on the Alabama page, Bradley, circled in faded pencil. We're eleven miles south of Mobile Bay, six miles west of Dauphin Island. We can't read the faded nautical markings on the atlas well enough to give you our exact longitude and latitude location, but surely that's close enough. Now that you know where we are, COME GET US BEFORE MANGO

DIES. (Either by Zika or Fantasy.) (Because Fantasy is mad.) (And a little drunk.) (But she finally admitted I was right about Mango.) She pointed the vodka bottle at me. "You grew up in Balamamba, Dablis. Don't they teach state histhory in Malabamma? Don't you memember anything abouth a gold island from the sixthies?" Off the top of my head, I remembered three pieces of Alabama history from the sixties: the Civil Rights Movement, Harper Lee, and *Gilligan's Island*. Unlike the first two, *Gilligan's Island* wasn't real. It was an old television show from the mid-sixties. But Alabama claims it as history because the inspiration for the show came from a chartered cruise ship on its way to a private island below Mobile Bay caught in a tropical storm at sea.

Wait a minute...

Backup Has Arrived

BY NELSON MILLER
WEBMASTER @ BiloxiTruth.org
Former Staff Investigative Reporter with Gulf Coast Herald
Wednesday, May 13, 12:17 p.m.

Welcome, new followers, all 423,000 of you, including my old employer, Gulf Coast Herald, along with my replacement, Tiffanee Jones. Are you still going by Tiffanee? Or should we call you @TiffeeRadNewsBabe? I'm thrilled to see what you're doing with my reporting, TiffeeRad. Good luck with this one. Best of luck finding an interpreter to explain everything to you so you can claim it as your own work and regurgitate it as barely comprehensible. And while I'm at it, congratulations on breaking the story of Cinderella's other slipper on the barge in Heron Bay, Alabama. I say that partially to remind you, Readers, calling in tips to my old Gulf Coast Herald phone number won't result in coherent news.

Greetings from one of three cramped study cubicles behind Adult Contemporary Fiction at Thomasville Public Library in Thomasville, Alabama. Passed out beside me, after a late breakfast of three Arby's Fire Roasted Phillys, two orders of potato cakes, an extra-large Jamocha Shake, and four Bud Lights to wash it all down, is Cosmo Booker. Between us, his gun. In the study booth a plexiglass window away on our left, observing from behind an ancient, battered copy of *The Scientific Journal*, is Reginald Erb, husband of the Bellissimo's Fantasy Erb. Through the plexiglass window in the study booth to our right is the Bellissimo's Baylor. If you follow me at all, you know Baylor, who goes by the single name, is Vice President of Security Jeremy Covey's right arm. Which is to say Baylor spends his days and nights swinging from the branch just below the top of the tall Security tree at the Bellissimo.

Readers, how many times have I told you the Bellissimo knows what they're doing?

Baylor and Reginald Erb took their places in five-minute intervals just after Cosmo Booker and I arrived. Were they already following Cosmo Booker? Were they following me? I don't know, and frankly, don't care. I'm glad they're here.

They made no attempt to apprehend my then inebriated, now passed-out companion when they arrived. Nor did they try to communicate directly with me beyond knowing and reassuring nods to let me know I had the full force of the Bellissimo behind me. I trust that it's their intent to follow us to the missing women without interfering unless necessary, and that, I can only assume, is because Baylor, Mr. Erb, and the Bellissimo resources behind them don't want to jeopardize my precarious relationship with Mr. Booker, combined with the fact that they surely realize I stand to learn as much from him on the road in Fantasy Erb's former car—I doubt she'll want it back—as I do about him in the libraries.

Bravo, Bellissimo. Gulf Coast Herald, take note: This is how to have an employee's back. And I don't even work for the Bellissimo.

A word or two about Mr. Booker.

Cosmo Booker, whose given name was Cosmoses Broussard, was raised by his father, Christopher Broussard, on the outskirts of Las Vegas, Nevada, in a motorhome behind Broussard's putt-putt golf course featuring poorly depicted and executed Las Vegas landmarks. Christopher Broussard, a habitual and heavy drinker, died of unknown causes in his sleep when Cosmo was fifteen years old. Cosmo hid his father's body inside the pyramid on the golf course's Luxor Las Vegas 2-par hole, then took off in the family home, a 1984 Tifton Allegro RV, to start a better life as a golf caddie named Cosmo Booker—a surname he'd stumbled across in the process of pawning his deceased father's personal effects—hustling experienced golfers on short-game bets and barely squeaking by. He worked his way east for the next several years, his destination Mississippi, where he believed his father's estranged family once had roots, and reached the Welcome to Biloxi sign just as the block cracked on his motorhome engine. Cosmo's mobile home was suddenly immobile, but just as offshore gambling was legalized. Not quite legal himself, Cosmo used the last thirty-two dollars he had to his name to purchase a fake ID and began hustling local golfers and blackjack players on casino riverboats.

The next twenty years of his life were more of the same, until six months ago when his luck seemingly changed. Cosmo was notified his only living relative, one Charles Broussard, a man he'd never heard of, died, leaving his entire estate to my boozy companion. My first question was how an estate attorney tracked him down, as he'd changed his name and his permanent residence was a motorhome parked behind an abandoned strip mall. Cosmo explained that was the beauty of incarceration, a seldomly acknowledged benefit of time spent in, out, and around the Criminal Justice system, the law (as Cosmo put it) knows your real name and they can always find you. He feels certain Publishers Clearing House will have equal success finding him should they ever need to. A hustler from way back with visions of sudden and immediate wealth, Cosmo, who, at the time, had nothing to his name but a set of mismatched golf clubs, a broken-down motorhome, and the shirt on his back, was suddenly the proud owner of a private island off the Alabama coast and property in Mississippi. Confused by the ancient handwritten deed to the property and unable to identify the island, Cosmo turned to *Craigslist* for help. He found it via UpSeek, a research freelance site primarily used by professional trivia players. The woman he hired, Mango Matisse, helped Cosmo hone in on his two skills, blackjack and golf, to raise enough capital to research the deed and locate the island.

"She told me we needed to go to the Cayman Islands first because that's where my family was last, but all we did when we got there was drink Jägerbombs until we ran out of money."

"Then what, Cosmo?"

"Then we ran out of money."

"Before you ran out of money, were you able to learn anything?"

"Only that when my dad was young, he ditched his family for my mother, they took off for Vegas, and as soon as I was born, she ditched us."

"I'm sorry, Cosmo."

"Don't be," he said. "My dad was a drunk."

"Did you learn anything else while in the Caymans?"

"We found the name of a blind dude who was keeping up the old railroad stations."

"Keeping up the old railroad stations?" I asked. "How so?"

"By trusting."

"You discovered a blind trust had been paying property taxes on the old Broussard railroad stations?"

"If you say so."

"Another long-lost Broussard?" I asked.

"Nope," Cosmo said.

"Then how is this person connected?"

"Connected to what?"

"Connected to you. Connected to your family. Connected to the old railroad stations."

"He's not," Cosmo said, "that I know of."

"Then why would he pay the property taxes?"

"Dude," he said, "I don't know why anyone does anything anymore."

Upon their penniless return to Biloxi, Mango, with at least a modicum of curiosity about the unknown benefactor who, for some reason, was keeping what was left of Broussard Railway's properties off the auction block, tracked the man down. He agreed to meet with her. Apparently, it went well, and afterward, she presented Cosmo with a new plan. She convinced him the only way forward was to bring in the mysterious railway benefactor as a third partner, an investor who would provide a much-needed capital infusion. That, according to Cosmo, was when everything went off the rails. Distracted by his upgraded living conditions (upgraded being a relative term) and cash in his pocket for all the Bud Light he could chug, along with promises of great fame and fortune, it was too late to turn back when Cosmo sobered up enough to realize he was no longer holding the reins.

"Who is this investment partner, Cosmo?" I asked. "What is his name?"

"I can't tell you."

"Why not?"

"Because I won't get my part of the ransom money if I tell."

I didn't have the heart to tell him that he'd never see a penny of the ransom money.

"Have you met him?"

"Once," Cosmo said, "in the very beginning."

"When was that?"

"A long time ago."

"How long?"

"Six weeks, maybe?"

"Can you tell me anything about him?"

"He said he'd been waiting all his life to meet a Broussard."

"And you didn't find that alarming?"

"No," Cosmo said, "he let me pick out my own RV. And she's a beaut."

"Then what?"

"Then he bought me a new barge and rented me a Ditch Witch."

According to Cosmo, he and Mango Matisse began exploration of the ravaged island off the Alabama coast shortly afterward. I asked what they were looking for. Cosmo said big treasure. Two weeks in, Mango, who'd done all the exploring while Cosmo, in his new "luxury" motorhome, drank all the Bud Light, told him there was no treasure, big or small, the island was worthless, and the illegally seized property in Mississippi was his best bet. Cosmo believed it when he was told the quitclaim deed from 1932 for a ten-mile-wide, four-mile-deep stretch of the Mississippi coast proved the land was legally his. Land upon which the Bellissimo Resort and Casino now sits. Land Cosmo was mistakenly led to believe that Salvatore Casimiro had obtained illegally, making Cosmo the rightful owner of the land, and by extension, the billion-dollar business on it. And Cosmo believed it when he was told the quickest means to that glorious end would be to abduct Salvatore Casimiro's only daughter, Bianca Casimiro Sanders.

Cosmo, opposed to the kidnapping plan, more because it involved temporarily relinquishing his new motorhome than anything else, struck a deal with his partners to buy his way out the only way he knew how—blackjack and golf. Failing to place on the leaderboard at Golden Oaks' PGA Tour Qualifying Tournament meant he had to go through with the abduction.

"Why, Cosmo?"

"Because it was the only way to get my casino."

"The Bellissimo?"

"It's mine," he said. "That's my land it's on."

A lamb to slaughter, Readers. A lamb to slaughter.

"Tell me about the kidnapping, Cosmo."

"It didn't work."

"I believe it did."

"Okay," he conceded, "but it didn't work right."

"How was it wrong?"

"It wasn't her."

"You didn't abduct Bianca Sanders?"

"I don't know if I did or not."

"How could you not know?"

"When's the last time you saw Bianca Sanders riding around in a regular car? That's how I knew it wasn't her. Mango was tricking me. And I think she was cheating on me."

"So you were romantically involved with Mango Matisse?"

"We was getting there."

"Is that why you abducted her too?"

"No," he said. "That was part of the plan. She's the kidnapping supervisor."

"What, exactly, is she supervising, Cosmo?"

"She didn't say."

Nudging Cosmo's firearm on the table between us an inch in his direction, I asked why he'd endangered the women's lives.

"I didn't shoot anybody," he said. "Alls I did was shoot. Not at anybody. And if I was going to shoot any of them, it would've been Mango."

He's in way over his head, Readers. He's been used, duped, misled, set up to take the fall, and he's stirring beside me.

Any information about a desolate island off the coast of Alabama would be much appreciated.

Rest easy, Mom, and keep your seat. The Bellissimo sent reinforcements.

Fantasy Is Off to Light Our Rescue Fire!

Dear Bradley,

Honestly, I can't believe it's come to this. I can't believe how long we've been here. I can't believe, when everything is stripped away, what matters and what doesn't. Finding forty gallons of water and shoes matters. Finding a way to light a rescue fire matters.

We poked through the golf garbage looking for a book of matches. There were none. The whole time we were poking, me in my duck boots, Fantasy in her new peep-toed golf shoes, the stove was right behind us. We didn't realize it because we were in such states of exhaustion, excitement, and vodka. We were exhausted because we had every single right to be. And we were excited because we had enough water to live a few more days, Mango wasn't dead, we had at least a general idea of where we were, we had shoes on our feet, and we were about to light our rescue fire. The combination of all that was probably how we missed that we were searching for a way to ignite a fire all around an obvious source, the same way we cooked mac and cheese, the stove.

We tore Missouri out of the atlas (sorry, Missouri), rolled it tight, lit it, then used burning Missouri to ignite a tiki torch dune-brush branch. I watched Fantasy from the doublewide door until she and the tiki torch were out of sight, then I made lemongrass tea for Mango. I stirred it with the gold fork. I went in the bedroomette to check on her and found her awake. Weak as a kitten, ghastly pale under the rash and camphorweed paste, still with the fever, she hadn't moved an inch, but her eyes were open.

She took in my new outfit, the Waffle House cup, and the gold fork.

I pulled up a chair.

(I sat on the tiny sliver of wood between the two skinny closets at the foot of the bed. I think there's supposed to be a small television there.)

First, I said, "How are you feeling, Mango?"

She croaked, "What happened?"

I told her she'd probably contracted Zika virus from a mosquito. She asked how long she'd been out. I told her at least ten or twelve hours. She asked if she was going to die. I told her she'd feel better when her fever broke.

"Is there anything you want to tell me, Mango?" I slowly waved the gold fork. She followed it with her eyes. Then I pulled the printed article Casino Nelson wrote from the waistband of my golf skirt. "You've known who we were all along." She stared straight through me. "What is it you want us to find?"

When she opened her mouth, I truly thought she might give me a straight answer, but instead she told me human brains were 73% water.

I got it.

I held her head and tipped the lemongrass water to her lips. She gulped, sputtered, coughed, and drank almost all of it, then turned away from me. I left the bedroomette with the gold fork, lest she make a miraculous recovery during the night and gouge our eyes out with its long gold tines while we slept, wondering if Mango not answering my direct questions meant anything. I tried to think of any other time on this grand adventure when faced with cold hard truth she couldn't deny she'd kept quiet instead of trying to throw us off with nonsense trivia, and if that in and of itself was some sort of Mango affirmation. Before I could decide, a monstrous clap of thunder stopped me in my tracks. It was immediately followed by a lightning bolt that struck so close it shook the entire doublewide. Thoughts of Mango were replaced by thoughts of Fantasy. Out there alone.

Seniorifics!!! Are You in the Mood for Some BANK?

BY TIFFANEE JONES
GULF COAST HERALD **SENIORITA** STAFF REPORTER
Wednesday, May 13, 5:18 p.m.

#CURRENTSTATUZ
#PROMOTED
#PAYPAYRAIZE
#BANGINGTHEBOZZ

Winky winky winkin' at you, LuvMan BossMan TyTyTownie!

How'z this for climbin' the Corporation Ladder, Lady ShawShaw?

This gurl's comin' atcha with a shout-out to all the throwbacks. Here's a woot-woot PSA just for the oldiez but goodiez fuddy-duddies. Here's the Daily. The Scooper Pooper. There's $50,000 up for grabs to any old geezer who remembers an old island off LA. [*Lower Alabama*] All you Life Alert Geritols put on your thinking pieces and dig thru the noodles in your noggins for intel about an island that was maybe weather bombed about a million years ago. Any old beach bummers out there? If you can memory lane an old island off RamaBama Roll Tide, the PoPo will put some scratch in your Wells Fargo.

Now, back to my BooBoss for some more #SEXTRACREDIT! (Old Fart, you ain't never getting your playcheck back. This gurl loves this gig.) (And Old Fart didn't figure out 'bout the island even tho he speed-dialed it in before me. Cause I was busy doin' the mattress mambo with #BossManTyTyTownie. Your **SENIORITA** Newschick knew it before Old Fart did.)

I sowwy, José. TyTy promised your gurl a big paypay raize for doin' the dirty.

Night

Ish

Dear Bradley,

I didn't have to go far to find Fantasy and get her back in the doublewide before she was struck by lightning. Her tiki torch had burned out before she could light our rescue fire. She was at the door before I'd stopped honking. We decided to (shoot vodka) wait out the weather. Half an hour passed, and I was judging the time by vodka shots since I had no way to tell time, except the sun, and by then, we were banging around in the semi-dark, but there'd been no more thunder or lightning. Fantasy and I pulled dish towels from the windows, secured them to the ends of two pieces of driftwood—more robust than dune-bush branches—siphoned gas from the doublewide tank to soak the dish towel curtains, then lit Oregon at the stove, and ran burning Oregon outside to light the gasoline-soaked dish towel curtain tiki torches. We checked on Mango one last time (snoring for the first time all day) (so maybe her fever was breaking), then made our way to the dead shark by tiki torch.

"It's not that bad," Fantasy said about the appalling smell. "You get used to it."

Bradley, it is that bad, I don't want to get used to it, but I was pleasantly distracted by Fantasy's handiwork. She had dune brush trees stacked almost four feet high with all kinds of kindling beneath stretching the full length of the dead shark and right in front of its body, so not only could I not really see it, but the wood, for the most part, absorbed a lot of the smell too. That could have been which way the wind was blowing, and it was raging, but then again it could have been because Fantasy built such a great dune tree barricade in front of it.

I guess you could say we did a little victory dance. Mango had woken up, barely, but barely awake is still awake, so maybe she'd live, we almost knew where we were and had a much better grasp of why we were there, we had fresh clothes, we'd been knocking back vodka shots, and we were about to be rescued.

We danced our ways to opposite ends, lit both, then the middle, tossing Fantasy's tiki torch on top, keeping mine to guide us back to the doublewide. When we got back there, Mango was right where we'd left her, snoring, and by then the fire had caught and we could see the glow of it on the beach. We climbed on top of the doublewide, via the doublewide hood and cracked windshield, then stood on the roof and admired the inferno we'd created knowing, as long and as hot as the fire would burn, the chances of someone in Mobile Bay eleven miles away seeing it were slim, but the chances of someone on Dauphin Island, only six miles away, were better. And the chances of it being seen by water were best. We felt very confident we would be rescued in a matter of hours, so confident, we couldn't decide between cooking and eating an entire box of mac and cheese each or waiting on real food. When we were rescued. In a matter of hours. Maybe less. And that's when it started raining.

Not just a little rain either.

More rain than I've ever seen in my life.

The sky opened up, Bradley. It just poured rain. Big, fat, relentless sheets of rain we could hardly see through to get back into the doublewide.

I'll write to you again when I can breathe.

From: baylor@bellissimo.com
To: davis@bellissimo.com
Day: Thursday
Subject: Hey

It's me again. Baylor. On your laptop. It's three in the morning and I'm at a rest stop in Alabama with Reggie and some hitchhikers I picked up. Old ladies. Old as your old grandmother old. They're all sleeping. I thought I'd tell you what happened in case you can read your email. What happened was by the time me and Reggie gassed up and hit the road, and this was after Reggie got us road snacks in case we didn't have time to stop and eat and he's excellent at road snacks—we have hot pork skins, Gatorade, beef jerky, sunflower seeds, trail mix, little donuts, and Monster Ultra Black energy drinks—Cosmo was way ahead of us. We caught up with him on I-65 North in Alabama. I was like...this is familiar. You know why? Cosmo was following Newspaper Nelson who was on his way to Pine Apple. Pine Apple as in *where you grew up*. Not a coincidence. Newspaper Nelson was looking for Bea your ex-mother-in-law. And Cosmo was looking for Newspaper Nelson. Since everybody was following everybody already, I told Reggie we'd better lay low. It's at least a day and a half later, and we're still laying low. First, we went to a library where we stayed forever, more about that in a minute, and now we're pulled over at the Conecuh County Rest Area because of massive rain, the kind of rain hydroplane nightmares are made of. It went like this: Pine Apple, a little library for about a hundred hours, rain, and now the rest stop. Cosmo and Newspaper Nelson are in Fantasy's destroyed car four parking spaces away and they're asleep. And I made the call on the hitchhikers myself because Reggie is asleep too. I wasn't asleep. So I went in the rest stop building because I'd had about ten Monsters, and that was after I backed out and blocked Newspaper Nelson in so he wouldn't leave without me, and there were all the little old ladies soaking wet and trying to buy the rest stop desk dude's car because they needed to get to south Alabama and their old lady van didn't have enough gas. The desk dude was telling them he could get roadside assistance to put gas in their old lady van for them, and they were telling him they didn't have the money for gas. If they didn't have the money for gas, how were they going to buy the dude's car? You know what it sounded like to me? It sounded like they stole the van and were trying to ditch it. The thing was, I knew those old ladies. I didn't know know them, but they were pulling into the library parking lot earlier when me and Reggie were pulling out. And they were driving an old lady home bus. One of the old ladies was driving it. Next thing I knew, they were behind us. We were holding back from Newspaper Nelson and Cosmo, and the little old ladies were holding back from us, like ten cars. I don't think I would have noticed them except how often do you see old ladies driving their own old lady home bus? Like the old lady home says raise your hand if you can still drive and whichever old lady raises her hand gets to drive the bus. I couldn't see that happening. Which is part of the reason I think they stole it. Then it started raining and the old ladies pulled into the rest stop right behind all of us. In their old lady home bus. You should see their phones. Flip phones with no Wi-Fi. I had a gut feeling about these little old ladies, because they were looking for an old island off the Alabama coast. And if you can read Newspaper Nelson, you already know we are too. And if the old ladies stole the old lady home van they'd probably steal the desk dude's car and end up in jail before they could get anywhere else, so I told them I was headed to south Alabama and they could hitch. There's seven of them but they're old lady shrunk. One of them screams because she can't hear. And we're in Reggie's Tahoe. There's plenty of room even with all our road snacks. I explained to the old ladies I was following somebody who goes to libraries, and if we detoured and went to a random library instead of straight to the coast I could drop them at a library and they said cool, because they're all in an old lady book club.

Most of the old ladies went to sleep, everyone else was asleep, but I drank too many Monsters to sleep. One of the old ladies was still awake too. I don't know what she drank. She's asleep now but she wasn't earlier. I was telling her about July. About how July and I want to get married but we can't seem to close the deal. She told me there was something holding me back. I was like, "Little Old Lady, I didn't make it snow the time we didn't get married, because I got snowed in at an airport." She was like, "Yes, you did." Because if I'd really wanted to get married, I'd have checked the weather before I went up north right before the wedding. "You need to search your heart," the old lady said. "What is it your heart wants most?" I told her my heart wanted to get married so the rest of me could stop with the weddings. The old lady said for me to dig deeper. You know what I dug up? I want most what Brad has. And don't take that the wrong way, because I don't mean I want *you*. That's sick. But how you and Brad are married. That's what I want. And not throwing shade on Fantasy and Reggie, but you know how they're always up and down? I don't want that. I think it's because Fantasy's such a hard ass. From the outside, it looks like Reggie's the bad ass because he's so big, and he can get so mad during the NBA playoffs, but you should hear him talking to their boys on the phone. He's so kumbaya with them. Fantasy's always threatening to pull everybody's hair out of their head, but Reggie's really cool with the boys. After all that, me telling the old lady I want to be married like you and Brad are married, as opposed to how Fantasy and Reggie are married, she said I passed. I didn't even know it was a test. But very cool that I passed. Then she says, "What does July want most?" I told her babies. So the old lady says, "Tell me about your childhood. Your parents. Your family." I'm going to cut to the chase here, Davis. This old lady is telling me that me growing up without a family and not even having a whole name is why me and July aren't married. Because I'm afraid there's something in my DNA that will be bad for kids. And in my heart, because I really do love July, I don't want to do that to her. According to the old lady, the big holdup on the weddings is that I'm deep down afraid to have kids. And here's what I want to ask you. Could she be right? I mean, can you very secretly be afraid of something and not know it? I told the old lady I wasn't afraid of babies. I asked her how I could be afraid of babies when I wasn't afraid of shoot-outs. For the most part, I dig shoot-outs. The old lady says maybe because I FEEL in control of shoot-outs and I wouldn't FEEL in control of babies. Are you buying any of this? I don't FEEL anything except I wish it'd stop raining.

Last update because all this email and rain is finally making me sleepy, Brad was on the news. I didn't see it, but it's all over my phone and the news. He came up seven million short on the fifty million and poor dude went on TV begging for seven million dollars to buy you back. Big press conference. He slapped up a picture of Cosmo saying we had him. I don't think that's what he meant to say, but that's how the stupid news took it. And we don't have him. Newspaper Nelson has him. I don't know if Brad got the money or not. I haven't talked to him or No Hair since I called to tell them to back off talking about Cosmo on the news because Newspaper Nelson can't blaze a trail to you without him. And I'm right behind him. With Reggie and a bunch of old ladies. And here's how I know we're headed straight to you. At the library, Newspaper Nelson slaps a note on the window between us. (Dude made me as soon as I walked in.) The note said Cosmo wasn't innocent, but he wasn't guilty either. He was dumber than anything else. Then he slaps up a note that says there's a treasure island somewhere. At first I thought that was a book, because it sounded familiar, but I think it means there's an island with treasure on it. Is that where you are? On a treasure island? Is it close to where they found Bianca's other shoe? I think that's where we're headed, if it'd stop raining and everyone would wake up, so keep your seat because I'm on my way. I texted July and told her it was probably best if we didn't have any kids and would she be okay with that. What'd she say back? Nothing.

Peace out.

Middle of the Night

Or Maybe Early Morning
Don't Know, Don't Care

Dear Bradley,

This will be the last time I write you, if for no other reason, this is the last takeout menu in the doublewide. I guess I could write to you on Maine, or Idaho, or North Dakota from the atlas, but I've run through the golf pencils too with no way to sharpen them. And I almost have nothing left to say. Live the rest of your life knowing you and our daughters were the best part of mine. It's still raining, it's going to rain forever, it's raining so hard the wood will be too wet for us to try to light our rescue fire tomorrow night, we're down to six boxes of mac and cheese, and Fantasy and I got into a big fight about absolutely nothing. I said, "We should have built the fire on the south beach," and that was all it took. She lit into me. Because it was my idea to build it on the north beach, closer to land. She'd said if it wasn't for me, she wouldn't have had to spend her day wallowing in shark guts. (Her words.) It went downhill from there. She says I can never make up my mind. I'm a straw-grasping conspiracy theorist thinking there's anything worth anything on this island. Her husband didn't have the resources or public platform or a vault or a direct line to Governor Wilson to get us off this island while my husband had all of that. Why were we still here?

None of which matters because it's going to rain forever.

The vodka is gone.

Bellissi Baldie Wearing Dope Necktie Off to the Graybar Hotel!

P.S. Give Me a RingyDing José 'Cause BossMan Ditched Me

BY TIFFANEE JONES
GULF COAST HERALD SENIORITA STAFF REPORTER
Thursday, May 14, 7:45 a.m.

This gurl needs to take a pauz for the cauz. My new Clark Kent gig is bustin' my balls, and I been up all night knockin' back breakup brewskis. Me and my gurls wanted to go to the Bellissi 'cause the Bellissi is turnt up and the bestie for a breakup throwdown, and we wus ready for a fantabulouz fiesta while we slot bombed the poker machines, but it was CLOSED FOR BIZ. We wus all, "Whaa?" There wus nobodies but the Boys in Blue blankying the place. Why? They heard the Bellissi had the MIA Tiger Woods desperado everyone is looking for under wraps and they wanted the Bellissi to give him up. Whaaaaa? The golfie who took BaBa? At the Bellissi? And your gurl has whooped out her cellie instead of going to my crib and sleepinating, because that's what us newsbabes do, to tell you a big bald man with a punk corporate noose around his neck left the Bellissi wearing silver bracelets because he refused to give up the golfie's locationary. Did your headline gurl ask him a loaded question before he took a dive into the backend of a blue-light lawrider? Affirmative. I said, "Where you get your dope tie, dude? I want to snag one for my poppa for Old Man's Day." Cause old bald dudes luv necki nooses and that's my paternal too. Baldie said, "On an island off the Alabama coast." Which was head slap, like, "Dude. Everybody's researchirating an old island! Old islands ROCK!" Your newschick's on it. Me and my crew are moving the party to an island off RamaBama just as soon as we get a nappipoo and some caffeination. Anybody got the MapQuest for the island everybody's giving a shout-out to? Ciao, love you lotties like jelly totties, you **SUCK** Bossman TyTyTownie, and Hot José, pleaz come wiff.

Day Five

Dear Bradley,

It's noon. I'm writing to you on Left Texas (Texas is two pages) with the stub of a golf pencil somewhat sharpened with the gold fork Fantasy found to tell you Mango's gone. So is the moldy inflatable mattress that fits the kiddy bed I spent the night on in a vodka coma after my showdown with Fantasy. Sometime during the night, neither Fantasy nor I remember exactly when, Mango woke up and stumbled through accusing us of trying to kill her ("Did you know first-degree attempted murder charges carry a penalty of life in prison?") which we barely heard because we were passed out vodka sleeping, and now she's gone. So is the moldy blow-up mattress. I'm assuming Mango took it to use for an umbrella.

Hours and hours later, Fantasy woke up when she heard me wake up. Her hair, after drowning in the rain, was standing straight up a foot off her head. She and her hair raised up from the bench. "Davis, I'm sorry."

I said, "Me too."

We hugged it out, promised each other we'd never get adultnabbed or shoot vodka or build a fire beside a dead shark again, then nosed around for Mango. No Mango. Now we're listening to the rain pound the doublewide, thumbing through the books I found under Mango's bed, and waiting for her to return. We have the windows cracked, airing this place out. If it weren't raining sideways, we'd have them all the way open, because what mosquito would be out in this kind of weather? It's hard to believe Mango's out in it.

Where are you, Bradley? Where are you?

Editor in Chief Denies Allegations and Apologizes for Confusion

BY VINCE BRUNNER
GULF COAST HERALD ASSISTANT EDITOR IN CHIEF
Thursday, May 13, 12:15 p.m.

In a public statement, Gulf Coast Herald Editor in Chief Ty Towns unequivocally denied having an inappropriate relationship with Senior Staff Reporter Tiffanee Jones. Mr. Towns is on record with the following statement: "I did not have sex with that woman." Mr. Towns, a respected journalist whose goals are to deliver the news South Mississippi needs to know while maintaining a safe workspace for all Herald employees, regrets that Miss Jones, two shifts of employees at Motel 6, and four DoorDash drivers collectively misinterpreted his admiration of her excellent reporting as sexual activity. "I'm sorry they were confused," Mr. Towns said.

A Little Breathing Room? Please?

BY NELSON MILLER
WEBMASTER @ BiloxiTruth.org
Former Staff Investigative Reporter with Gulf Coast Herald
Thursday, May 13, 1:17 p.m.

To my 2.7 million followers, please stop following me. Not you, Mom. Stay right where you are.

To Tiffanee Jones's parents, if you're out there, now might be a good time to step in.

To Shawnta Kimball, disgruntled Investigative News Desk Director at Gulf Coast Herald, siccing the amoral class bully on the naive new kid is no way to get him back for what he did to you.

Now on to business at hand.

If it weren't for the unending deluge of rain and the fact that Cosmo Booker sleeps for four solid hours after a super-sized fast-food meal—most recently a late breakfast courtesy of Long John Silver's consisting of a Variety Platter of fish, chicken, and shrimp, with a side order of grilled salmon tacos accompanied by coleslaw, hush puppies, buttered corn, two slices of strawberry swirl cheesecake, and washed down with six Bud Lights—this gig would be up. If Cosmo Booker weren't sleeping off his fish and beer buffet, he would see exactly what I can barely see in my rearview mirror: the miles of you behind us. He would hear what I'm hearing: honks, beeps, and the never-ending squeal of your brakes as you jockey for better positions. On flooded roads. You're risking your own lives and ours. And to the Alabama Department of Transportation, the digital message boards directing me to Heron Bay aren't helping a bit. Do you not understand that when he's awake, Cosmo Booker is looking out the same windshield I am? The man already knows where we're going. He does not need to be reminded by electronic message boards at every overpass. I too know where we're going. The Heron Bay tip (reported by my Gulf Coast Herald replacement, Tiffanee Jones) was called in to my personal cell phone and retrieved illegally from AT&T servers by (what a prince of a guy) Ty Towns, Gulf Coast Herald's sorry excuse for an editor in chief. So I know, Readers, I know. I know a barely seaworthy construction flatboat with what is believed to be Bianca Casimiro Sanders's second shoe was found hidden in five hundred acres of coastal marsh in Heron Bay. I already know. What you, Readers, need to know is that the missing women aren't in or on Heron Bay. It may very well have been their last stop, but the women are on an island south of Heron Bay. Readers, Hurricane Katrina, and many storms before and after it, resulted in several clusters of uninhabited barrier islands in the Mississippi Sound and beyond totaling literally hundreds of islands, some the size of a suburban backyard, some the size of Rhode Island. **The missing women could be on any one of them. Do you want Cosmo Booker to catch on before he discloses which island? Neither do I. So back off.**

Stop with the posters and banners displayed in your windows directing me to Heron Bay and wishing me luck, and please, I beg of you, stop hurling floral bouquets and designer shoes in tribute to Bianca Casimiro Sanders along with fast-food offerings for Cosmo at us. I appreciate the sentiment. I really do. Do you appreciate the fact that you're littering? Which is secondary to the fact that I'm trying to drive in the pouring rain? And a Happy Meal hitting the windshield at seventy miles per hour is the equivalent of you hurling a happy boulder? If you really want to help, Readers, please, take the next exit. For your safety, for ours, and especially before Cosmo Booker wakes or sobers up enough to realize we're being followed, as, may I remind you, *he is the only person who knows the exact location of the abducted women.* I implore you, concerned citizens, authorities, interested parties, and especially media and voyeurs, retreat.

Wish Us Luck

Dear Bradley,

Greetings from Right Texas.

I'm leaving the letters I've written you in the doublewide. I've zipped them inside the waterproof mattress cover on Mango's bed. (Wear gloves.) If something happens to me (as if enough hasn't happened to me already), if I don't make it back, which is to say if the doublewide isn't here for me to make it back to, I want you to have closure. I want you to know how deeply I love you, more with each breath I take, and that will be true until I take my very last. (Breath.) I want our daughters to know how very much I love the pure light that pours from their baby blue eyes, every blonde curl on their head, and the unbridled joy that radiates from them at all times. I want everyone to know how much they mean to me.

Just in case.

Bexley Anne Cole and Caroline Quinn Cole, your mommy has loved you since before you were born and will love you with everything she has forever and always. Please take care of Daddy.

To my own Daddy, know I've used every survival skill you ever taught me to make it out here in the wild, and my only regret is that I never went fishing with you. If I had, I wouldn't have lived my last few days on mac and cheese. I know what you've been doing, Daddy, looking for motive. You've tried to find the story behind the story—who has a good enough reason to do something like this?—and I know you will. When you do, you'll make sure justice is served, and then, Daddy, please put just as much heart, effort, and energy into looking for peace with what happened. You'll eventually find it too. You're my hero.

Mother, you are a wonderful mother. I wish you'd been in a better mood about it, but I'm the mother I am because of you. Thank you.

Granny Dee, I love you. If something happens to Cyril, please don't marry again. Five dead husbands is enough. And know that you saved Mango's life. (If Mango has drowned, that's all on her. Not you, Granny.)

Meredith, the coffee mug I gave you for your birthday last year? World's Best Sister? I meant it. I love you dearly. I'm sorry to leave the responsibility of Mother and Daddy all to you, especially as they age, but according to you, I did that long ago. One last thing. When you were fourteen and I was fifteen and you accused me of taking your Add-A-Pearl necklace and I swore on *The Fresh Prince of Bel-Air* I didn't? I did. I was mad at you. Maybe I was mad at Danielle Sparks for inviting you to her birthday sleepover and not inviting me, or maybe I was mad at both of you, her for inviting you and you for going, but you were right. I took your Add-A-Pearl and hid it. Instead of hiding it somewhere in or around my bed, like I always do, I cleverly hid it in bedding that time. It's in the linen closet upstairs in Mother's sewing room. I tossed it way in the back of the top shelf no one can reach. It's somewhere behind Grandmother Davis's old quilts and doilies.

Riley, I love you. Take care of your mom, and really take care of your grandparents and your little cousins, Bex and Quinn. If I could pick out my only niece in the history of only nieces, it would be you. And ask your mother for the Add-A-Pearl necklace when she finds it. Tell her Aunt Dabis wants you to have it.

To my mother-in-law, Anne Cole. Anne, Bradley is a grown man. It's far past time for you to treat him like one. He loves you too much to ask you to stop parenting him as if he were still twelve years old. Do you know who you're hurting, Anne? Yourself. You're only hurting yourself by not accepting the fact that your grown son can no longer be The Man in your life. Bradley and I both dread the day you realize his world doesn't and shouldn't and can't revolve around you. Which is not to say he doesn't love you dearly, Anne, he absolutely does, but he's an adult. Stop cutting the crusts off his sandwiches. Stop calling him your Little Bradley Boo Boo. Redecorate his old room, because—newsflash—he gave up the Teenage Mutant Ninja Turtle dream long ago. And stop sending him home from your house with his clothes ironed to within an inch of their lives. His favorite jeans he wore to your house last year that came home so stiff they could stand on their own? I had to donate them to Goodwill after five rounds in my washing machine set on the industrial waste cycle because the starch still wouldn't wash out. And please stop feeding him information about single women in Tumbleweed who would be wonderful stepmothers to our daughters. It's offensive. He's an adult, Anne. An adult who loves us both. If I don't make it out of this alive, how Bradley moves on with his life is up to him. HIS decisions. HIS choices. And know that if you use my death as an opportunity to move into my home, I will haunt you from my grave.

Bianca, embrace your age. Stop fighting it so hard. Growing older is an honor and a privilege. And if you haven't already, the time has come for you—YOU—to let everyone know you're not missing. That it's me.

July, Baylor truly loves you. Elope.

Baylor, July isn't going to wait on you forever. She's past ready for the next step. And get off my computer.

No Hair, thank you. For everything. And get Baylor off my computer.

Candy, you're a good, good girl. Keep your people sisters safe and your people daddy company.

OH MY GOD I AM ABOUT TO START BAWLING.

Bradley, the rain is coming from the south and it's all the way up the three doublewide steps and at the door. When it started inching in, we started packing. We threw everything on the rocks just outside the bathette window and we're about to jump out after it. If the water rises just one more inch, and I'm sure it will, the doublewide will surely float away and sink in the ocean. We don't want to float away and sink in the ocean with it. We've packed our blankets, the five boxes of mac and cheese we have left, our saucepan, three of our spoons, and our golf clubs. Why haven't we packed water? We're taking the empty vodka bottle with us, but we haven't filled it with doublewide water because there's plenty of water outside. It's rained twelve feet in twelve hours. And in those twelve hours, Mango has not returned. There's no way, considering she probably still had a fever when she left with the blow-up mattress, that she's survived. We're off to find higher ground (the mountain) and her body.

I don't know what else to say.

From: baylor@bellissimo.com
To: davis@bellissimo.com
Day: Thursday
Subject: Hey

Hey, Davis. It's me. Baylor. I downloaded a keyboard light and sound effects app to your laptop and you're going to love it. You have seven keyboard colors to choose from plus any custom color you want to add and nine light effects, like fade or rainbow. There's one called shooting star, but it gave me a raging headache. The sound effects are cool too. The app picks songs from your playlist based on the mood of the words you're typing and the faster you type the faster the song. You didn't have any tunes, so I loaded you up with my Spotify playlists. I had to delete a few thousand pictures of your kids, which gets you down to a few million, but your laptop is way cooler now. I might have accidentally screwed up your bank account. Sorry about that. It's more your fault than mine because you spend too much money at Target. I like Target too. That's where I got the Death Star firepit last year. But I don't like Target like you like Target. They kept emailing you because you didn't pay your bill before you got kidnapped. I tried to pay it for you, that's when I guessed your checking account password too many times and you got locked out of your bank, so I went ahead and paid your Target bill on my debit card. You're welcome.

If you're reading Newspaper Nelson, you won't know where we are. He can't tell because too many people are reading his articles and finding us, but I can tell. We're at

Bayou La Batre Library in Irvington, Alabama. Your living room is bigger than this place. It only has two little rooms with tables and chairs, no windows between them like at the last library, so me and Reggie are in one of the little rooms beside Newspaper Nelson and Cosmo in the other. We can't see them. Our hitchhikers are in the Tahoe. They're playing cards. Those old ladies bet big too. We probably ought to get them to the casino when all this is over. The one who can't hear is about to drive everyone else crazy with her yelling, but other than that, those old ladies are cool. It's Thursday afternoon and it's still Bible raining. You know when it rains so long in the Bible? That's this rain. Lucky break with the rain though, Fantasy's car looks a little better. I don't know what Cosmo painted it with, school paint, maybe, but the rain is washing it off. Let her know her car isn't camouflage anymore. It isn't white again, but it isn't camo either. It's basically trashed. She's going to need a new car.

Listen to how we got here. Remember I told you it was Bible raining. Newspaper Nelson ditched 99% of the people following us by flying off the road, splashing through a median and a field, then pulling into the carwash behind a gas station. He gave me a heads up he was going to do it by hitting his right blinker three times. Absolutely dope move hiding in the carwash because who washes their car during Bible rain? It was a smooth move too, because half the people behind us didn't know about it and kept going, and the half who saw us and took the real exit were too late because Newspaper Nelson was already hiding in the carwash. When Me and Reggie and our hitchhikers flew off the road behind Newspaper Nelson, you'd have thought we were at a cross country waterpark with all the yelling those old ladies did. They're, like, thrill seekers. Or maybe they don't get out much. We laid low across the street from the carwash at a Circle K. Reggie went in and got all the hitchhikers snacks. He got them decaffeinated coffee, squeeze tubes of kid yogurt, bananas, raisins, graham crackers and peanut butter, and Boost protein drinks that taste like strawberry milkshakes. This is for sure, Davis, no one is better at road snacks than Reggie. After about an hour, and it took the whole hour for all the old ladies to go to the bathroom two at a time, the coast was clear. Newspaper Nelson pulled out of the carwash, got Cosmo two large pizzas at Papa John's, took a left for a two-lane, and we ended up at this library.

We sat there for about a million years. Reggie was shaking his foot. I think he's nervous about Fantasy. Which I understand. I was about to say dude, stop shaking your foot, when there was a tap on our door. You know me, I drew my gun. Then eased open the door.

It was Newspaper Nelson.

He said, "Pardon me. Do you know where the men's room is?"

I said, "No."

He said, "Thanks."

That was it.

I found the men's room behind the desk where you check out books. There's no person. It's the honor system. You write down what book you took on a clipboard. I went in the men's room behind the checkout desk and looked around. Nothing. Nowhere to hide anything. Then I saw the towel thing by the sink. Crooked towel sticking out. Just gut feeling, I pulled it. It was a note from Newspaper Nelson, because he is a sharp dude who knows how to hide things. It said this library didn't have the resources to find the island, but the next one does. So we're on the move again. And that might sound like the big news, but it isn't. The big news is when me and Reggie and the hitchhikers pulled out of the library parking lot after Newspaper Nelson, you won't believe who fell in behind us. You wouldn't believe me if I told you, so I'm not going to.

And the worst news, I still haven't heard from July. I have called her a hundred times and she hasn't answered the phone even once. My old lady marriage counselor says July must be thinking about what she needs to say to me and how she's going to say it. Give her time to get her thoughts together. How much time? What thoughts? Then she said the thing to do while I'm waiting on her to say something to me is to say something to her. I reminded her I've been trying to say something to July since Saturday and she won't take my calls. So my old lady therapist tells me to say something to July in a much bigger and very different way. What very different way? It's not like I speak another language. I took two semesters of French at LSU, but I don't remember enough to "unequivocally declare my undying love" in French. I have never needed to talk to you and Fantasy more than I do right now. And, oh, hey, No Hair's in jail because he wouldn't give up any info on Cosmo. If your husband wasn't barricaded in the lobby of the empty casino sitting on fifty million dollars waiting to pay the ransom (finally pumped it up) (but no word yet from the dude who's supposed to pick it up), I think they'd have him locked up too. I found Bianca's emergency vacation phone number in your email. I dialed it. Talked to her for a while. She's cool.

Peace out.

U.S. News Thursday, 5:00 p.m. ET

Rain Halts Maritime Search for Missing Women

By Jennette Massey

HERON BAY, ALABAMA (Reuters) – Torrential downpours, engorged tributaries, and perilous flying conditions have temporarily halted search and rescue efforts for three missing Mississippi women now believed to be on one of the many uninhabited barrier islands in the Mississippi Sound off the Alabama coast. Maritime first responders, to include Coast Guard forty-five-foot utility boats, HC-144 Ocean Sentry planes, and MH-60 Jayhawk helicopters will resume visual and thermal canvassing of the area as soon as weather conditions allow. In the meantime, they wait, along with tens of thousands of others who have convened, all intent on finding the women. Heron Bay is located in south Mobile County across from Portersville Bay. Together, the bays make up five hundred acres of coastal marsh, maritime forest, and piney flatwoods, managed as nature preserves to protect the tidal marshes between them. Heron Bay is a nearby unincorporated community by the same name. It's seven miles north of the popular Dauphin Island, but with an elevation of ten feet, it's home to little more than three thousand souls. Search and rescue crews have swarmed the small area. Starbucks, Chick-fil-A, and Chipotle have established mobile operations on Heron Bay Loop East. A temporary Missing Persons headquarters has been set up at St. Michael's Catholic Church. Authorities and volunteers have canvassed door to door seeking information regarding sightings of a Fleetwood Storm 28MS Class A Motorhome initially believed to have been hidden somewhere in the vast snake-ridden marshes of the community. After exhaustive efforts to locate the motorhome, a maritime search of nearby barrier islands was organized, now delayed by inclement weather. Coast Guard Sector Commander Marion Maxwell said, "I'm confident we'll find the motorhome. When we find the motorhome, we'll find the women. As soon as it stops raining."

REAL CELEB TALK * HOLLYWOOD GOSSIP AS IT HAPPENS * VIDEO OF BIANCA SANDERS SURFACES

BY CARLITA MARTINDALE

HOLLYWOOD, CALIFORNIA. Production halted! Sources close to my heart tell me sets are dark, concessions closed, and actors are holed up in trailers during what should have been the bitter end of the plagued filming of *Mission: Impossible 14 – Rehabilitated*, in which Ethan Hunt, senior field agent for Impossible Mission Force, stops with the nose candy long enough to take down Plutonian invaders who crash landed their spaceship on Wrigley Field. Why did filming abruptly stop? Because Bianca Casimiro Sanders, wife of Mississippi casino mogul Richard Sanders, called in a favor to Executive Producer Penney Paquette. What manner of dirt might Bianca Casimiro Sanders have on Penny Paquette to warrant the unbridled wrath of the film's temperamental star?

I'm working on it.

This, I do know, the debt was settled between the two women by way of video editing. Bianca, yachting in the South of France with her husband, finally learned what the rest of us have known for days—she's been kidnapped. Unhappy with the quality of the video recorded on a smartphone by her chief stewardess aboard the unnamed and exact-location-undisclosed private yacht, Bianca called Penny Paquette via satellite phone demanding the full force of the *Mission: Impossible 14 – Rehabilitation* production team to redirect their efforts from the movie to editing and enhancing Bianca's video before it airs tonight at seven o'clock EST on E! Below is the transcript of Bianca's segment hours before its (edited) television debut. Production of *Mission: Impossible 14 – Rehabilitation* is set to resume tomorrow. I'll let you know how it goes.

I, Bianca Casimiro Sanders, being of perfectly sound mind and body, as you can very well see, was devastated to learn of my kidnapping and the fifty-million-dollar ransom demand following, which, I understand, was immediately raised. In cash, no less. It is my widely held belief that cash is for amateurs, but in the case of my abduction, I'm willing to make an exception. As for the amount of the ransom demanded, one is reminded of Julius Caesar, who was once so incensed at the pitifully low amount requested by his captors for his safe return, he insisted the price on his head be raised as he believed his self-worth to be much more than his abductors were demanding. And if my exclusive private Italian education serves me well, as it continues to do even as I approach my fortieth birthday, I believe Caesar subsequently beheaded the fools who initially thought so little of him. After all, what is the monetary value of one's life? As I ponder that, and urge you to as well, I beseech you, dear devoted family and friends from all corners of the world and all walks of life, rest assured, I am safe. Enjoying time with my beloved husband, Richard.

I fear, alas, that it is my assistant, David[1], who has been seized. And not accidentally. I believe David[2] sacrificed herself on my behalf. That is David's[3] job, to throw herself in harm's way for me. I am distraught, distressed, and somewhat confused. Once or twice a year, in the most forgiving light, from afar, and through the rosiest of colored glasses, it could be said by those who know us intimately,

---

[1] There is no record of anyone named David on Bianca's staff
[2] Still can't find a David
[3] No one in the newsroom can find a David

which is very few people, that David[4] favors me. I fail to understand how the criminal behind this vile act was so easily fooled, as he certainly does not know me. Intimately or otherwise. One only need blink to realize their grave error. Unlike me, David[5] has not followed a strict skin care regimen her entire life, compounded by the fact that David[6] often frolics in the sun without any protection from ultraviolet rays. She prepares her own carbohydrate-laden meals, often (and I've witnessed this personally) including one of several variations of white potatoes. David[7] does not follow recommended water consumption guidelines, preferring instead to ingest twice that in caffeinated beverages. To my knowledge, David[8] has never employed the expertise of a personal trainer. Our respective glutei maximi alone tell that sad story. The visual chasm between us is wide, leaving me no choice but to assume her abductor may have ocular difficulties. And that observation from me may very well be the key to finding David[9]. The perpetrator surely has extremely poor eyesight. There is but one thing to add, and that is in spite of her many faults, I care deeply for David[10]. I wouldn't know how to go on without her. As such, I plan to forfeit what is left of my glorious holiday to return to the Bellissimo as soon as those intent on doing me harm are apprehended and incarcerated so that I might be by David's[11] side when she returns. And to David[12], if your abductor is allowing you access to network television, I hope, with all my heart, you enjoy this interview, and I also hope to see you soon.

---

[4] David WHO?
[5] I give up
[6] My sister, #1 Bianca Fangirl, says there's no David
[7] Yoo-hoo, David
[8] Broken record
[9] Getting comical
[10] David, raise your hand
[11] Can't wait to meet this David
[12] Seriously?

COMING FOR YOU <u>TYTYTOWNIE</u>!!!

BY TIFFANEE JONES
GULF COAST HERALD SENORITA STAFF REPORTER
Thursday, May 14, 6:00 p.m.

I assidently zonked out all day instead of islandating 'cauz it was raining bitches. I coulda sawed more logs 'cept my cellie rang and it wuz hottie toddie BellissiBoss BradMan Cole with an invite. Your trusty newschick took off in turbo greased lightning speed for the Bellissi 'caus I thought it was a Bellissi exclusie, and that's how this gurl gets her payday, but it was some guidance counselor for—pause for you to guesstimate—hurry up and wait—ME! I did a parkie at the Bellissi door, 'cause there wuz still no driver BooBoys, busted in the glass doors by my lonesome 'cause there wuz still no door BooBoys either, and your gurl found herself in a ghostbox again. The Bellissi was like the outskirts of nowhere. No people slam. No Motown sound trip for my earmuffs. No after partae. I was like, "WHAAAAAA? STILLZ????"

BellissiBoss BradMan hoofed my way. He held out his hand to press some flesh, knock me some skin, and truthation, it was the solo time anybody has ever made this gurl feel like a pro. Lickety splickety I put BellissiBoss BradMan in my friend zone. And that's phatty newz, 'cause your trustie newschick was thinking I might have to go totes lesbionic after what **SLIMEBUCKET TYTYTOWNIE** did to yours truly. Until BellissiBoss BradMan showed me the flipside to remind me that one bad apple don't spurl the whole bunch, gurl. And that's xactly what BellissiBoss BradMan wanted to Dr. Phil me about.

TYTY SCUZBAG, who BradMan knew I was mangry at. He said, "Tiffanee, you have a voice. A strong and powerful voice. Millions of people are on the edge of their seats waiting to hear from you." (Legit? This gurl wazn't in the know.) "Every time you post a story, people read it so fast the servers at Gulf Coast Herald crash." (For realz? No one told this gurl. José, you too mad to informinate me?) BellissiBoss BradMan said, "What your boss did to you was wrong. Not to mention against the law. He needs to be held accountable. My advice is for you to urge Ty Towns to show his face and make it right."

I wuz like, "Whaaa?"

Here's the dirty: BradMan thinks somebodies at Gulfy Coast Herald corporational headquarterz has ulterior motives with **MOI** directly connectified to the missing gurlz, and **TYTY SCUZBALL** knowz all about it. If he showz his **YUGLY FACE,** we will get informationalz 'bout the lost gurlz, and he will get paybackz for his bad behaviorz.

(For realz?)

After BradMan 'splained all that, I was like, how's that gonna go down? 'Cauz **TYTY SLEAZEBALL** went Bermuda Triangle. He's like a weapon of mass disappearance.

BellissiBoss BradMan was like, "I believe if you appeal to your readers and ask them to find Ty Towns for you, they will. Have them bring him here. I'll make sure he apologizes for mistreating you and faces criminal charges so it doesn't happen to anyone else."

I was like, but what if he sends his manetary who does all his grungy work?

BellissiBoss BradMan was like, okey-dokey, that doggie will hunt too, 'cause **TYTY FLAKENSTEIN'S** work hubby would know his locale.

So, like, SEARCH PARTAY! If you know **TyTyTownie's** twenty, don't iPhone bomb me. Bring him to the Bellissi. 'Cauz me and BellisiBoss BradMan are going to truthinate him about this shituation. Schnoz to schnoz. Time for you to face the muzak and spill the beanz, TyTy.

Missing in Action

BY NELSON MILLER
WEBMASTER @ BiloxiTruth.org
Former Staff Investigative Reporter with Gulf Coast Herald
Thursday, May 14, 11:55 p.m.

For the first time in my two-plus-decade journalism career, I'm on the verge of being at a loss for words. I don't know where to begin. I suppose Cosmo Booker's calorie count wouldn't be a bad place to start, because anticipating the need to accommodate Cosmo's insatiable appetite when he woke was where it ended.

After two large Papa John's Epic Stuffed Crust meatball pizzas with extra pickled jalapeño peppers and a six-pack of Bud Light, Cosmo slept in the passenger seat beside me between Bayou La Batre Library in Irvington, Alabama, and Citronelle Memorial Library in Citronelle, Alabama. I don't think it was necessarily the pizza and beer that had him sleeping so soundly, I think it was the relentless rain. Travel was slow and visibility at times zero on the dark standing-water-only backroads between the two libraries. Before I tell you what happened, let's recap what we already know through research and in conversation with Cosmo, and face hard truths.

The short version: Cosmo Booker is more victim than perpetrator. He's an accomplice; he fired a weapon on Bellissimo property; he abducted three women. In spite of all that, his criminal misdeeds don't appear to hold a candle to the crimes committed against him.

The twist: Someone else is pulling the strings.

The bitter truth: The missing women may never be found.

Summation: I've spent the last two days of my life with a golfing, gambling, beer-guzzling pawn named Cosmo who was betrayed by an opportunistic grifter named Mango after she teamed up with a mystery investor who could have a Broussard-related hidden agenda and who wound up pushing all the buttons. We don't know his name and the women are still missing.

The light at the end of the tunnel until an hour ago: Cosmo knows where the missing women are.

The light extinguished: I don't know where Cosmo is.

And here we are.

Or, rather, here I am. At Sonic – America's Drive-In. Across the street from Citronelle Memorial Library in Citronelle, Alabama, where I hoped, with Cosmo's help, to physically locate the island. I pulled in and parked near the restaurant knowing that when Cosmo woke, he'd be hungry. I'd have to feed him first. My entourage in the Tahoe didn't arrive for twenty additional minutes, having taken several detours along the way to intercept a tugboat of an older model car that kept popping up in our rearview mirrors. Once there, Baylor and crew parked opposite me. After their comforting arrival, I joined my travel companion for some much-needed sleep, as did the Bellissimo's Baylor, who'd put in as many rainy road hours in the past forty-eight hours as I had, only to be awakened half an hour ago with a knock to my window.

I started the engine and cracked the window, assuming it was someone requesting we find somewhere else to loiter.

Nope.

It was the driver of the tugboat Bellissimo's Baylor had run off the road several times on our way here. The man spoke to me. I couldn't hear him. I lowered my window farther. He coldcocked me. He had an admirable right hook. By the time my vision returned and the siren blaring in my ears lowered by a single decibel, the tugboat driver had made his way to the passenger door of the Volvo. He yanked it open and unceremoniously relieved me of Cosmo Booker.

It was only then that he introduced himself. His name is Edward Melvin Crawford II. He said I could call him Eddie. He's the son of Silver Single Beatrice Crawford, proprietor of formerly Mel's, currently Bea's Diner in beautiful Pine Apple, Alabama. I won't share his parting words, but I will share his parting sentiment: Eddie Crawford intends to collect the reward money for finding Cosmo. (Reward money that, to my knowledge, hasn't been offered.) How's that for an update? I've lost Cosmo Booker.

I am also unable to reprint Bellissimo Baylor's and Reggie Erb's strong reactions when they were rudely awakened to the scene of Cosmo Booker slipping from our collective grasps. They promptly took chase after the tugboat (a 1979 Lincoln Continental) leaving a downed row of Sonic menu housing and speaker units in their wake. I had no choice but to follow, because there went my mom and the other seniors missing from Caring Star.

U.S. News Friday, 7:13 a.m. ET
Heron Bay Residents Wake Up to Haunting Discovery
By Jennette Massey

HERON BAY, ALABAMA (Reuters) – Hopes were dashed in the search efforts to locate and recover three Mississippi women who have been missing for six days and are now feared dead after Heron Bay residents Jimmy and Elaine Murray woke to the startling sight of a motorhome floating in their backyard. "I was trying to sleep," said Elaine Murray, "but I kept hearing something banging on the back deck. We knew the water was up from the rain, happens all the time, and stuff washes up with the water. Mostly gas cans. Sometimes tires. Lots of times our neighbor's stuff washes over to our yard and all our stuff washes over to theirs. When the water goes down, we trade back. I knew from how loud it was that whatever washed up this morning was big. I told Jimmy to get up and see what it was. He said it was probably a gas can. I said, 'Jimmy, that might be a gas tanker, but it ain't no gas can. Go look.' He came running back from the kitchen telling me it was those women everybody's looking for. I told him women banging on the porch wouldn't make that much noise. He told me come see for myself. I did. It was that motorhome in the news. The one that's lost. It ain't lost anymore. It's bobbing like a big ole apple in my backyard."

After being secured by authorities, who didn't breach the doors or windows for fear of disturbing evidence, the Fleetwood Storm 28MS Class A Motorhome is being relocated to shore by tugboat then loaded onto a flatbed trailer and transported to the soccer field at Anna F. Booth Elementary in Coden, Alabama, where forensic teams will be waiting in what appears to be a tragic end to the riveting story of the abduction of three women from Biloxi.

From: baylor@bellissimo.com
To: davis@bellissimo.com
Day: Friday
Subject: Hey

Hey, Davis. It's me. Baylor. I'm sitting in the middle of the woods with three slashed tires and a busted axel after off-road chasing your maniac ex-husband. What a tool. I'd like to know what kind of stupid pill you took when you married him. I mean, I know you were young, like high-school young, but the thing is, Davis, you're smart. I know you're smart. Everyone knows you're smart. You're too smart now to have not been smarter back then. How could you have done something so dumb? I spent half of last night trying to chase Eddie's sorry ass off the road and every time he came back for more. He's like a disease that won't go away. Everything gets better then BAM here comes the disease again. Last night when I was sure I'd lost Eddie for good, I caught up with Newspaper Nelson and closed my eyes for ten minutes. I woke up nine minutes later and there he was again, Disease Eddie, and now he has Cosmo. I thought he was chasing after us to help get you, which at first I thought was nice, stupid, but nice, but my marriage counselor said him chasing us while we were chasing Cosmo indicated his motives weren't that "pure" and it would be better to lose his ass. She was right. He was only chasing us because he wants the reward money for finding Cosmo. And here's how stupid Eddie is, Davis, nobody's offered a reward for Cosmo. So twisted. And now we're stuck in the woods because of trying to run him down and get

Cosmo back before the police get him. Here's why I'm writing to you—do you have any idea where your asshole ex-husband would hide in Mobile County? I lost him in the woods in Grand Bay. Everything here's flooded, including the woods—trees down everywhere, and I hit one too hot. That's bad news, because Fantasy's Volvo was already trashed and now Reggie's Tahoe is trashed, and how are their boys going to get around if their parents don't have cars? Ask me how mad Reggie is about it. He isn't. Reggie is cool. He's not cool about Fantasy being gone for so long, but he's cool about the Tahoe.

My phone is dead, and Reggie's has one bar left. I wanted to try July again, not that she'd answer, because she still won't talk to me, but since we're stuck in the woods with no snacks and nowhere to get snacks even if we had a way to get snacks, I thought I'd better use what was left of Reggie's phone to call No Hair and ask for a truck to tow us out. When he answered I said, "Dude, I thought you were in jail." He said, "Then why did you call me?" I said, "How did you get out?" He said, "I made bail." I said, "Cool."

No Hair said he'd send a tow truck.

And snacks.

He hasn't heard from July either.

Then I called Brad with the last juice left on Reggie's phone to ask him where he thought your asshole ex-husband would hide in Mobile County. He said, "What kind of question is that, Baylor? My wife has been missing for six days and you want to talk to me about her ex-husband?" Then I told him Eddie the Disease had Cosmo. I said, "Come on and help us find Eddie." Because we all think it's past time for Brad to get out of the Bellissimo. He's set up camp in the lobby at the front door like you're going to walk in any minute. He said he couldn't come chase Eddie because he's at the Bellissimo with @TiffeeRadNewsBabe (she's a piece of work) waiting for the big boss to show up. Don't get your feelings hurt about that because everyone's after @TiffeeRad's boss. Makes sense to me. In the middle of nothing making any sense at all. So I'm going on and on telling Reggie what's going down while we wait on the tow truck and our senior hitchhikers are chiming in every three minutes. Because they say Ty Towns doesn't fit the profile. (Truth. They said, "Ty Towns doesn't fit the profile.") I know Newspaper Nelson can't stand the guy, so he's probably buying into the Ty Towns business, and I know @TiffeeRad is hoping it's true, because he made that big play-for-pay move on her that she told the whole world about, but the real reason everyone's looking at Ty Towns is because Brad is looking at him. My marriage counselor said, "That doesn't necessarily mean Bradley Cole thinks Ty Towns is responsible. Ty Towns may very well be a means to an end, Baylor. You need to read between the lines." I said, "What lines?" Then she went on and on about that being a problem in my "relationship" with July, that I took everything too literally and didn't recognize "subtext." I said, "I read the article about Brad drawing out Ty Towns twice and it said the same thing both times. Brad Cole wants Ty Towns. Trust me, if Brad thinks he did it, he did it." Then my marriage counselor said, "Brad Cole must be onto something and Ty Towns is key to it. He may very well be looking for someone connected to Ty Towns, Baylor. If that's the case, this is about to be over."

If she's right, Davis, after all this running and chasing and pumping intel out of Cosmo with more junk food than you can imagine and enough Bud Light for an LSU playoff game while the whole world looks for you, it might be your own husband who saves you. Maybe he was the smart one to stay at the Bellissimo and figure everything out. I was thinking about all that when Newspaper Nelson pulled up. I didn't know it was Newspaper Nelson at first, because he'd ditched Fantasy's Volvo. He was driving the old lady home van we'd left at the rest stop in Conecuh County. Turns out my marriage counselor is his MOTHER. We're off to find Eddie and Cosmo. I hope you're not dead in that trailer that washed up.

Peace out.

U.S. News Friday, 3:02 p.m. ET
Scene Guard Tent Breached
By Jennette Massey

HERON BAY, ALABAMA (Reuters) – Mobile Forensic Lab Units swarmed the scene tent hastily constructed to house the motorhome recovered from rising bay waters earlier this morning in hopes of learning the fate of three Mississippi women missing since last Saturday. After hours of no update and no one allowed in the scene tent or even on the soccer field at Anna F. Booth Elementary School, Pine Apple Police Chief Samuel Way along with his daughter, thirty-five-year-old Meredith Way, stormed the crime scene perimeter in hopes of news of Chief Way's daughter and Meredith Way's sister, Davis Way Cole, wife of Bellissimo President and CEO Bradley Cole. Chief Way and his daughter Meredith emerged fifteen minutes later with what looked like a length of yellowed plastic folded into thirds under Chief Way's arm. In response to endless press pool questions shouted at them, Ms. Way made the only statement: "I know where my sister hides things." When asked if the Ways would face charges for their actions, Mobile County Medical Examiner Dennis Goodwin said no. "Four crime scene investigators have taken the motorhome down to the studs looking for digital, personal, physical, or trace evidence, finding none, which makes sense considering everything inside is waterlogged, then Davis Way Cole's sister walked in and immediately found what looks to be the only evidence the motorhome had to offer." When asked if the women's bodies were inside the scene tent, Dr. Goodwin said, "I'm not at liberty to say."

MANHUNT UNDERWAY
By Cameron Briggs

MOBILE, ALABAMA (AL.com) – A manhunt is underway for thirty-two-year-old Cosmo Booker after he escaped an ambulance transporting him from Providence Medical Group on Rangeline Service Road to Providence Hospital on Airport Boulevard. "I don't know what happened," paramedic and driver Kent Moody said. "It was a quick transfer, less than a mile, so I was solo. I turned a corner, the back doors flew open, and there he went." Security cameras showed Cosmo Booker, lead suspect wanted by everyone everywhere in the disappearance of three Biloxi, Mississippi, women being dropped at the entrance of the Providence Medical Group an hour before his escape. Footage shows Mr. Booker being pushed from the passenger seat of a 1979 two-door Lincoln Continental with Alabama plates registered to Edward Melvin Crawford II from Pine Apple. Footage also showed Mr. Booker in severe gastrointestinal distress. Providence Medical Group is home to a network of primary care and specialty physician offices, unequipped to treat medical emergencies, and Mr. Booker certainly fell into that category. OB-GYN Valerie Maldonado stabilized Mr. Booker enough for transport to the hospital for treatment for what she said presented as a pancreatic episode, possibly acute pancreatitis, and while doing so, recognized him. She immediately called authorities who, after hearing the details of Mr. Booker's symptoms, did not want to transfer the patient/prisoner in a squad car. "We have to clean our own squad cars," Officer Owen Williamson said. Dr. Maldonado called EMT Services for the transfer to the hospital for further treatment and certain admission. Cosmo Booker somehow escaped en route. Mr. Crawford, who'd unceremoniously deposited Mr. Booker at the front door of the doctor's offices, was immediately apprehended and taken into custody for "harboring a fugitive and barbaric treatment of said fugitive." Mr. Booker is believed to be on foot. He was last seen wearing a pink Labor and Delivery gown featuring ducklings.

Arrest Warrant Issued for Gulf Coast Herald Editor in Chief Ty Towns

BY VINCE BRUNNER
GULF COAST HERALD ACTING EDITOR IN CHIEF
Friday, May 15, 6:30 p.m.

It is with heavy hearts we at Gulf Coast Herald, in our efforts to report the news, find ourselves in the unenviable position of being the news. Ty Towns, our widely respected Editor in Chief, is wanted for questioning in the disappearance of three Biloxi women and faces multiple workplace sexual misconduct charges after thirty-four women (so far) have filed assault complaints against him just today. Biloxi Police Department Public Relations Officer Holly Griffin said, "Women are lined up around the block to press charges. We don't have time for this." In his absence and until he is cleared of all wrongdoing, I will assume the duties of Editor in Chief. Gulf Coast Herald will cooperate and assist the authorities in any way we can to facilitate the capture of our temporarily suspended Editor in Chief. Gulf Coast Herald's parent company, Global Media, Inc., is offering a $5,000 reward for any tip, information, or sighting of Ty Towns that leads to his apprehension. Please contact me directly: 228-911-NEWS or vbrunner@coastherald.org. And count on Gulf Coast Herald for the news you need to know.

BaBa Sanders in Another Galaxy Far Far Away AND Golden Gurls 'Bout to Mob the Bellissi!!!!

BY TIFFANEE JONES
GULF COAST HERALD STAFF REPORTER
Friday, May 15, 7:15 p.m.

I was hanging with BellissiBoss BradMan sippin' java, waitinating on **TyTyJerkly** to show hiz face, and eyeballing the freak show on E!, this gurl'z fave telly channel. The episode was called *BaBa Sanders & Space Invaders*. BaBa looked her usual GORGE, but I waz like, "HUH? WHO ARE THE GREEN GALASTICS SHOOTING SPACE BOMBZ AT YOU, BABA?" BellissiBoss BradMan splained that E! musta had technical difficultiez. He said, "Tiffanee, I can assure you, Bianca is not in space. That's Wrigley Field behind her. And the aliens, while I can't explain them, appear to be Hollywood special effects. Something must have gone wrong with the editing of Bianca's interview." The whole time me and BradMan were doin' the hurry up and wait for **SlugHead TyTyTownie** and we were both textually frustrated. My dumbphone was blazy with ringy-dings from Karens who were same boating it with me about **TurdHead TyTyTownie**, and BellissiBoss BradMan was phone deaf from his cellie blowin' up too. This gurl doesn't know who was callin' him until Old Fart dialed him in. Comprende? Old Fart who is neva gonna wrassle my newschick gig away from me dialed BellissiBoss BradMan's digits!!! He sayz, "BradMan, keep your seat and save one for me 'cause I'm road raging it on the Alzheimer's Express with a bunch of ultra senioritas who know xactly where the lost gurlz are!!!" I sayz, "Huh?" I pointed at the telly. "Check it, BradMan. BaBa's already raised her hand. She's locationed." Then BradMan splained to me that it wuzn't BaBa who was lost in the woodz anymore. It was his wifeypoo!!! And some random old gurlz have the Where's Waldo on her!!!!!

LOST AND FOUND

BY NELSON MILLER
WEBMASTER @ BiloxiTruth.org
Former Staff Investigative Reporter with Gulf Coast Herald
Friday, May 15, 7:27 p.m.

I'm on my way to the Bellissimo Resort and Casino, and before I tell you why, let me just say, well, well, well, how the mighty have fallen. Sorry for your troubles, Ty Towns.
    NOT.
    For what it's worth, Ty, my mother doesn't think you're the mastermind behind the kidnapping of Davis Way Cole, Fantasy Erb, and Mango Matisse. She thinks someone you've wronged set you up to take the fall, and that list is too long for even me to tackle.
    Hello to my new 5,882,039 followers.
    @TiffeeRad, below you'll find your next story. Please, have at it.
    Update: There have been no reported sightings of Cosmo Booker. How is that possible? He's roaming the Mobile, Alabama, streets in a pink hospital gown, and from what I understand, not one stitch else. Do Mobile residents not look twice at a nearly naked bearded man wearing a pink duck gown who, not knowing more greasy food will only exacerbate his already grave condition, is most likely rooting through dumpsters behind fast-food restaurants in search of a snack? He needs to be in a hospital. He needs a lawyer. Someone please help the man.

Continuing Coverage: The wandering residents of Caring Star Senior Center are alive and well and with me, including my own mother. I'd say, "Hi, Mom!" if she weren't behind me playing high-stakes Gin Rummy with one of her oldest friends, Beulah Hildreth. You might remember Caring Star Senior Living Center's Transportation Manager, Antonio Rhodes, saying at the time of the residents' disappearance from Rock and Brews Casino in Biloxi that he was in possession of one resident's HearGo Rechargeable Hearing Aids, because, as she explained to me, the ambient noise of surrounding slot machines interferes with her ability to hear the bells and whistles of her own? That was my mother's friend, Beulah Hildreth. Hold that thought, please, because it will come in handy as you read on.

While I'd rather not say exactly where we were, I will tell you this, because of mechanical trouble with the Caring Star van and a desperate need to recharge our batteries, we've been off the road most of the day. Bellissimo's Baylor, Fantasy Erb's husband, Reggie, myself, and seven fugitives from Caring Star Senior Living Center secured and occupied four connecting motel rooms for most of the day, catching our breaths, replenishing our wardrobes at a nearby Kohl's department store, showering, emptying the motel vending machines, and regrouping.

I spent two of those hours at Dot Laney Memorial Library in Ariton, Alabama, then rejoined my fellow outlaws to share what I'd learned from obscure research catalogs, periodicals, and historical databases without the benefit of Cosmo Booker's input.

A large part of me missed him.

Brace yourselves for what I learned.

In 1955, Cornelius Broussard and his wife, Coraline, purchased and retired to a private island after abruptly selling their Biloxi home, waterfront property, and livelihood, Broussard Railways. The Broussards, with their sons Charles and Christopher in tow, built an island estate, followed by a small island resort, then commissioned the construction of two opulent cruise ships originating in the

Cayman's with a single destination, Broussard Island. A year later, their efforts having been wildly rewarded, they doubled down just as their youngest son, Christopher, Cosmo's deceased father, stole away during the night with his girlfriend of one day, Cosmo's birth mother, never to be seen or heard from by the family again. The remaining three Broussards carried on, renovating and expanding the resort to include luxury bungalows surrounding a grand hall and purchased a third cruise ship. They changed the name of the island. They enjoyed huge success and an idyllic life until 1961 when the island was destroyed by a tropical cyclone. Forty-two lives, almost all Broussard employees, were lost, including that of island owner Cornelius Broussard. The death toll could easily have been 542, but mercifully, none of the Broussard cruise ships were in port and no guests were registered at the resort when the "very severe cyclonic storm" came and went in just eighteen minutes devastating the island. Help didn't arrive for two weeks. When it did, what was left of the Broussard family, namely the wife, Coraline, and the oldest son, Charles, were shocked to learn life beyond their destroyed island had escaped nature's wrath, the deadly cyclone having targeted only their patriarch, employees, home, livelihood, and family fortune. Leaving all the dirty work to the first and only responders, mother and son fled under the cover of darkness to escape whatever their responsibilities might be to the families of those who'd perished. They had nothing left with which to make reparations. They hid in the Caymans, changed their surname to Booker, and by all accounts lived out the rest of their lives in near poverty and total obscurity. Until Charles Broussard Booker died six months ago. And Cosmo Broussard Booker inherited what was left of the once prosperous family.

At the end of my story in the relative quiet of the motel room, Beulah Hildreth, who could finally hear without the background noise of the road, spoke up. "I KNOW EXACTLY WHERE THE GIRLS ARE."

We brokered a deal with the motel owner trading Bellissimo Baylor's Precision 8000 TASK Premium Mobile Workstation for the motel's maintenance van (worth considerably less than the laptop) and are on our way to Bradley Cole at the Bellissimo. To tell him where his wife is.

ALABAMA TODAY Friday 9:21 p.m. ET

SMASH AND GRAB SUSPECT MOST LIKELY COSMO BOOKER
By Cameron Briggs

MOBILE, ALABAMA (AL.com) – A Walgreens, CVS Pharmacy, and a Winn-Dixie Superstore located in a one-mile stretch of Government Road in Mobile were all broken into after nightfall. Surveillance video shows the same naked man, his head and face covered in what appears to be a loose pink headdress, entering all three closed businesses with a crowbar to the glass storefronts. In all three instances store alarms alerted authorities, but all three times the suspect had fled the scene by the time police arrived. All three stores were wiped clean of Pepto Bismol. Store managers found empty Pepto Bismol bottles and packaging strewn in the aisles and their shelves depleted of the ultra-coating pink medicine used to treat digestive issues. No additional property or inventory was reported damaged or missing at the three stores. Police suspect the perpetrator was thirty-two-year-old Cosmo Booker who escaped from an ambulance earlier today en route to Providence Hospital. Pepto Bismol's parent company, Proctor & Gamble, now joins the long list of those searching for Cosmo Booker. P&G Product Marketing Manager Lanita Blais said, "Pepto Bismol is far and wide the largest selling and most iconic item we sell. It even beats our Febreze and Pantene lines to death. We love that the Pepto Bismol Bandit was wearing pink while guzzling what we refer to as 'The Pink That Pays.' We think he'll be a YouTube sensation."

From: MotherOfBradley@aol.com
To: BCole@Bellissimo.com
Date: May 15, 8:30:16 p.m.
Subject: Our Promising Future
Sent from the Internet

Beloved spawn, I am packed. I will arrive at noon tomorrow and am prepared to stay indefinitely. Your inability to commit to a date to return home combined with the lack of substantial communication between us has convinced me you need me there. You know how I abhor mobile phone messages because all sentiment is lost in brief exchanges on electronic devices, and it has reached the point I must be by your side so that we may speak in person. As your mother, it is my duty to <u>hear</u> your words, to <u>look you in the eye</u> as you speak them, not just read them on a small phone, so that I can know for certain you are at peace and have closure with the loss of your wife. Susan Dodger's son, Kevin, will keep a watchful eye on the house and tend to the gardens while I am away. Rest easy, Son. Mother is on the way. I will be at your side as quickly as Pastor Landry's automobile will deliver us.

Us, you ask?

Read on, beloved son!

Who, Bradster, would you imagine is accompanying me? Would you care to venture a guess? None other than Paster Landry's daughter, LeeAnn! She has taken a leave of absence from her management position in the lumber department at Home Depot in Houston to accompany me! You will hardly recognize her, as she is sturdier and healthier than in the oil portrait I had commissioned after you two lovebirds were crowned Homecoming King and Queen, although still so beautiful. Glowing, I dare say. And not to be fresh, but she's very buxom too. Her personality is nothing short of effervescent, she's a fabulous conversationalist, and as I can attest, a skilled and gifted chef given last night's delicious Tex-Mex feast at Pastor and Sissy Landry's home. It was a glorious Welcome Home Dinner prepared by the guest of honor herself! To which I was invited! LeeAnn, always with such a good head on her strong shoulders, agrees with everyone else I've consulted, that it is far past time for a memorial service to honor your former wife. A proper farewell needs to be organized and executed right away. Tomorrow is not too soon. Bradster, your deceased wife's remains might not be recovered for years. You simply can't wait that long to move on with your life. If you are in any way hesitant, just think of our darling twins! It is in their best interests! And think of your former wife! Let her sprit move on to the next realm! May she rest in peace!

With an unprecedented amount of love and excitement at seeing you soon,

Your Devoted Mother

From: baylor@bellissimo.com
To: davis@bellissimo.com
Day: Friday
Subject: Hey

Hey, Davis. It's me. Baylor. And I'm not on your laptop. I'll tell you why I'm sending you an email from my phone instead of your laptop later. You'll like the story better if I tell it in person, and that might be in a few hours. One of these old girls with us thinks she knows where you are. The one who can't hear. Beulah. I was talking to my marriage counselor about how crazy it was that the one who couldn't hear any of the questions was the one sitting on all the answers, which sent my marriage counselor off on a rant about communication in relationships. Did I listen to July? I told her I listened to July all the time. Mostly about did I want pizza or Thai, but I listened. My marriage counselor said think back on the other three times July and I didn't get married. How did July react? What did July SAY? I told her those times July was cool about it. Like when we didn't get married in Hawaii, she said she didn't want to get married so far from home anyway. And how she was okay with missing our Christmas wedding, because she said when you go back later and look at pictures with everything red and green, you don't like them. And how last summer when we didn't get married it was probably a good thing because there wouldn't be any way to not invite your ex-mother-in-law, Bea, who was in town. My marriage counselor said, "That's because the first three times July saw the glass half full. What was it about your wedding last week that might have caused July to see the glass half empty?" And that was when it hit me exactly what was wrong with July. This time her glass was all the way full. She had too many glasses of wine. Or tequila. Who knows. You know how she's such a lightweight when it comes to drinking? How she drinks one glass of wine and falls asleep? That's what's wrong with her. She had ten glasses of wine, or twenty Coronas, or fifty Jolly Rancher Jell-O shots, and she has a massive hangover. I knew I'd figure it out if I tried hard enough. The wedding was supposed to be on Saturday but wasn't because all hell broke loose. July went to New Orleans Thursday to stay with her parents and check on the flowers and go out with her college friends. I was busy tying up loose ends at work so I could take a week off for our honeymoon and didn't talk to July except text messages until I was on my way Saturday morning. And we didn't really talk. I called to tell her happy wedding day finally. She said she wasn't really awake yet and didn't feel like talking so she'd see me at the wedding. But then there wasn't a wedding. And since then she hasn't answered my calls and her mother keeps telling me she doesn't feel like coming to the phone or she's asleep. And I have figured out why. Because she DOESN'T feel like coming to the phone and she IS asleep, because she has a HANGOVER. I bet she shot too many Jolly Ranchers when she was out with her college friends, and since she's not a pro like me, she's still hungover. And that's it. July has a hangover. So we were on our way to Biloxi to meet up with Brad and figure out if Old Beulah had any idea what she was talking about when I dialed July's dad to make sure. If I hadn't been so busy looking for you, I'd have thought about calling him before, because unlike July's mother who packed her up and moved her out of my whole life, he's cool. I said, "Let me ask you something. Do you think July has a hangover? Like a week-long hangover?" He said I'd have to talk to July about that. I said July wouldn't talk to me, and he said he wished he could help me but he couldn't. Then I remembered he's a real estate attorney, or a property lawyer, one of those. While I had him on the phone, I told him he could help me. I ran it by him what Old Beulah said, thinking we could save some time when we got back to the Bellissimo. He said, "Give me a minute." Then he said, "What year?" I said 1961. So, three things, Davis: July has a massive hangover, we're on our way to get you, and Cosmo's family owned an island exactly where Old Beulah said it was. As soon as we get you home, I'm going straight to July's parent's house, because I know every hangover cure there is. There are a bunch of us coming to get you, but not No Hair, because he got a lead on Ty Towns. I feel sorry for that guy when No Hair gets ahold of him. And Cosmo isn't coming with us either, because that poor bastard is his own worst enemy.

FROM THE DESK OF BRADLEY COLE

Dear Davis,

Above all else, answering Bexley's and Quinn's questions about where their mother is and when she will be home has been the hardest. Harder than my fear for you or my personal heartache. Harder than pacing the floors night after night trying to reconcile what happened, how it happened, and why it happened. Harder than sifting through the endless calls from the media, psychics, and certain sightings—how did you get from Golden Oaks to Cairo, Egypt, in an hour?—and harder than obtaining fifty million dollars by hook and crook with which to purchase your freedom.

Your mother, sister, and niece kept Bex and Quinn so distracted the first two days that it wasn't until I tucked them in at night that they asked. It almost destroyed me to make promises to our daughters I didn't know if I could keep. By the third day, they'd overheard too many hushed conversations, they'd picked up on the panicked energy in every room, on every face, in every heart, and their suspicions grew to fear. To distract them, Meredith had two Barbie jeeps delivered. Davis, the jeeps have 12V batteries. I haven't clocked the girls because I haven't had the time, but wide open, Bex and Quinn's favorite speed, I think they raced through the empty mezzanine—buckled in and wearing their glitter bike helmets—for ten straight hours at no less than three miles per hour stopping only to trade depleted batteries for fully charged. By Wednesday, the thrill of the jeeps had worn off and the girls grew quiet again, so Meredith had a playhouse delivered. A playhouse, Davis. A child-

sized pink playhouse. She had it set up in our foyer. Our whole foyer. It's two-story, fully furnished, it has hardwood floors, a skylight, a loft bedroom, working lights, running water in the kitchen, a wide back porch, and an attached garage. At the end of that long exhausting day of decorating and redecorating, Bex and Quinn did not fall asleep without asking where their mama was.

Part of the problem has been our third twin. Our dog. I don't know how Candy knew, but she knew. On Saturday night, my head spinning and heart breaking, having barely accepted the idea of you having been kidnapped, still staring at my phone thinking you'd call any minute, waiting for you to walk through the door, your mother, who'd been there long enough to prepare a buffet (ten minutes) asked about Candy. At the time, she was holding what looked like a dinosaur leg bone. To give to the dog. I found Candy in our closet. Had it not been for the thump of her tail against the back wall, behind our luggage, behind the chair you are forever asking me to stop lobbing clothes onto, behind the stack of boxes you insist are too nice to throw out, you'll need them one day, there was Candy. She'd pulled your bathrobe from its hook, gathered the clothes you'd changed out of before you dressed for the Golden Oaks awards luncheon Saturday, found the white slip-on Keds sneakers you wear eight days a week, then made a bed of them. She was waiting patiently. For you. On the fourth morning of your absence, your mother, your sister, your niece, and I, after finding the girls' beds empty and frantically searching for our daughters over and under every square inch of our home, the life draining from my very soul as I reached for my phone to have an Amber Alert issued for our daughters—Davis, our daughters were missing—I found them sleeping in the back of our closet with Candy. Our dog was their pillow, your bathrobe their blanket. I'm telling you all that to tell you this. Later that morning, your sister contacted the Old English Sheepdog Rescue Network of Biloxi and facilitated the adoption of a four-

year-old one-hundred-and-thirty-pound beast the girls have named Cotton. As in Cotton and Candy. He'd been surrendered to the shelter having outgrown his previous owners' seven-thousand-square-foot home. Davis, his paws are the size of manhole covers, his girth that of a small car, and he's covered in a shag carpet of fur so dense and thick it's a challenge to find the dog beneath. We will certainly have to hire a professional, with heavy equipment, to groom him. He's a lot of dog, Davis, who somehow manages to squeeze into spaces much smaller than himself. He can wedge into the backseat of a Barbie Jeep (a good rider) (although speed is greatly reduced) and inside the garage of the playhouse (with nowhere to go once he's in), which has been relocated to our living room. Our living room, you ask? The same maintenance crew that installed the playhouse in the foyer returned, dismantled it, and reassembled it in our living room, because, I was told, we needed the foyer for the wedding. Davis, Cotton and Candy are to be married in two days. Sunday. A short engagement, I agree, but I'm not in charge. Catering is preparing a four-tiered wedding cake, Special Events has worked around the clock decorating the foyer (the theme is Lady and the Tramp), Christina Aguilera, who arrived with her band as scheduled, unaware and having not been told the casino was temporarily closed, will provide music, Candy's veil and Cotton's tux are complete, and all we need is you.

All that said, my much better half, I'm on my way to pick you up, because the wedding can't go on without you. July, who I understand has been a little under the weather this week, will be with the girls overseeing the final wedding preparations as the rest of us make our way to you. Our guide is an elderly woman named Beulah who has been where I believe you are. Her hearing is long gone, but her mind is still sharp. She honeymooned on an island below Mobile Bay when she was in her mid-twenties. She has detailed memories of a specific landmark on the now-deserted island, a gold wall, the same gold wall you described in your letters that have mercifully made their way to me thanks to your father and sister locating them in the, as you say, doublewide motorhome. Believe it or not, Beulah is all we have by way of navigation to and on the island. She remembers very little—a grand home, a gold wall, resort cottages—but the more she talks, the more she remembers. With her help, I hope to be where you are in a matter of hours. I understand the smart money would pass on Beulah's knowledge to trained rescue and medical professionals, but Davis, you and I don't have time for that. Not only do we have Cotton and Candy's wedding, I believe someone else is trying to reach you as well. Overwhelmingly popular opinion, everyone's but mine and your father's, in fact, says it's one man. Your father and I believe it to be another. Not only have we been unable to convince anyone else, we've been unable to identify or draw the other man out either. As such, two additional traveling companions of mine will be a Gen X correspondent for whom I and everyone else could use an interpreter, and Nelson Miller, who lost his casino-beat reporting job to the Gen Xer. I think these two adversaries are unaware of the fact that they each hold a piece of the puzzle, the last two pieces, and in the same room, or airbus copter as it were, I hope and pray the final questions will be met with answers. Because I can't let the person ultimately responsible for this nightmare find you before I do.

I love you, I need you, I miss you, and this I promise—I will buy you ten new laptops if your sister doesn't bankrupt us with outrageous gifts for the girls first, I will cook the mac and cheese for Bexley and Quinn from now on, and I'm bringing coffee.

All my love, every bit of it,
Bradley

U.S. News Saturday, 8:22 a.m. ET
Maritime Search Resumes
By Jennette Massey

HERON BAY, ALABAMA (Reuters) – Clearing skies and receding waters are allowing maritime rescue efforts to resume in the search for three missing Biloxi women. Coast Guard forty-five-foot utility boats, HC-144 Ocean Sentry planes, and MH-60 Jayhawk helicopters prepared to deploy after Mobile County Medical Examiner Dennis Goodwin announced earlier this morning that the motorhome found floating in a Heron Bay resident's backyard did not contain the bodies of the three missing women. Davis Way Cole's mother, Mrs. Caroline Way, was on the scene. "I knew she wasn't in that trailer," Mrs. Way said. "Let me tell you something about Davis. That one knows how to get herself out of a pickle. She's been getting in pickles since the day she was born, and she always finds her way out. I knew she wasn't in that trailer because I raised her better. She'd know to climb a tree and wait on the water to go down before letting herself be washed away. Now I hate to think of her stuck up in a tree, and I can't wait to hear what she was thinking when she let herself be hauled off by the Pepto Bismol Outlaw. I plan on speaking to her about that when I see her right after I explain why I had to leave my sweet granddaughters with their nanny, who I call January, June, or July, like in the song "Shine On, Harvest Moon." Normally Davis wouldn't mind the girls staying with their nanny, except not when the nanny's feeling puny. That girl can barely hold her head up. But she's like part of our family and she dragged herself out of bed because her family needed her. I left her with two tins of soda crackers and a case of ginger ale. I told her to look at the bright side. Her feeling so puny only means her baby's going to have a full head of hair. I felt puny when I was pregnant with Davis too, and my mother-in-law had me eating red raspberry leaves from her garden. Not the raspberries. The leaves. They made me feel worse than I felt before, and Davis was born bald as an eagle. Now with my second daughter I knew better. I nibbled on soda crackers and sipped ginger ale. I felt a lot better, and Meredith was born with a beautiful head of hair. There was Davis without enough hair to hold a barrette beside her tiny baby sister who had a full head of hair. Everybody loves a baby with a full head of hair. And the reason I left my sweet granddaughters with July at all was because Davis's husband and a girl I don't know who goes by Rappy Tiffy and no telling who else are gone looking for her on an island. In case everybody gets crossways and Davis shows up here before any of them find her there or yon, we thought someone from the family ought to be here to welcome her if she swims up. Which she just might do any minute. Mark my words. My daughter knows how to take care of herself. You wait and see. She'll pop up any minute. And she'll probably be hungry. I have a pot roast and a strawberry shortcake waiting on her."

When asked exactly where Davis's husband and company were looking for her daughter and the two women who disappeared with her, Mrs. Way said, "I wouldn't know exactly."

When told a search party led by the Bellissimo's Bradley Cole was conducting their own rescue operation, Coast Guard Sector Commander Marion Maxwell said, "That's never a good idea on or over open water. By not coordinating with State Emergency Services, they're putting themselves in as much danger if not more than the missing women." He went on to say it didn't look particularly hopeful for his own operation. Without the marker of the motorhome, previously the visual target for the rescue teams, recovery efforts would have to rely on thermal imaging to detect heat signatures. Commander Maxwell said, "There's good news and there's bad news with that. If the women are still alive, our equipment will spot them. But it will also spot animals. We'll see a thousand alligator heat stamps before we see one woman heat stamp."

State sanctioned search efforts will begin south of Mobile Bay, and if needed, will expand to all barrier islands in the Gulf from Brownsville, Texas, to Key West, Florida, until the women are located. Dead or alive.

Hola

This is José from the mailroom at Gulf Coast Herald. It is Saturday morning which is Donut Day at Gulf Coast Herald. The donuts are to make us feel good about working on Saturday. They do not. My job here is to sort and deliver the mail, but we do not get very much mail. Mostly casino flyers and pizza coupons. So I work all over. If a leg on a desk breaks, call Mr. Fix Things José. If someone needs a pickup at Goodyear because they had a blowout and dropped their car off for a new tire, call José Uber. If there is not a photographer to go on your interview throw a camera at José of All Jobs. You get my draft. The newspaper is mostly online. We still deliver newspapers to the casinos and to old people who do not have computers or maybe they have computers but do not know how to download the Gulf Coast Herald website so they can read the news. Tech is hard for old folks. Like my abuela who is always calling me to fix her television when she kills the remote. All I do is reset the remote and she thinks I am a genius. She is the only one.

At night I bus tables at the Holy Cow! at Cash Cow Casino behind Walmart and I get grief there too. I work two jobs because I am saving to get my media degree from Miller-Motte so I can get a real news job. The problem is English is not my first language. I can speak it fine but writing it is hard because there are so many rules and there are not very many of them that make since to me especially words that sound the same but are different words. How does any body learn how to right those? Sometimes I think what I need more than school is some kind of break already and I might finally have one. I am the only one who showed up to work today at

Gulf Coast Herald News. It is all me. This place looks like somebody called in a bomb warning and I did not get the letter. Even my boss Vince is not here and that hombre almost lives here. The newsroom is empty. The copyediting room is empty. The ad department is empty. Nobody is printing the Sunday newspapers. Even circulation is not here, and those guys are always here because they do not get paid unless they sell newspapers and more people answer the phone about newspapers on Saturday than any other day. The worst news is that the new reporter Tiffanee is not here. I was about to give away my dream of being a news reporter and go full-time at Holy Cow! because the money is better until she started working here. She is the reason my dream is still alive and I keep showing out every day. In Hot Chica World, she is queen. She is the hottest chica of all hot chicas going back to the beginning of hot chicas. And the hottest chica in the world is not here either. And if you are reading this Tiffanee, I am not mad at you. It is important to forget and forgive. It is not your fault he put the sheep over your eyes. I wish you were here write now to help me tell this news because there is nobody left except me and you. I am sorry for getting off the track. I will get back to my story. I asked myself what would happen that would make everybody leave. Usually it would be something at one of the casinos, but they are all closed. Except Cash Cow. And what made me think that was the last time this place cleaned out like this was when the Bellissimo gave away ten Range Rovers. I did not win one. My abuela knows a lady at her church who did. But the newsroom could not be empty because of that, because like I said the casinos are closed. Then I decided exactly what probably happened. Some body called the tip phone and said where our old boss Don Juan Ty was and everybody and their hermano here at Gulf Coast Herald left to find him for the reward money. They knew first because the call came into the tip phone and that way they got first bullet at the reward money. Makes since to me because of how they do things here anyway, which is to only give you the news they want you to have. They hideout the rest of it. Like if what I said happened, you will read in the paper **Smart Gulf Coast Herald Copy Editor Found Ty Towns** and you will not read **Because He Was Standing by the Phone**. They tell you exactly what they want you to know and not any more words. But guess what? I am the only one here and that leaves only me to tell you the news, and I do not owe the city or the mayor's girlfriend or Hard Rock any flavors. I do not have to keep any secrets. No one is paying me under the tables. I work two jobs and I barely get paid on top of the tables.

So here is the news. Three big helicopters almost too big to be helicopters left right before sunrise from the roof of the Bellissimo. One went one way one went the other way and one went straight over the water. I know about them because I was across the street at the Waffle House between my Holy Cow! shift and my Herald job. You might be wondering why I did not eat at Holy Cow! since I work there, and the answer is because I have seen the kitchen. That is why. My abuela did not raise an idiot. I eat at Waffle House where I can see what they are doing in the kitchen. I was at Waffle House waiting on my waffle after my steak and eggs when the roof of the Bellissimo lighted up in three places. Me and the Waffle House waitresses and the two cooks went out to the parking lot to watch. To me it looked like two of the helicopters had no people and one was full of people, but it was hard to tell and that was probably the plans so anyone trying to follow them would not know which way to go. The helicopters took off at the same time and lighted up the sky better than any Bellissimo fireworks I have ever seen, and I never miss Bellissimo fireworks. By then it was time for my day job. I went to Gulf Coast Herald to ask if anybody knew anything about the helicopters, but no body was here and it made me think this is my chance. If I can figure out who was in those helicopters and where they were going it could lead to a real news job. I was thinking about going back to the Waffle House and interviewing the waitresses then I changed my mind because they saw the same thing I saw. And their shifts were probably over.

While I was deciding not to do that, I remembered my waffle that I never got to eat after my steak and eggs and that made me think of donuts. Because it is Saturday. Donut Day. I went into the breakroom to see if anybody brought donuts before they cleaned out, and no one did but big surprise there was Don Juan Ty. There goes my good idea that everyone else at Gulf Coast Herald was not here because they were looking for him. And get this he is dead. So police when you read this I have a dead man in the breakroom. Come get him. And to the people who own the newspaper, please give the reward money for finding Don Juan Ty to my abuela. I did not touch anything. I looked but I did not touch. I especially did not touch the railroad spike in his head. His eyes are very wrong. They are poking out. I am not going to show you a picture because it would be too ugly. So now I am hitting DISTRIBUTE TO ALL SUBSCRIBERS and adios muchachos. Hey, Tiffanee.

VACAY!!!!!

BY TIFFANEE JONES
GULF COAST HERALD BABEBOSS STAFF REPORTER
Saturday, May 16, 9:20 a.m.

Member I wuz at the Bellissi with BradMan? Member? We were waitiating on **TyTyTurdly**? Next thing I knew I was gizzone. BradMan said, "Tiffanee, would you like to accompany me to a remote island?" I wuz like woah boy, you gotta ball and chain. This gurl don't do hitched if she knowz about it first. He said that was a non-romantic misunderstanding. He wuzn't coming on to your gurl. He wuz axing if I wanted to ride in his swagcopter with him to get his wifeypoo. He sayz to me, "We'll be traveling in a comfortable sixteen-passenger helicopter with air-to-ground Wi-Fi should there be any news to report. I should also tell you Nelson Miller and his mother will be with us." I wuz like, "Old Fart and Old Mama Fart?" BradMan said correctamundo. 'Cauz some Old Gurl from Wrinkle Town who is with Old Fart and Old Mama Fart sayz she had the skinnie on where BradMan's wifeypoo wuz. So your gurl philosophied about it for a NY mini, then said, "M'kay! Let'z giddy up!" 'Cause vacay is vacay. And your gurl needs an island vacay. And it turnt out to be woot-woot good newz about Old Gurl knowing where BradMan's wifeypoo iz, 'cause **TyTyDeadie** ain't talkin'. Dead sleazeballz tell no tales. And **CosMan the Golfster** can't tell where wifeypoo is neither 'cause he was sicko and looking for a clinical crib for medicinal porpoises, but he assidentally stumblinated on a looney bin instead after it wuz wikileaked by Hot Boi José at Costa di Herald about

TyTyDeadio riding the midnight train to Slab Town. **CosMan the Golfster** musta got the heebie jeebies thinkin' he'd be the next one pushing up daizies so he found a M*A*S*H unit and crybabied UNCLE. But it wuzn't a house of medical assistanz. It was a Nut Hut. **CosMan** was nude-beachin' it so they obvz thought he was from Nut Town. Then they assidentally gave him a drugsplosion of Quaaludes. They said he's gonna be shuteye for dayz. Do ya feel me? Old Gurl from Wrinkle Town is the only one on the down low. She'z the only one who knowz where BradMan's wifeypoo iz. So we wuz flying the friendly skyz in a loopieloop foreva which wuz all aesthetically appleasing till your gurl wuz peepin' tom out the window and saw Jawz. I said, "Whoa, there'z Jawz. And he's floatie." Old Gurl from Wrinkle Town 'bout gave me a busted eargasm when she jumped me to eyeball Jawz then roar squealed in the blingholders on the sides of my noggin, "THAT'Z IT."

We been here foreva.

If wifeypoo and her homies are here, they're incognito.

Or they might be hidin' out becauz this place is so fugly.

So, me and Old Girl from Wrinkle Town wuz doin' the snail trail at the back of the line. Old Gurl was zonked and my dogs were barkin' from doin' the boogie on sheshells by the sheshore. So I sayz, "It'z Flaming Cheetos out here. Can somebody turn on the air condrizzle? Old Gurl here is sweating balls." So then BradMan says, "Tiffanee, take Beulah back to the airbus and stay there." I sayz, "M'kay." Then I sayz, "COME ON, OLD GURL. LET'S ME AND YOU RETURMINATE TO THE SWAGCOPTER 'CAUSE YOU NEED SOME BEAUTIE RESTFULNESS." She sayz, "M'KAY," and when we rearrived, who else wuz already in swagcopter on his iCaller trying to pooperscooper this gurl'z story? Old Fart.

I sayz, "You can't have your gig back, Old Fart."

He sayz, "I don't want it back."

Then I sayz, "Kewl."

Then he sayz, "Let me ask you something, Tiffanee."

I sayz, "M'kay."

He sayz, "When Ty hired you, did you not suspect that he had ulterior motives?"

I sayz, "Huh?"

He sayz, "Tiffanee, you had no experience. You stepped into an investigative job so very ill equipped considering the assignment you were handed. And not to be disrespectful, but your version of the King's English isn't anyone else's."

I sayz, "Huh?"

He sayz, "Did you not realize you were taking on the responsibility of three women's lives? Did you not suspect you were being set up? Did you not find it suspicious that Ty would hire you for such a big job?"

I sayz, "Huh?" But then I sayz, "Windows update, Old Fart. **TyTyDeadDoorbell** didn't nine-to-five me."

He sayz, "Are you saying Ty Towns didn't hire you?"

I sayz, "Don't make me rewind, Old Fart."

He sayz, "Tiffanee. If Ty Towns didn't hire you, who did?"

I sayz, "I don't memember hiz name."

He sayz, "What do you remember about him?"

I sayz, "His office was coolio—" and I was 'bout to tell Old Fart mucho more about the coolio decorationz but didn't 'cauz Old Gurl and Old Mama Fart wuz flippin' their lidz looking out the peepholes for the Bellissi. I gave Old Fart a breaky and said to them, "Old Gurlz. We're not in Kansas anymore. The Bellissi is like way back yonder."

Then the Old Yeller who got us here flabbergasted, "WE'RE NOT LOOKING FOR THE BELLISSIMO. WE'RE LOOKING FOR THE CASINO. THERE'S A CASINO ON THIS ISLAND. A GOLD CASINO."

Isle of Aurum Chalets and Gambling Hall

Dear Bradley,

How do you like my new stationery?

I found it in a perfectly preserved bungalow from the early sixties. One of no telling how many perfectly preserved bungalows from the early sixties that are buried under sand on the other side of the gold jungle wall. The bungalows, should you be looking for our exact location, are only accessible from the shark beach unless you want to jump off the gold jungle wall.

Please don't do that.

You'd land in sand and sink.

Go down the shark beach several miles until you can see the end of the island in the distance. Stop. Look to your left. Past the sand you'll see a small but thick collection of island trees, like a little island forest, about ten trees wide and twenty trees deep. Between two of the trees just to the left of the middle there's a water inlet you can't see until you're on top of it. You'll need a small boat, a canoe, maybe. Once in, the overgrowth is so dense there's no air or light; it feels like the tunnel to middle earth. Once out, you'll be on a lake. I'd call it a bay, but the tide isn't reaching this water. It's pane-of-glass still, not a ripple on it, just like a lake. A lake with water so clear you can see all the way to the white sand floor. Look for the schools of red and purple fish. And while you're at it, look for the striped orange and yellow birds in the trees. There are thousands of them, bright chirping birds. Above the red and purple fish, under the yellow and orange birds, and across the still water on the other side of the lake is a casino, Bradley. A casino. Behind the casino are bungalows. This island was once home to a casino and bungalows at what used to be a resort. Fantasy and I are locked in one of two bungalows that have been partially dug out of the sand. And we're very locked in. The door is barricaded with an iron pipe and there's sand everywhere else. There's so much sand where we are that if you were to climb a fifty-foot ladder on the shark beach to see past the trees and over the lake, you'd think there was nothing on the other side but a mountain of sand. Even from the middle of the lake, you can't see the casino or the bungalows because everything is so monochromatic. It looks like the buildings once had gold façades, but with time and the elements having taken their tolls, the colors are barely distinguishable from each other until they begin taking on angular shapes.

To say this place is hidden is an understatement. Maybe it wasn't way back when, but at some point, every grain of sand in the ocean beyond held a convention at this resort and liked it so much they stayed. Some manner of weather event, an island sandstorm, maybe, if there's any such thing, buried the casino and the bungalows, and since then, the island has grown all over itself. It can barely be seen by land; I can't imagine it could be seen by air. You'd see a mountain of sand. We're at the base of the mountain, and the sand won't budge for us to get out a window or the backdoor of the bungalow, and how hard do we want to try? We could start an avalanche and bury ourselves completely. The bungalow is our new island prison, Bradley, but it won't be for long, because if our prison guard keeps us locked up much longer, we'll run out of air.

Just when we thought things couldn't get worse.

We're on our way out to fill our lungs soon because our casino shift is about to start.

How familiar does that sound?

Fantasy's stretched out on one of the two twin bungalow beds trying to sleep. I said, "Do you want to sleep away what could be the last few hours of your life?" She said, "Do you have anything better to do while you wait to die?"

I did.

You.

I found stationery in a little Mad for Mod desk. I also found playing cards, dice, matchbooks, brass room keys, a shoeshine kit, and a Parker's Electro-Polished Point pen. After drawing endless circles that were doing nothing but making depressions in my new stationery, ink sputtered out of the pen. My point? Sand preserves things, and my better thing to do while I wait to die is write you.

Finally, Bradley, someone arrived.

It wasn't you.

It wasn't the crazy golfer.

It's someone I don't know. I have no idea who this man is. I've looked for him in every corner of my brain and still can't find him. I do know he didn't come to rescue us. I think he intends to kill us. He doesn't look like a killer, he doesn't have the countenance of a killer, but after we find and crack the vault full of gold he thinks is in the casino, I can't imagine he'll let us live. I don't know where to start, so I'll tell you how we met.

Flood night, whatever night that was—I've completely lost track—Fantasy and I jumped out the bathroomette window of the doublewide and gathered our supplies to make our way to higher ground. It wasn't like finding Mango wasn't a priority, but it was pitch black and pouring rain sideways, like buckets of water being thrown at us from every direction, so looking for Mango, or even for our hands in front of our faces, wasn't an option. When we steadied ourselves enough to step off the rocks, we landed mid-calf in thick sandy mud with water rushing above it to our knees, and we could smell the water. We knew the smell. It was runoff from the marsh behind the sea oats. We were wallowing in marsh water runoff. Which meant the shortcut to the gold jungle wall, or I should say to higher ground, wasn't an option. If the water coming down the hill and over the marsh was flowing hard enough for us to be standing in it as far away from the marsh as we were, chances were we'd never be able to navigate our way around it. We'd drown in the marsh, then our bodies would sink to the bottom and never be found. Fantasy yelled above the roar of the rain, "THIS MEANS THE WAVES AND

RAIN ARE COMING FROM THE SOUTH, DAVIS, THE SHELL BEACH. WE'LL HAVE TO GO TO THE SHARK BEACH."

I was in no position to argue, had no sense of direction whatsoever, and was no longer worried about the dead shark, so I yelled back, "LEAD THE WAY."

We used a golf club as a lifeline between us so we wouldn't lose each other. She held the grip and I held the head. We'd traveled two feet, maybe, when it sounded like the island split down the middle. Before we could even wrap our brains around plunging into the dark sea through the split island abyss, the doublewide shot by. If we'd been a foot closer, it would've knocked us down. It wasn't the island cracking in two that we'd heard over the storm, it was the doublewide being lifted from its perch and carried out to sea. It sounded like it took everything in its path with it—trees, rocks, and there went my letters to you along with our only shelter. We made it out just in time. When we realized we'd survived, we were ridiculously disoriented, turning in circles, which was hard to do with the golf club between us, and Bradley, at that point, the golf club we were holding on to for dear life—and I mean those words—was all we had left in the world. Somewhere in there I'd lost my grip on the blankets and our saucepan and she'd lost hers on the vodka bottle and the boxes of mac and cheese. She yelled, "IF ONE THING DOESN'T KILL US TONIGHT ANOTHER ONE WILL."

It felt that way, Bradley.

At that point, both of us so disoriented, we stood still until we could determine which way the water was hitting us (every single which way) and went in the opposite direction hoping it would lead us to the shark beach. What had been a fifteen-minute walk before took hours to reach. We were somewhat confident we'd arrived when we felt packed sand beneath our feet. We weren't sure we were there until we ran into what was left of the firewood from our failed rescue fire. Reduced by 90%, washed away, but a collection of wood, even a small collection in the blinding rain, was enough of a landmark for us to know we'd made it to the other side of the island. And we were right about the tide bringing the water from the south, because while the monsoon rain was still coming down, we were only standing in it up to our ankles. And it wasn't trying to knock us down.

"NOW WHAT?" Fantasy yelled.

"WE STAY PUT," I yelled back. "WE WAIT FOR MORNING."

She yelled, "HOW'S THAT GOING TO HELP?"

I yelled, "WE'RE TOO CLOSE TO THE WATERLINE, FANTASY. ONE MISSTEP AND A RIPTIDE COULD DRAG US OUT TO SEA."

She yelled, "IF YOU INSIST."

Dirt, sand, and no telling what else, alligator bodies, maybe, had been carried by storm water and wedged themselves under and around what was left of the firewood. It was, for the moment, somewhat stable. We climbed it.

I said, "I DON'T SMELL THE SHARK."

She said, "HOW COULD YOU IN THIS DOWNPOUR?"

We linked arms before I let go of my end of the golf club, then she used it to stab in the dark for the shark cadaver. She never landed on it. It was comforting to know we weren't waiting out the weather with the dead shark. It must have ridden the storm train out with the doublewide.

We huddled together on the two-foot-tall stack of wet wood in the pelting rain—like liquid nails falling from the sky—waiting for daylight. It was just as comfortable as it sounds like it would be, but at least, after the most treacherous hike in the history of hikes, we'd lived long enough to die sitting down. We sat like statues on the logs, afraid to move the smallest of muscles lest we unsettle the wood and be washed out to sea with everything else, but we were breathing. Sitting and breathing. As close as we were, we couldn't see each other. We could feel each other—shoulder to shoulder, knee-to-knee—we knew the other was there, but we couldn't see through the storm. Neither of us spoke. I don't know what was going through her mind while mine raced with the singular thought of survival. After all we'd been through, thinking so many times it couldn't possibly get worse, it did. Don't take this the wrong way, Bradley, don't think this diminishes my love for you and our daughters, which has, if anything, grown in ways I didn't know were possible, but at that exact moment, my world was reduced to one person, Fantasy, and my goal in life was for us to live through the night, both of us, because there was only one way left for it to get worse and that would be to lose each other. Every secondary need and every other thought was swept from my mind by the storm. The only thing remaining was for us to stay alive. I was afraid if she fell asleep she'd never wake up. I was afraid if I fell asleep I'd never wake up.

We both fell asleep.

Have you ever woken up on a stack of wet firewood, Bradley?

I have.

I don't recommend it.

Mango woke us. She shook my shoulder. At first, I couldn't see her for the sun. "Did you know—" she poked me "—that tropical storms are between tropical depressions and tropical cyclones on the severe weather scale?"

Fantasy and I scrambled, the logs rearranging beneath us from our sudden movement, trying to decide if we were awake or asleep, dead or alive. Fantasy fell into the woodpile; I tumbled to the sand. Sometime during the night, I'd lost a duck boot, and I knew that because I cut my bare foot on a jagged dune tree branch on the way down. Fantasy's golf shirt had ripped from her body and was left anchored by one button at her neck. Like a cape. Like a ravaged superhero cape. She climbed out of the woodpile and stood on top of it, the morning sun beating down on her, hands on hips, wearing one of Mango's red silk bras that didn't come close to fitting, with a wrecked superhero cape billowing behind her.

It was surreal.

Before my brain could register that we'd found Mango and she was still alive, it registered she wasn't alone. Beside her, a man. At first glance, he wasn't exactly foreboding. He was shorter than Mango by a few inches, mid- to late fifties, maybe even in his early sixties, pale to the point of translucent, thin hair, thick middle, wire-rimmed tinted glasses on a wide beak nose, and so inappropriately wearing office clothes—khakis and a short-sleeved button-down shirt with loafers on his feet, all he needed was a pocket protector. He looked like every person in a red vest behind every Customer Service desk at every Costco. He looked like everyone's odd uncle from Kansas who no one wanted to sit beside at Thanksgiving. He looked like every assistant in every office since the beginning of offices. He had a bulky, and obviously brand new, outdoor backpack hanging off his left shoulder, then I saw what was in his right hand. A gun. It was a girl gun. He had a clumsy grip on a Smith & Wesson J-Frame revolver, the world's most popular carry and conceal, for all the good it does, which is very little. A J-Frame is notoriously hard to aim, Bradley. He didn't look like he'd ever held a gun before, so he probably couldn't hit the side of a barn with it. And his answer to the question I asked on the morning after Fantasy and I miraculously lived through the night gave me more hope than anything else had since we'd been stuffed into the doublewide basement. I said, "Who are you?" He said, or he spat, rather, "You can call me The Conductor."

The Conductor of what? Did he have his own orchestra? Did he drive a trolley? It didn't matter. What mattered was Mango had mentioned him—those words, The Conductor—days earlier, right before she told me Cosmo's name, and I thought they were the same person. They're not. And The Conductor doesn't want us to know his real name SO HE WON'T BE CAUGHT. Granted, it was only a thread of hope, but by that time, my heart was skipping from one beat to the next on threads of hope. And his anonymity hope thread meant we still had a chance. I looked down the beach a half mile or so and didn't care what his name was because I spotted a barge. Or I should say I spotted the very tail end of a barge. Mostly hidden in miles of thick ivy growing wild on the beach was a barge. A way out. An escape route. From what I could see, it wasn't crazy golfer Cosmo's barge we'd ridden in on. Or The Conductor had replaced the lawnmower engine with two new outboards. It was obviously how he'd arrived, and it would be how Fantasy and I would depart. He must have seen my hope and patted his right pant pocket with the barrel of his girl gun. "Sparkplugs."

Bradley, we weren't dealing with a genius, otherwise he wouldn't have told us the barge was inoperable without the contents of his pocket. So there was something on the island he wanted. And no one was leaving until he found it.

This was greed.

I couldn't see it in his eyes behind the tint of his glasses. I could, however, see panic everywhere else. I could see dueling pulses pounding at his temples, he wasn't breathing so much as he was panting, and he couldn't stop clearing his throat. It was worse when Mango opened her mouth. Did we know there were women pirates too? So she thought she and The Conductor were partners, but it didn't look that way to me. Because every time she took a breath to give us more useless information, his head would twitch, or one of his shoulders would pitch forward an inch, or he'd dig a loafered heel deeper into the sand. What did all these nervous gestures mean? They could mean he'd just polished off his third pot of coffee. They could mean he ate Adderall for breakfast. But then again, they could mean The Conductor was sick to death of Mango and was mad at her that it had come to this. He clearly didn't want to be there, and he didn't strike me as someone who'd ever been in charge of anything more important than organizing the office Christmas party, yet somehow found himself on a devastated island in charge of us. So after being Cosmo's prisoners, then the island's, we found ourselves prisoners of an angry man in over his head and ready to get whatever it was he was there to do over with quickly. At the time, we had no idea what that might be, what it had to do with us, or the exact nature of his and Mango's relationship. All we knew was that he was a THIRD player in the adultnabbing game who, like Cosmo, and like Mango, operated one offense at a time and probably had no idea how quickly the battered, bruised, and half-naked island women he was hiding sparkplugs from and holding at gunpoint could turn the tables on him.

He used the barrel of his girl gun as a pointer to direct Fantasy off the woodpile. He said, "Move, Taco." Then he ushered me down the beach. "Go, Tuesday."

He called us Taco and Tuesday. Just like Casino Nelson. Forget me trying to convince myself we had the mental upper hand. The Conductor knew exactly who we were. Finally, we were face-to-face with the man who'd read between the lines. We were finally dealing with the head of the snake. And it was good to know with certainty that Bianca hadn't been kidnapped. It was a bit of closure to know someone thought enough of Fantasy's and my skillsets to kidnap us. At the time, we didn't know which particular skills he was interested in—our breaking and entering prowess? Our investigative skills? Our surveillance talents? Our behind-the-curtain knowledge of casino operation? All of the above?

He stood on the beach impatiently shifting his weight from loafer to loafer while I tied Fantasy's golf shirt back on her body, then shooed us down the shark beach past the hidden barge with his girl gun.

Over her shoulder, trying to keep the lines of communication open, Fantasy said, "Feeling better, Mango?"

Mango said, "Did you know it can take up to six weeks to fully recover from a severe illness?"

(Translation: Mango was better, but not all the way there yet.)

Fantasy asked her, "Where's the shark?"

Mango answered, "Did you know a ghost ship was found floating off the coast of Myanmar nine years after it disappeared?"

(Translation: The shark's body is floating nearby. She predicts it will be there another nine years. I predict it will decompose before then.)

Fantasy said, "Were there ghosts on the ship?"

The Conductor jammed the barrel of his gun between Fantasy's shoulder blades. "Shut up."

She shut up.

I found it odd he used so few words, as if he had an allotted amount and didn't want to waste them. Or maybe he just didn't like us.

The feeling was mutual.

It was our first trip down the shark beach, our first close look, and our first hint at how pretty the island may have once been. Let me interrupt myself to say, had we known, we'd have climbed the dead shark, gotten it over with, and set up camp on the north beach because it was so much nicer. No jagged black rocks, no sharp shells, and soft white sand under my bare foot. The coves all held water so clear and still it made me think of paddleboat excursions, or canoeing, or picnicking. The same flowers we found behind the sea oats and past the marsh were growing wild and free in huge ribbons where sand met land. Even the air on the shark beach was nicer. It was vacation air—cleansing, cool, and seaside scented. And the destroyed resort at the end of the beach, through the woods, and over the lake was proof that we were at the location of what was once a beautiful destination. At the edge of the lake entrance beside a four-man raft with a teeny little outboard motor was the blow-up mattress from the doublewide. It was partially inflated. One tube of the four was taut. Full of air, it would have the buoyancy to pretend it was a raft. Mango, obviously knowing the whole time that the resort was there and tired of waiting for us to find an alternate route to it, which is to say a path that didn't include scaling a dead shark, had made the decision to ditch us, brave the shark body, and strike out alone for the casino on a mattress raft. I shielded my eyes from the sun and turned to Mango. "Thanks a lot."

Mango said, "Did you know the faster you move the slower time passes?"

(Translation: Mango ran out of time.)

Fantasy said, "We save your life, and this is how you repay us?"

Under normal circumstances, I'd have called Fantasy out on that one, because the whole time Mango was sick Fantasy stayed as far away from her as she possibly could, but just then The Conductor fired a shot through the air.

He said, "Silence."

So he knew how to pull a trigger.

One round down, four to go if the cylinder was full.

We boarded the motorized raft, crept through the tunnel to hell, then set out on the beautiful lake having no idea where we were going except across it, because at that point, we still couldn't see anything on the other side but sand dunes as tall as buildings. The closer we got to the sand dunes, the more we could see that the one in the middle had been disturbed. We crept closer and could make out color variations, then distinct shapes, then structures.

Fantasy cut her eyes at me like, "Where are we?"

I cut my eyes at her like, "I have no idea."

Finally, we docked, which was to say The Conductor stopped the plastic boat beside a driftwood log the length and circumference of a telephone pole and in front of a building with broken and cracked windows partially obscured by sand. Then he unzipped his backpack, threw a stretch of rope at me, and told me to tie up the raft. Had he not had the girl gun in his hand, I'd have lassoed him around the neck with the rope, but from one foot away, he'd surely make the shot, and I wasn't in the mood to be a gunshot victim on top of everything else and still didn't have a good feel for whose side Mango was on. Would she help me hang him with his own rope or would she tip my dead body over the side of the raft for burial at lake after he shot me? I was reaching for the rope when Fantasy's hand flew out in front of mine. She said, "Let me."

The Conductor waved permission with his gun.

Fantasy tied the rope around the driftwood with some manner of Houdini knot. Way more knot than necessary. She might be able to untie it, but no doubt The Conductor would have to shoot it off because his soft office fingers would never loosen it. Even if it only took him one shot, we'd be two rounds down and three to go. Even if his backpack had endless ammo, we could take him all the way down as he fumbled rounds into the cylinder. All that to say this, Bradley: we were desperately looking for the chance to ambush him, but the odds weren't in our favor. Not only did he have the gun, we weren't exactly operating at maximum capacity. I couldn't remember the last bite of food either of us ate, the last drop of water either of us drank, and we'd slept on wet logs in a storm. We were running on pure adrenaline and had no idea what was next. What was next was a long trip through a narrow tunnel carved out of the sand that led to a perfectly preserved bungalow from the early sixties. From his backpack, The Conductor produced a plastic flashlight and shoved us through the door, then a bar—it sounded like iron or steel— clanked down on the other side. He locked us in.

I clicked on the flashlight and saw twin beds. On the foot of one of the beds was a room service menu. A Hawaiian Ham Steak dinner was $1.50. A Fried Spring Chicken dinner with hot biscuits and honey was $2.25. A pot of coffee—coffee, Bradley—was $0.50.

We stood the flashlight on its base in front of the dresser mirror and, with the reflection, could almost see. Fantasy read the room service menu over my shoulder then crossed the small room to pick up the dead phone on the nightstand between the beds. The rotary-dial phone was gold, as was most everything else, and covered in a fine film of sand. The telephone receiver was connected to the bulky base with a gold cloth cord. She had the mouth end on her ear and the ear end on her mouth when she said, "Room service? We'd like four Spring Chicken dinners and five pots of coffee."

We fell on the sandy beds.

The most comfortable beds so far in our island world.

"Do we take this place apart looking for weapons?" I asked.

"You think there are swords in here, Davis? Maybe a cannon?"

I dropped over the side of the bed. "The bedframes are metal."

"What are we going to do with a bedframe?" Even though the room was mostly dark, she had an arm lobbed over her eyes. "We could smash the mirror for the glass," she said. "Because seven years bad luck might mean we'll actually live seven more years."

The gold walls might be plaster. The gold furniture was mostly molded plastic, maybe acrylic, mixed with wooden pieces, and the accent colors were cobalt blue and tangerine orange. Everything was mid-century: sleek lines, geometric shapes, and with an architectural feel. You should see the television. The brand is Capehart-Farnsworth. It's a 661-P. It's in a maple cabinet the size of an oven. The top half is the television, the bottom half is the speaker, and it's missing one knob. In the bathroom I found a linen closet. In addition to bath towels and bedsheets galore, the top shelf had four glass bottles of Old Spice aftershave, four tins of Jean Nate talc, four aerosol cans of Aqua Net hair spray, and four hundred individually wrapped miniature bars of soap. There were two gold sinks, a gold bathtub, and tiny gold tiles on the floor. Let me just say this: the whole experience was like stepping onto the annihilated set of *Mad Men*.

There was a knock on the door. The iron bar clanked away, the door cracked, then a sliver of daylight and Mango stuck their noses in. Behind her, with his girl gun, The Conductor. She said, "Did you know the longest game of poker lasted for more than eight years?"

By that, she meant it was time for us to go to the casino.

The sand-cleared entrance was no more than five hundred feet down another narrow sand tunnel path to our left. I was busy wondering who'd done all the excavation work and how they'd managed it when I thought I heard the chop of helicopter rotors. Sound was so muted in the sand tunnel, I cut my eyes at Fantasy like, "Did you hear that?" She cut her eyes at me like, "Hear what? We're in a sand subway. I can't hear a thing." The Conductor, at the back of the line and watching our exchange, shoved Fantasy to move her along. She bumped into me, which pitched me into Mango, and I laid her flat. As I helped her up, I whispered to her, "Mango, you have to help us escape." She looked me dead in the eye and said three words that weren't, "Did you know—?" She whispered, "Find the gold." Then we all looked up because there was no doubt about it, a helicopter was circling the island. I know it's you, Bradley. I can FEEL you.

From: baylor@bellissimo.com
To: davis@bellissimo.com
Day: Saturday
Subject: Hey

Hey, Davis. It's me. Baylor. Where the hell are you? We've been here five hours already and we don't have all day. I need to go. For one thing, I know where July is, she's keeping your kids at your house, and I know the code to get in your door. She'll have to talk to me face-to-face. Unless you've changed the code. The second reason you need to show yourself is because No Hair's locked up again. He was locked up a few days ago because he wouldn't give up Cosmo, and they dragged him in again because he's wanted for questioning in a homicide and they're threatening to keep him the whole forty-eight. I told him the first time if he didn't dial it down something bad was going to happen and he didn't listen. I know and you know he didn't nail that guy. And that guy definitely got nailed. With a nail. A railroad nail. Brutal. The strange thing about that? Your dad has been working a railroad angle this whole time, because Cosmo's family used to own a railroad. If we could find you, you could say you don't believe in coincidences, but then you'd say this is too big of a coincidence and you might side with your dad on the railroad business. For sure, there isn't a railroad on this nasty island. If there is, I'll have to look for it later, because it looks like we're going to have to blaze out of here. And that's mostly because two of my old lady hitchhikers are with us and they're dragging, plus we need to ditch @TiffeeRadNewsBabe. She never shuts up. I don't know where she learned to talk. No one understands a word she says. I was talking to my marriage counselor about July not returning my calls telling her how to get over her hangover and asking her if she thought it was possible July didn't even want to get over her hangover, and she was telling me maybe it wasn't July's choice to get better or not get better. Maybe it was a "journey" July was on and reaching the natural end of the "trip" was part of the process July had to go through. I told her July wasn't on a "trip," because she's never even been in the same room with drugs that I knew of, then I asked her if she was saying July was an alcoholic. She said she "wasn't suggesting anything of the sort," but it made sense to me. You know how you go so far you scare yourself? We see it all the time in the casino, people in too deep. So I sent July ANOTHER text that if she needed to go to rehab I'd deal with it because I love her, and what did she say back? Nothing. Then I started worrying if July went to rehab and stopped drinking, which is crazy, since July never really started drinking, will I have to stop drinking too? I mean, no Stellas for the rest of my life? To be with July I have to be like a rehab alcoholic too? O'Doul's is crap, Davis. All fake beer is crap. Then here comes @TiffeeRad, who I wasn't even talking to, and she said I needed to newsification myself because everyone knew July was spermiated. Whatever the hell all that means. Which sorta leads me back to wherever the hell are you?

When we first landed, part of me hoped you were here so this would all be over. Then we got a good look at this place and I changed my mind and hoped you weren't here, because this island is mostly trashed. It was probably wrecked before the storm hit, the same storm we were in, but for sure it was worse down here. We know you were here because we found pieces of a motorhome. We found one flat tire, looks like a spare, and a piece of a side panel wedged between two short trees. Finding motorhome parts is too much coincidence for you to not be here, even by your coincidence rules, but WHERE? Did you catch a ride home already? We know you didn't leave in the motorhome because it turned up and you weren't in it. Your letters were. Brad won't let anyone read them because they're personal, but he says for sure this is where you were and still are. He says he can FEEL you. We've been here five hours now and I don't FEEL you, so we're taking a break back at the chopper. Brad is on the phone trying to bust No Hair out and the rest of us are trying to decide how to talk Brad into calling the Coast Guard. We wanted to find you ourselves, so we could take you straight home instead of all the red tape, but for that to happen you're going to have to show up soon. It's not like this island is all that big. We've been down one beach that was solid shells, and we've been up through the middle of the island, where we found a gold wall behind branches and vines, which Brad says is positive proof you're here, and then we started down the other side of the island and found a shoe. It's a girl boot. Brad's dragging it around like he's looking for your foot. We're all back at the copter with satellite Wi-Fi and cellular and the girl boot trying to get one of our attorneys on the phone to post bail for No Hair and knocking off the mud before we hit the other side of the island. We'd have hit that side first, but it was the one we could see best when we flew in and we didn't see anything but a decent looking beach, a nice bay that looks like a lake, and the biggest sand dune I've ever seen in my life that would be excellent for off-road four-wheeling. We were going to try it anyway, but now we see smoke. So we have to make a run back to Biloxi to get everyone who isn't us back to safety and for sure call in the Coast Guard, because it's a lot of smoke. We think something is on fire because of the storm, and we think it's coming from the huge sand dune. The thing is sand doesn't burn. It melts. Once the sand dune starts melting, all the sand underneath will melt. I'm no mad scientist, but I don't think it would take much for the whole island to sink. What I'm saying is you have about ten minutes to raise your hand before we have to leave. I don't want to be the one to tell you this, but I FEEL like I should, your husband is staying. I'll be back as soon as we drop off everyone else and I bust No Hair out of City lockup. If there's anything to come back to.

Peace out.

Isle of Aurum Chalets and Gambling Hall

Dear Bradley,

And now we know.

The Conductor thinks there's gold in the casino.

(There is.)

Mango's known all along but couldn't find it because she didn't know where to look. The Conductor wants it. He claims it's rightfully his. And now it's Fantasy's and my job to find it. It's why we were abducted and why we were dumped on this godforsaken island. The Conductor is tired of waiting. He's here to oversee the job himself and not happy about it. Mango doesn't get that he's most unhappy with her. It's so obvious to us she's in danger, yet she seems totally unaware. Every time she opens her mouth he gets a fingernails-scraping-the-chalkboard look on his face and every time she misses it. She just won't stop. Octophobia is fear of the figure eight. Fingernails grow faster on your dominant hand. Apple seeds contain cyanide. We keep shooting her put-a-lid-on-it-Mango looks. She doesn't seem to understand that the minute he has the gold, he'll have absolutely no use for her.

Or us.

The difference is we get it.

We spotted the gold the minute we stepped in the casino and around the Ditch Witch. I only know it's a Ditch Witch because it says Ditch Witch on the side. It's obviously how the sand was excavated to get us this far. It looks like a small tractor but with a scoop at one end and a snowplow looking blade on the other. Without a single word, The Conductor and his girl gun climbed into the driver's seat and lowered the blade to block the exit. He clicked on a spotlight at the top of the orange frame above his head and the casino lit up. Bradley, this casino was frozen in time, and that time was Elvis, Rat Pack, and Marilyn Monroe. Like the bungalows, it was built of solid plaster to withstand the island weather. It mostly withstood the sand too. The floor has several inches of sand carpet—it'd crept in, especially through the broken windows along the north wall—but other than that, and like the bungalow, everything above the floor had no more than a fine dusting. The casino is one rectangular room, probably twelve thousand square feet. There are five retro blackjack tables in a circle in the middle of the floor with semi-circle craps table bookends, seating areas around bars on both sides of the gaming tables, a restaurant that looks out over the lake with tables still set with Franciscan Starburst china and gold flatware, the same pattern Fantasy dug up on the other end of the island. In the middle of one of those tables, a perfectly preserved first edition of *To Kill a Mockingbird*. It still has a sticker on the spine. "Signed by Miss Lee $3.95." (There's your gold, Conductor. Add it to the Bianca ransom I assume you've already collected and go away.) And what else? All the gold. Side by side on a waist-high shelf along all four walls stopping only for the front door and the restaurant entrance are slot machines. There must be two hundred of them. They're small by today's slot-machine standards and made of cast iron. With their pure gold payloads, they probably weigh a hundred pounds each. They have cast iron one-arm-bandit pull handles on their right sides. The play windows, no larger than postcards, are in the middle of the machines, slightly left, three little faded reels, all retro cherries, and the payout tables, the size of a business card, barely legible, are slightly right. Below the coin slot at the top, a window says, "Isle of Arum Gambling Hall. $1.00 Token."

A steep bet back in the day.

A steep bet for a huge jackpot.

If you know how to read a slot machine payout table.

I dodged old casino furniture. "I don't see gold."

Fantasy chimed right in. "There's no gold."

(There was so much gold.)

The Conductor said, "Find the vault."

Mango said, "Did you know the vault door at Fort Knox weighs more than twenty tons?"

They think the gold is in a vault and they can't find the vault. Idiots.

Fantasy said, "We need to eat. We can't find a twenty-ton vault door until you give us food and water."

I jumped in before Mango could with, "And you need to let us contact our families." Which is not to say I had any reason to believe he had a phone that would work in the middle of exactly nowhere, or that I'd ever try that trick on you, like a few weeks ago when I told you we needed a weekend away and you countered with a night out alone, which was all I was after in the first place, and it worked. (Both times. Remember us and that bottle of Silver Oak cabernet we drank on the balcony of an empty Magnolia Suite?) From his backpack, The Conductor didn't toss us a satellite phone, but did toss what we were really after: Nature Valley Dark Chocolate Cherry Fruit & Nut bars and Dasani bottled water. We made quick work of both. I'm sad to say it was the best meal I've had in a week.

Fantasy searched her fingers for chocolate and cherry crumbs. "Where have you already looked for the vault?"

Mango said, "Did you know the movie *Vault* starring Theo Rossi is based on a true story?"

"Have you checked the walls for hidden doors?" I asked.

Mango said, "Did you know there's a hidden gold mine in the Superstitious Mountains of Arizona?"

"Is there an office anywhere?" Fantasy asked. "There has to be an office."

Mango said, "Did you know that most people have coat closets at home larger than their offices at work?"

"All casinos have cashier desks," I said. "They wouldn't have exchanged cash for slot machine coins on the casino floor."

Mango said, "Did you know that airports collect a million dollars a year in coins left in security bins?"

I asked, "Is there a locked door anywhere?"

Mango said, "Did you know if you dream about a locked door it represents a missed opportunity?"

We kept it up hoping The Conductor's head would explode. He couldn't begin to answer one question before we hurled the next, not that he wanted to answer even one. I think he was up to ten words at that point and didn't want to be forced to use any more, making me wonder again what his preferred form of communication was. Charades? Sign language? The written word would be my guess. From under the hot spotlight on the Ditch Witch, sweat poured down his face. His shirt was soaked. When he finally spoke, it was the same three little words. "Find the vault."

Fantasy kicked the leg of a blackjack table. "How are we supposed to find anything in this mess?"

Mango said, "Did you know messy rooms inspire creativity?"

I said, "Trust me. There's a count room."

Mango said, "Did you know it would take eleven and a half days to count to a million?"

Fantasy said, "There's too much furniture in our way."

Mango said, "Did you know the most expensive chair in the world sold for twenty-eight million dollars?"

I said, "They had to do their accounting somewhere. There should be an office with desks, ledgers, typewriters, adding machines, pens, pencils, notepads."

Mango said, "Did you know it would take five hundred million Post-it notes to wrap around the world?"

Fantasy said, "Maybe the vault is in the restaurant."

Mango said, "Did you know the world's largest restaurant is in Syria?"

"What's up there?" I pointed to the plaster ceiling. "Could the vault be above the casino?"

Mango piped up with, "Did you know—" but The Conductor interrupted her with a shot fired straight into an old chandelier exactly where it was anchored above our heads. (So much for him not knowing his way around a J-Frame.) Fantasy and I were halfway prepared for an outburst from him. Mango wasn't. She dove under a blackjack table.

Two rounds down, three to go.

As we knocked glass shards and plaster dust out of our hair and off our shoulders, I said to him, very calmly, "There are rooms off this room. Case in point, restaurants have kitchens. There has to be an office somewhere. That's where the vault will be."

He waved his gun as in "proceed."

"We need to move the furniture out of the restaurant."

He spoke. "No." Because, of course, he could see out the broken windows too. He didn't want us that close to an escape route.

We went to Plan B, which was keep him busy. Fantasy took the front of the room, I took the back, Mango crawled out from under the blackjack table and sat cross-legged in the middle of it. And why not? She'd spent endless days with us and possibly weeks before looking for the gold and hadn't found it. Why bother looking again?

Fantasy took round one. "It's too dark."

The Conductor redirected the spotlight.

Thirty seconds later from the back of the room, I said, "I need light." I got it.

"I think I have something here," Fantasy said. The spotlight swung her way.

Then me, thirty seconds later, "I might have found a hidden door, but I can't see it."

Until he caught on. "You." He pointed the gun at me. He arced the barrel through the air all the way to Fantasy. "Work together."

From the blackjack table, Mango said, "Did you know the ideal workplace team is between four and nine—?"

People, she would have said, had The Conductor not blown her head off her neck.

Mango was dead.

The payout hopper bins inside the old slot machines full of solid gold coins will have to stay where they are for now, Bradley. He's locked me and Fantasy in the bungalow again. He said he'd be back in an hour and it would be our last chance.

He means it.

The last chance part.

And we believe him.

We have the Capehart-Farnsworth television cabinet at the front door. Inside, behind the screen, we have the four cans of Aqua Net hair spray along with everything else we could find in the bungalow that might have combustible properties with the metal bedframes holding everything in place. We've taken the phone apart and have the cloth cord stretched out as a fuse. We have three books of matches. We're about to blow the door off the bungalow. If this goes wrong, you'll find me and Fantasy stuffed in the bathroom linen closet, not under the mattresses we placed on top of the bathtub. We're hoping that's where he looks for us after the blast, and the minute he does, we intend to ambush him from behind. So far, we've done nothing but wait for our chance to escape from him only to decide he's going with us. We didn't really care who he was before he blew Mango's head off, we just wanted off the island. Now we care. Now we're wondering who else he's killed. This man, whoever he is, is riding out of here as OUR prisoner on his own barge, because he needs to pay for what he's done. For the first time since this all started, I don't hope to see you and Bexley and Quinn soon, I KNOW I'll see you and our daughters soon. Or I'll die trying.

I love you.

If I make it out, I'll leave these letters in my other boot on the beach. All of me hopes you'll find them. We're lighting the telephone cord fuse.

Hola

This is José from the mailroom at Gulf Coast Herald again. It is three o'clock Saturday afternoon and I am the new boss. My abuela is very proud and I am very happy to do something to make her proud. She was proud of me before because I taught myself English when I was little from watching *Buffy the Vampire Slayer* and because I stay out of trouble, but now she has a better reason. The people who own the newspaper sent out an email to everyone who works in the office except me and told them not to come back until further notice. Maybe I did not get the email because Everyone's Lunch Truck José does not get office emails, but maybe I did not get it because the newspaper owners want me to tell you the news until further notice. So here is the news until further notice.

The police came and took dead Ty Towns off. They did not clean the mess up in the breakroom from where he died. After I answered the same questions many times and passed a test they ran on my hands and they could not find blood on my clothes with their ray gun, they told me to get out. I told them I could not get out because I was the only one left to answer the tip phone when people called about the missing women. They said they did not hear the phone ringing. I said that was because the phone was ringing way downstairs. So they said go way downstairs and answer the tip phone and stay there. I told them I could not do that because the office with the tip phone was locked up like a prison. The policeman said how do you know that. Have you been in prison? I said no I have never been in prison. Then I said I knew the office was locked up because it is beside the mailroom and I work in the mailroom. The policeman said show me. I showed him. We could hear the phone ringing through the door. He told me to step away then he blew off the deadbolt. Which was cool. He looked around and whistled. Then he said do not touch anything. I told him I had to touch the phone. He said do not touch anything else. I did not touch anything else. I already knew not to touch anything in that office. I answered the tip phone. Most of the calls were stupid like one from a lady who thought I was the turkey tip phone who asked me if she could thaw her turkey in the swimming pool since the water was cold and the directions on the turkey package say thaw the turkey in cold water. I told her frozen turkeys do not float. So she could put the turkey in her pool to thaw it but put it on the steps so it does not drown to the bottom. She said thanks. Then a kid called because his mom would not give him a beer. I asked how old he was. He said twelve. I told him to go do his homework so he could grow up and get a good job. He did not say thanks. Then a man called who said he was Cosmo Booker. I know that name. Everybody knows that name. I said, "Where are you?" He said he was in a janitor closet at a looney bin. I told him English was not my first language and asked him to explain looney bin. He did. That was when I knew for sure the man on the phone was exactly who I thought it was, because how many people named Cosmo are locked up because they are loco? Not many. I asked him why he was in the janitor closet, and he told me he crawled through the ceiling to the janitor office to get clothes and to use the phone. Then I asked him if he was calling to tell me about the missing women, which he should know about because he is the reason the women were missing. He said no. He said he called because he needs money. I wondered why he was calling the tip phone for money, but since I had already talked to a lady about a turkey and to a kid about a beer I should not be very surprised. I told him I had twenty-seven dollars from bussing tables the night before at Holy Cow!, my other job, and he asked if he could have it. I said come get it. He asked if I could bring it to him. I asked where the loco hospital was. He told me. I told him I would have to use some of the twenty-seven dollars to put gas in my truck, and if I gave the rest of the money to him I wanted to interview him for a news story. He said okay but only if I would give him a ride. I asked him where he wanted to go. He told me anywhere. I asked him how I would know it was him, and he said he would be the person behind the loco hospital by the garbage bin wearing a janitor uniform and no shoes. So I am leaving to interview Cosmo Booker and give him a ride somewhere. I will forward the tip phone calls to @TiffeeRadNewsBabe. I do not think she got the email to not work until further notice either, because she is too hot to get that email. The owners would be put in a loco hospital if they told her not to work until further notice, because when she writes a story and it goes life, the computers here go loco. Everyone loves to read what she writes. Her last story has already been shared four thousand times and it is a very new story. I hope she does not mind me sending the tip calls to her, but I will not be here to answer the phone. Everyone and their hermano wants to talk to Cosmo, but I am the one who gets to which is job securities for me. I am not hitting the DISTRIBUTE TO ALL SUBSCRIBERS button right now because I do not want anyone to find Cosmo before I do. I am hitting the SCHEDULE FOR DISTRIBUTION TO ALL SUBSCRIBERS for 4:30 this afternoon which is in one hour and fifteen minutes. That will give me time to get gas and drive to the loco hospital to get Cosmo. Adios.

GET OFF THE WATER

WEBMASTER @ BiloxiTruth.org
Former Staff Investigative Reporter with Gulf Coast Herald
Saturday, May 16, 3:14 p.m.

To my 9,770,312 followers, please, help me spread the word to everyone in the southeastern United States who owns a Sea-Doo, GET OFF THE WATER. Readers, let's go over this again. The Gulf of Mexico is home to hundreds and hundreds of uninhabited barrier islands. Some the size of your garage. Others the size of Dallas. After a frantic, frustrating, and heartbreaking week for so many in the search for three abducted Biloxi women, the hunt was narrowed to a twenty-five-mile area in, around, and directly south of Mobile Bay, Alabama. The specific remote island was finally located and searched earlier today only to discover two of the three women had managed to escape and are missing yet again. Evidence suggests one is injured. The charred and headless remains of the third woman's body have been recovered and airlifted to the Department of Forensic Science in Auburn, Alabama, for positive identification. The body was found early this afternoon in what was formerly the Aurum Gambling Hall on what was formerly Isle of Aurum, eleven miles south of Mobile Bay, Alabama, six miles west of Dauphin Island, and don't even think about it, you rubbernecking lookie-loos in your rental speedboats. You will be stopped before you get anywhere near the island by Alabama rescue teams, Coast Guard and Air Force rescue crews, Mississippi Bureau of Investigation's

State Crime Information teams, Georgia mobile crime lab techs, or Florida arson investigators.

How do we know the other two women escaped? The contents of a women's Sperry Duck Boot left on the beach in addition to K9 ALERT Search and Rescue dogs said as much. Why do we believe they left the island by water? The boot was found by Bellissimo President and CEO Bradley Cole in the wake of a deep impression on the beach indicating the departure of a flat-bottom boat. It could be a Jon boat, a deck barge, a pontoon boat, or a large gondola for all we know. Evidence suggests the unidentified vessel is approximately thirty feet by twelve feet, a virtual needle in an ocean haystack. To all of you swarming Mobile Bay: **YOUR DRONES ARE CREATING DANGEROUS FLYING CONDITIONS FOR SEARCH AND RESCUE AIRCRAFTS IN ADDITION TO INTERFERING WITH RADIO BEACONS POSSIBLY EMINATING FROM THE WATERCRAFT THE WOMEN ARE ABOARD. AND YOU VOUEYERS AND MEDIA IN YOUR RECREATIONAL AND FISHING BOATS ARE IMPEDING COAST GUARD SEARCH AND RESCUE VESSELS.**

Please, if you care at all about the fate of the two women we hope are still alive, move your party flotillas. Get off the water and let the authorities do their jobs. And to my mother and the rest of the Whodunnits, get back to Caring Star. The last thing I need to do right now is worry about you.

Need a VaCay from My VaCay!

BY TIFFANEE JONES
GULF COAST HERALD STAFF REPORTER
Saturday, May 16, 4:00 p.m.

Bustola. Terribad vacay! Your gurl'z never going back. The wurst wuz my pouty face 'cauz we didn't locationate Bellissi BradMan's wifeypoo before we had to u-turn 'cauz of a firedragon. When the swagcopter dropped me at the Bellissi I went to my crib to revamp 'cauz my threads were yesterwear and I wanted to look purty if I smacked into José, plus your gurl never double dooties her stylish garms. I redecked in phresh phashions and was on my way to the office to identifize the man who gave this gurl her kewl NewsBabe job when BRADMAN'S WIFEYPOO DIALED MY DIGITS.

I sayz, "Uhm, yello."

She sayz, "Uhm, yello. This is Davis Way Cole."

I sayz, "Who?"

She sayz, "My name is Davis Way Cole. I'm married to Bradley Cole, the president of the Bellissimo. My friend is injured, and we need help."

I sayz, "Who is this?"

She sayz, "DAVIS WAY COLE."

I sayz, "Get out."

She sayz, "I will not get out. Fantasy Erb and I have been missing for a week. Fantasy needs a hospital. We're trapped. I can't get my husband on the phone. I can't get my boss or my coworker on the phone. All Bellissimo lines are answered with a recording that says the casino is closed. I've tried to call everyone in my family and their phones are out of range. I've tried 911 five times and was hung up on all five times by dispatchers who did not believe me. I have very little time, so I've dialed the Gulf Coast Herald tip line. You are my last hope. Is this the Gulf Coast Herald tip line?"

I sayz, "Uhm, no."

Then she wuz gonner. I wuz like, "WHAAA? Rewind!" So I did the trackie dance on my cellie to locate her 'cauz I logicized her vacay wuz worse than mine and I should assistancize her. I wuz on my wayz to my vehicular when BABA SANDERS dialed my digits!

I sayz, "Uhm, yello?"

She sayz, "Forevermore. Who is this?"

I sayz, "I'm Tiffee Newschick. What'z your name puddintane?"

She sayz BABA SANDERS! And she thought she wuz calling the tippy line too!!!!

I sayz, "Get out!"

She sayz, "Pardon me?"

I sayz, "M'kay."

She sayz, "Whatever is your problem, young lady?"

I sayz, "I got no probs 'cept a bad vacay and Hot José is angrimated at me."

She sayz, "Is this Gulf Coast Herald? I called to speak to someone about my immediate need for positive press after defamation of my character from unfortunate publicity, and so far this has been a very fruitless conversation."

I sayz, "This gurl luvs fruits, 'specially in my cockytails, but I gotta circle back atcha, BaBa, 'cauze I'm busy doin' the boot scootin' boogie to rescue a chica named Davis."

Then she sayz SHE WANTS TO GO WIFF! 'Cauz that would improvinate her bad reputation from her Spaze Invaderz interviewz if she saved her bestie!!!! Me and BABA SANDERS are not returminating without BradMan's wifeypoo!!!!

BaBa is SO KEWL!

Tootles.

From: baylor@bellissimo.com
To: davis@bellissimo.com
Day: Saturday
Subject: Hey

Hey, Davis. It's me. Baylor. No Hair says to tell you hey. I'm at City lockup with him. Sandy Marini is the lead homicide detective on No Hair's case, and since we know her and she knows us and everybody knows No Hair didn't do it, she's letting me take your dad's place behind the glass of his interrogation room until it's a good time to spring him. What they're doing is keeping No Hair hoping whoever has you will think he's off the hook and surface. While he was here your dad was reading old case files about anyone associated with the old railroad trying to figure out who really did run a railroad spike through Ty Towns's skull and blew the Mango woman's brains out, because for sure that's who has you, and it looks like your dad might have finally found something in these old files. It's not like he hasn't been looking night and day. We've all been focusing on the island and the relatives and friends of the people who died on the island, but your dad has been saying all along it goes further back. He thinks it goes back to the railroad company they owned before they owned the island. He says the person who has you is a friend or relative of one of the people who got screwed by the railroad. You know that old railroad station on the back bay everyone tries to buy and turn into a casino, but the bank won't let it go because it's in a blind trust? And someone keeps paying the taxes on it, but no one knows who? Cosmo's family used to own it. Before they bought Trash Island where all those people died they sold a railroad and put a lot of people out of work with no warning, and half the railroad guys who lost their jobs went crazy, lots of others ran off and left their families, and one who had a wife and a baby committed suicide because of it. Do you think this whole thing is about someone who wants revenge because the railroad shut down? Your dad sure does. And just to let you know, he's off looking for old railroad stations. Guess where my old lady hitchhikers are. Just guess. They're here, being booked for criminal trespassing, criminal mischief, and contributing to the delinquency of a minor. I have no idea what happened. When I find out I'll let you know. Everybody's everywhere they shouldn't be. Sandy Marini and the rest of homicide left for dinner at the Half Shell a while ago and invited me, but I stayed here with No Hair and the old ladies. Sandy asked me not to go into the interrogation room with No Hair because it's all recorded, and if they have to submit video, they don't want to get tied up in court about it, so I talked to No Hair through the interrogation window squawk box.

And speaking of talking to people, your mother-in-law is a bitch. I don't mean your old mother-in-law, Bea Crawford, who is also a bitch but a very different kind of bitch. There are all kinds of bitches in the world, Davis. I'm talking about your new mother-in-law, Brad's mom. Anne Cole. She's the reason I have nineteen stiches above my left eye. I bet my eyebrow will never be right. I had an EMT who was dropping off at the drunk tank here stitch me up in the parking lot. Because of your mother-in-law. What happened was when we got back to Biloxi and I got my old lady hitchhikers in the back of a cab (should have driven them to the old lady home myself instead of trusting them to go where they were supposed to, because it turns out they didn't go home and now they're all here at City lockup being booked for mischief and the intake desk won't let me talk to them), I went straight to your place to make July talk to me. I did the door code and walked in and got attacked. At the time I was only half sure I was in the right place because your regular furniture is gone. I don't know when your mother-in-law and her bodyguard showed up or why she thinks it's okay to move your furniture while you're not there, and I especially don't know why she thought it was okay to bring her dog that is the size of a horse. Her dog is BIG and LOUD and it DROOLS. So I get in the door and look at all the new furniture that makes your foyer look like outside a spaghetti restaurant all over the place and I yelled, "JULY!" and here comes that dog. It doesn't even know me, and it was so glad to see me it took me down. I was up then I was down. That dog pinned me on the floor with his massive paws and started wet licking me. I couldn't even breathe because it has so much hair. And it has bad breath too. Then here comes your mother-in-law, Anne, with a golf umbrella— huge—and she starts beating me. And get this, your mother-in-law has a bodyguard who was egging her on yelling, "STOP THE STEAL! STOP THE STEAL!" like I was there to rob the place. And your mother-in-law was yelling back at her bodyguard, "THE ONLY THING HE'S STOLEN IS JULY'S INNOCENCE!"

If your mother-in-law's dog hadn't had me glued to the floor licking me, like taking a dog slobber shower, maybe I'd have seen the umbrella coming. I tried telling her I was there because I needed to talk to July, and she said July already got my message loud and clear and it sent her straight to her room crying. What message? The hundred messages I left on her phone? Crying about what? Why would I leave July alone if she's crying? Your mother-in-law didn't answer any of my questions. She just kept beating me with the umbrella telling me it was all my fault and the whole time her bodyguard was telling her to get me in the kidneys. Then your mother-in-law says if I knew what was good for me, I'd repent. For what?

What the hell have I ever done to that woman? All this was between her trying to kill me with a golf umbrella and the dog trying to drown me with slobber and her bodyguard yelling at her to jab my eyes out with the end of the umbrella. And your mother-in-law was trying. I didn't get out of that mess without almost losing my eyebrow. Not sure where you are, Davis, but brace yourself for going home. I never saw July and I didn't see Bex or Quinn. That doesn't mean they weren't there, that only means I didn't see them. I saw your mother-in-law, her dog, and her bitchy bodyguard who wouldn't let me past the front door. A woman named LeeAnn. I think she's a woman. Maybe not. I'll tell you this about her, if she's a woman, she could take No Hair. I mean it. She's sumo material. That was it. I was only there long enough to get attacked by a dog, beaten up by your mother-in-law, and yelled at by her sumo bodyguard. Now I'm really worried about July. July only cries when she's happy. She doesn't sad cry. She cries over love movies and about weddings and babies. But I've never had an eight-day hangover like July is having. Maybe the eighth day is the crying day? I don't know. I haven't had any decent sleep in so long I can't think straight.

Listen, one last thing because I need to figure out what message I left for July that made her cry and also what my old lady hitchhikers did to get locked up, Brad found your letters on the beach while he was waiting on the firefighters, and just in time, because he thought you were melting in the fire until he read your letters and saw where you'd left. In a million years, who would believe that when we were on one side of the island looking for you, you were on the other side. And it looks like you shoved off when we were all at the chopper trying to spring No Hair and figure out what to do next. Bad timing. When you blew up your hotel room, a chemical fire started in the sand and took just about everything out. I was already gone with my old lady hitchhikers and @TiffeeRad. Brad and Newspaper Nelson were running for the fire when they found your boot and a golf club. Brad read the letters in the boot while he waited on the aerial firefighters to dump foam on the sand, then had to gear up in aluminized Kevlar to get past the heat, and when he did he found two things. Three if you count the dead woman, Mango. One thing was all the slot machines. The gold inside is fine. There's a lot of gold. They say about six million dollars of gold. The other thing he found was blood in the hotel room you were in on a piece of metal from the bedframe, and we know it was from the bed because it says Kroehler Quality Beds. The mobile lab tested the blood and it's Fantasy's on one end but your fingerprints on the other. What happened? Is she okay? Homicide's back from dinner, July is crying, No Hair wants me to call your dad and see if he's found anything, my old lady hitchhikers are locked up, and it's getting dark.

Davis, show yourself. Turn up at a hospital with Fantasy, because that bedframe business had to hurt. Your dad has everyone he could round up looking for you at old train stations in three states, but it's getting dark. Davis, if I've never said it before, I'll say it now, you are very important to me. Most of what I know I learned from you. I really need you to be okay. If something happens to you, what's going to happen to me? No Brad, because he'll mope around for the rest of his life. No No Hair, because he'll be mad for the rest of his. No Fantasy, because she'll never make it without you if she's even okay from being stabbed by a bed, and no July, because something is VERY WRONG with her. All that and no you? Come on, Davis.

Peace out.

Dear Mommy,

Pleese come home.

We have a new playhous and a new dog.

Daddy is very sad.

July is taking a nap.

Gramwitch is here and she told us to stop callin her Gramwitch.

Love Bexly Anne Cole and Carolin Quin Cole

BROUSSARD RAILWAY COMPANY
BILOXI STATION

Dear Bradley,

Fantasy might die just three little miles from her home, from her family. If there were a window I could drag her to and wake her up enough to open her eyes, I think we might be able to see the top floors of the Bellissimo. My home. And my family. We're on the Back Bay. We're in the caboose of an old train wedged in the corner of the old Broussard train station. You know it. The big red brick building in the woods behind miles of electric fencing off Back Bay Road. Someone's always trying to buy it. It's dark inside the terminal. If it weren't for a beam of moonlight hitting the caboose through a crater-sized hole in the roof above it, I wouldn't be able to see at all. And if Fantasy's lips weren't so blue and her breathing so shallow, she might look like she was sleeping peacefully, but I know better. I think she's in shock. She's lost so much blood. She surely needs a transfusion. And fifteen tetanus shots. And something, anything, for her blood pressure, because it isn't right. I don't know if it's too high or too low, but one of the last words she spoke aloud that made sense was "sepsis," which I think has something to do with blood pressure bottoming out after infection hits the bloodstream, and the only reason I believe her is because I can't stop checking her pulse, and it's racing one minute and I can't find it the next. Bradley, she's in bad shape, and I'm writing what I'm sure will be my very last letter to you on stationery I found in the conductor's desk.

The Conductor.

Sound familiar?

I haven't traveled by train since I was a little girl, and I've never set foot in the caboose of a train, which, as it turns out, is the train's office. I don't know what I thought it was before, other than the cute red car at the end of the line, but it's an office. There's a huge iron stove, two sleeping berths, an icebox under a shelf of stacked bowls and coffee mugs, a small table with two chairs, and a desk. Beside the desk there are old jackets on hooks. On the desk there's a perfectly preserved Biloxi Daily Herald newspaper from November 6, 1955 with the headline, "Broussard Sells Railroad, 2,000 Out of Work" and a brass nameplate that says, "Conductor." Beside that, there's a smaller brass plate that reads "Assistant Conductor" and a baby boy's blue-striped hat. Behind that, there's a framed picture of a woman, Mrs. Conductor, I guess. So this was the conductor's office. And the conductor of this train must have been The Evil Conductor's father. In the father's desk I found stationery, a thirty-two-dollar bill from Biloxi Petroleum and Electricity, and an I'm So Sorry postcard, which read to me like a suicide note, from 1958 with a $0.07 stamp on it. It was never mailed from Mr. Conductor, Robert Brunner, to Mrs. Conductor, Vivian Brunner.

BRUNNER. Do we know that name?

Start there if you ever find this letter.

Brunner.

Who would think to look for us here? Who would ever, in the search for us, consider an abandoned railway station in our own backyard? I'll tell you who, Cosmo, because he was here recently, very recently, but there's no way he's still alive. It would be the ninth wonder of the world if Cosmo has skated through this. The only person I feel sure will walk away without a scratch is The Conductor. The brutal, heartless, murderous, greedy conductor, who for some reason holds me and Fantasy responsible for what happened to his family decades ago.

The caboose has three exits, four if you count the trap door in the ceiling, but I don't know how it could help, so let's concentrate on the three that can—one door on each of the long caboose walls and another in the back. One of the side doors and the back door are blocked because they're against brick walls. The Conductor barricaded the third door, the only real way out of the caboose, holding us hostage again to "take care of business." That was hours ago. I don't know if his business is sleeping in the old passenger car on the other side of the terminal or on one of the old benches near the ticket desk, or if he left us here to die while he goes back to the island for the gold he so desperately desires.

When we first arrived, all I wanted to do was stabilize Fantasy, and the thought of leaving her side wasn't an option. I don't think she'd be in the shape she's in had we not traveled so far so fast in such a short period of time. I was hanging on for my own dear life, hanging on to Fantasy for hers, and The Conductor was running for his. Because as we were leaving the island a chopper that looked just like one of the three Bellissimo copters flew over so close that had we looked up it might have grazed our noses. And here I am, several treacherous and terrifying hours later, a prisoner in my own backyard. This reorienting myself to new and more devastating detainee conditions seems to be what my life has become. What's next? Alcatraz? Guantánamo Bay? A holding cell in hell?

I've been alone with my thoughts and Fantasy's ragged pulse for hours. It's time for me to make a move, any move, but I wanted to write you first. I feel like I've done nothing but write you goodbye letters for a week. This will be my final goodbye letter. Because I think this is goodbye. If I don't at least try to get help for her, she won't live through the night, but I'm not sure I'll live through escaping the caboose. My best exit option is a small glass window between the icebox and the shelf of dishes, and my biggest fear is that he'll be waiting for me with his girl gun and I'll die half in and half out of the small window. Let's be more optimistic and say I live through the window, in which case I won't be able to get Fantasy up and out the same small window, so to get her to a hospital, I'll have to clear the window then open the blocked door, and I don't know what I'm up against. Whatever he scraped up to it was loud. When it made contact, the caboose shook. If I manage to move whatever it is and we make it out of the caboose, we have to exit the terminal, which won't be hard, because we entered through an open bay, but then there's the electric fence around the property, an electric fence for which The Conductor has a remote control in the same pocket he had the barge sparkplugs earlier. I seriously doubt he left the remote for me. Which means I'll have to find the power source. In the dark. And the fence is around at least ten acres. I'm at worst-case scenario, Bradley. But if I don't at least try, Fantasy and I will die in the caboose. I'd rather go down fighting.

I searched the caboose for weapons. The closest thing I found was a fireplace poker. So if we make it out, look for your five-foot-tall half naked electrocuted wife carrying her six-foot-tall half naked electrocuted best friend wandering the Back Bay roads trying to bum a ride to Biloxi Memorial. I'll be the one brandishing the fireplace poker. When I found the poker beside the stove iron, I discovered a golf tournament gift bag shoved behind it, which is why I believe Cosmo was here at some point. At first it was a godsend. Then it broke my heart. Inside there was a visor, an ink pen (this ink pen), a bottle opener, a ball marker, a koozie, and a golf towel. Everything is white and says Golden Oaks Golf Course in green. I dug through quickly, keeping the pen and towel, then tossed it back where I found it and heard a thud when it landed. I didn't remember anything thud worthy in the bag. I looked again and found a cell phone inside the koozie. It had one last breath of power.

I tried.

The saddest part of all of this is that we could've been home now. Or, rather, in a hospital with Fantasy now. We could have easily escaped the island this morning—our plan was so solid—had a metal spike from the bungalow bedframe not shot through Fantasy's right leg just above her knee. It happened when we blew the bungalow door.

We had to light the telephone cord fuse four times before it ignited, then it took forever to burn, but eventually it worked. The blast was ground shaking and deafening, but it didn't blow the bungalow door out; it blew it in. We bombed the bungalow bedroom. Had it not been for the mattress we'd dragged in the bathroom before we lit the fuse, we'd probably both be dead. There's very little linen closet left standing and there's no bedroom whatsoever. When the flying sand settled, I realized we were no longer behind the linen closet door. Because the linen closet door was gone. The mattress had blown off the bathtub and blocked the linen closet held in place by huge ceramic chunks of the bathtub. I felt for Fantasy and the first words she spoke will haunt me forever. She said, "Are you okay, Davis?"

She wasn't okay but asked if I was.

We were covered in sticky sand and plaster and who knows what else, with sand spilling in through holes in the ceiling. We could barely breathe. Even had it not been dead-of-night dark in the linen closet, we still wouldn't have been able to see through the sand. We beat past the mattress to dim daylight, and I immediately started scrambling over the debris and swimming through the sand between us and freedom until I realized Fantasy wasn't scrambling and swimming with me. I turned and saw the blood pouring down her leg. It was a shock—the red. At first, it didn't even make sense to me. I think my brain was trying to locate anything liquid and shiny red that might have been pouring down her leg other than the very obvious. We looked up from her leg, our horrified eyes met each other's, and we were forced to acknowledge the truth. She had a bed spike through her leg. The next three or four minutes would have been our escape, but they weren't. We'd planned on The Conductor hearing the explosion and taking the fastest path to us which would have been the sand tunnel to our right. Our plan was to go the other way, the casino route, past Mango's dead body and through the broken windows above the lake to freedom while he dug for us in the bungalow rubble. Fantasy and I realized, staring at each other, mouths wide open, blood trailing down her leg, we wouldn't make it to freedom faster than he'd find us. She slumped and tried to slide down what was left of the linen closet wall, her immobile injured leg stopping her. I crawled back to her and helped her onto the mattress.

It immediately turned bright red.

She said, "Get it out."

I said, "No."

"Davis, pull it out."

"Fantasy, no. I won't pull it out."

She said, "Look."

I looked.

"It's nowhere near my femoral artery." Her breath was ragged. "I won't hemorrhage. This is all the blood there'll be. I can't walk with it in my leg. Pull it out. If I can't walk, we can't get out. If you don't pull it out I will. Don't make me pull this thing out of my own leg."

I have no idea if she knew what she was talking about or not. I do know there was already too much blood. I was terrified to pull it out thinking there'd be even more blood. She begged, Bradley. I think the metal spike was scraping bone.

I didn't even close my eyes when I pulled it out. I kept my eyes on hers. We've been through everything, Bradley, so much, going back years, never dreaming we'd go through anything like what we'd been through the past week of our lives, and if it had come to this and she was wrong about the metal stemming even more blood loss and I would lose her three minutes after I pulled it out, I would damn sure look her in the eye while I did it. I told her I loved her, I yanked it out, her scream was deafening, but not so much that I didn't hear The Conductor behind me slowly clapping his hands. I turned to look at him. He met my eyes. He said, "Clever."

He was talking about the Aqua Net bomb.

Mercy upon mercies, he didn't stop me from tying a bedsheet-strip tourniquet above Fantasy's knee. With superhuman strength that came out of absolutely nowhere, I tied it tight enough to stop the bleeding, cutting off her circulation above the wound, and it finally stopped. Her injured leg was limp. She couldn't hold an ounce of weight on it, but at that point she still had enough strength to lean on me as I hobbled us over the rubble and out the wide bungalow opening with The Conductor and his girl gun at my back. One stagger out the door and we were almost knocked down by heat radiating from the sand to our right. We went left. We went through the dark casino, past Mango's headless and horrifying corpse, then out the restaurant windows—The Conductor would not help me get Fantasy out the window because he simply didn't care—and into the raft. Twenty excruciating minutes later we were on the barge. The last thing I did was pull off my single duck boot full of letters to you and toss it in our wake on the beach. For my efforts, he smacked me in the face with the butt of his girl gun. I haven't seen a mirror since the filthy cracked mirror of the doublewide, but I'm pretty sure I have a shiner. It's tender. It's raw. It's a concentrated representation of the rest of me, especially my heart.

We traveled by water at top speed for two hours, never cutting through the water on a smooth plane, always airborne on whitecaps then slamming down hard, it's a miracle we didn't capsize, all the way to the Biloxi Bay before he slowed down enough to not draw attention to us (and it would have only been bird attention—WHERE IS EVERYONE?) until he docked the barge behind the old train station. And here we are.

Fantasy's hallucinating.

She mumbles about Reggie and the boys, she's deliriously called out to her parents, and she keeps saying what sounds like "yello" like she's answering someone who's calling out to her. She's burning up with fever, but I have no excuse, because ten minutes ago I swear I saw a huge flash of light and heard Bea Crawford calling my name from a nearby tunnel. Or maybe my excuse is the blood pounding in my temples, because I honestly thought I heard Bianca too. Which means it's time for me to go, Bradley, before I deliriously drop in my tracks. I'm so sleepy, Bradley. I'm just so sleepy.

Know that I gave it my everything. Know, and make sure our daughters, my family, and Fantasy's family knows we did everything we could to find our way h

Bellissimo Resort and Casino Declines to Press Charges in Property Defacement Case

Source: WLOX CBS Biloxi
Saturday 16 May 7:18 PM EST
Biloxi, Mississippi

Seven elderly women ranging in age from 76 to 88 who purportedly paid a teenage boy to deface a billboard directly across the street from the Bellissimo Resort and Casino owned and maintained by the Bellissimo's advertising division will not face vandalism charges. Nor will they face contributing to the delinquency of minor charges, as the parents of the minor involved have also declined to press charges against the elderly women. Bellissimo legal representative Cory Soto said in a phone interview, "It looks like the ladies meant no harm. They were attempting to facilitate a reconciliation between a young couple having trouble communicating. And the Biloxi High School student who scaled the sixty-five-foot fixed ladder with three gallons of latex paint to write the billboard love letter at the elderly women's bequest was not only the captain of Biloxi High's climbing team, thus outfitted properly in a body harness with a rest lanyard, he was an enthusiastic participant. We will not press charges."

WLOX wishes the couple, who according to the defaced billboard are named Baylor and July, our very best.

PUBLIC NOTICE

GLOBAL MEDIA, INC. ANNOUNCES AUCTION OF ALL GULF COAST HERALD PUBLISHING HOLDINGS
Date of Auction: Monday, May 18, 2:00 p.m.

Auction Type: property, building, contents, subscriber list
Auction Location: Corner of Cavalier and Division Streets, Biloxi, Mississippi
Square Footage of Single Structure: 27,000 individual and open-floorplan offices on two levels, 9,000 production facility
Lot Size (Acres): 1.1
Primary Property Type: Commercial/newspaper print and distribution
Year Built: 1997
Parking Count: 62

Contents:
- 2008 Comet Newspaper Press and accompanying folders, grippers, stackers, and strappers
- Various office equipment and furniture including desks, chairs, file cabinets, computers, monitors, routers, desktop printers, backup drives, surge protectors, telephones, fluorescent lighting fixtures, various photography equipment, one umbrella stand
- Four 2018 International 4300 SBA box trucks, low mileage
- 1955 Lionel Standard Gauge Model Train Set in perfect condition, opening bid $250,000. Buyer must disassemble from current basement office location and arrange transport. Seller not responsible for any damage incurred during transit.

Isle of Aurum Sold and Trust Established for Families of Victims of 1961 Tropical Cyclone

By Jennette Massey

HERON BAY, ALABAMA (Reuters) – Pleading no contest and waiving his right to a trial on multiple felony charges, and before being taken into custody by Mississippi Corrections in Biloxi, Cosmoses (Broussard) Booker signed seven million dollars in gold into a trust established to locate and make reparations to the families of victims who lost their lives on Isle of Aurum during a swift and deadly storm in 1961. Afterward, he sold Isle of Aurum to Bellissimo Resort and Casino President and CEO Bradley Cole in a cash deal for $5.00. Mr. Cole, in turn, donated the island to Gulf Islands Seashore Preservation Group.

Hit and Run Driver Surrenders to Police

WLOX-TV Biloxi
By WLOX Staff
Sunday, May 17, 2:19 p.m.

According to authorities, Beatrice Crawford, sixty years old, of Pine Apple, Alabama, turned herself in to Biloxi PD detectives earlier today. In a statement, Ms. Crawford said, "This is all a misunderstanding and I'm here to straighten it out. I didn't do any hitting and running. What I did was bumping and rescuing. I'm one of the Pine Apple Rescuers from Pine Apple, Alabama. Our mayor and police chief had us all out looking for my daughter-in-law, Davis, in old train stations because he couldn't talk any other law enforcement into looking for her at the train stations. She's not my daughter-in-law anymore, but we're still thick as thieves. I help her out all the [deleted] time. I was on my way to the train station where I was supposed to be looking for Davis when I ran into my best girlfriend, Bianca Sanders, and some crazy [censored] who calls herself Baby Trippy. And that one's a trip all right. That Baby Trippy's blue jeans was threads. I mean it, just threads hanging on her skinny legs. She said it was the unconstruction look, and I say it's the stupid as [omitted] look. And I've never seen so much makeup in my life. Don't bother trying to buy any makeup around here, because that girl's bought it all already. I don't think she was wearing a bra either. I don't know that for sure. You'd have to ask her if she was wearing a bra or not, and good luck understanding what the [deleted] she tells you. I don't know where the [censored expletive] that girl is from, but they don't speak American wherever it is. They were looking for Davis too. I said, y'all come on and ride with me, because I got a shotgun and I'm a [*deleted*] deputy.

So let's get one thing straight. I was doing my law duties when I bumped that coyote. The judge needs to know that. And I wouldn't have bumped it at all except for my new tires. Big ass tires. They're thirty inchers. All terrains. Had to get new rims too. And my new tires have me so jacked up off the [*omitted*] road, I can't see what's right there in front of me, so you squirrels watch out for Bea, you hear? I was driving slow anyway. I was looking for somewheres to park Bianca's hoity-toity butt because she doesn't like my truck, and that's when I barely bumped into the coyote. And let's get this straight. I didn't kill that [*censored*] coyote. A hot fence killed that coyote. Alls I did was bump it. That coyote got right up after I bumped it then scurried off and hit that hot fence all by itself. The hot fence killed it. That coyote ran straight for that hot fence and fried like a chicken. The whole fence lit up the night like it was [*expletive*] high noon. That poor coyote sizzled like a slab of bacon. Which if you ask me is innocent. How the [*deleted*] was I supposed to know about that hot fence? It's not like I said, 'Now go on and run into that hot fence, coyote.' That coyote ran into that hot fence all by its lonesome. And if you don't do anything but bump a coyote who runs into a hot fence on its own, well you're [*omitted*] innocent. I like coyotes okay. I like all God's creatures. I even felt bad for it when I saw it frying on that fence like a pork chop, because that hot fence had some [*deleted*] juice. That coyote was fricasseed.

I yelled out the window I was sorry about him frying himself, and that was when a hobo climbed up on the roof of the train station. Everybody was screaming except that coyote because it was a goner. There was smoke coming off it. Then I figured out that hobo on the roof was my daughter-in-law, Davis, because she was yelling my name. She might have figured out it was me when she heard me telling the coyote I was sorry it fried itself and asking Bianca to shut the hell up, because they tell me my voice carries good. Davis had climbed up on that [censored] roof trying to get help for her friend, because she knew about the hot fence I didn't know about. So let's be real clear on this. I didn't know about that hot fence. And nobody gets locked up because they didn't know about a [omitted] hot fence.

After that I got busy on my rescue work. Because I'm a good human citizen from Alabama who helps people. I was busy helping get Fantasy to the hospital, because she was about to meet her maker. All her doctors say she isn't going to lose that leg, but I'm not so sure. I was at the hospital seeing her early this morning to ask her what she was going to do with her extra shoes if they end up taking that leg, and here comes the [deleted] law on me for hitting a man with my truck then running off. So I start explaining to them I was the law and alls I did was bump a coyote who jumped on that [omitted] hot fence by itself. I explained how it fried like a turkey leg on that hot fence and I explained my new tires. Turns out it wasn't a coyote. It was that old boy who locked up Davis and Fantasy at the train station, and blowed that other girl's head off, AND drove that railroad spike through that [censored] newspaper man's head. Vince Bummer, they said. And if you ask me, I should get a reward, because that there was one [deleted] twisted [omitted] psycho. Somebody ought to be giving me a citizen's award.

This is all a misunderstanding between me and the law, but I've been down this [omitted] road before. One, I got evidence. My bumper and my grill don't have a scratch on them. That's how not hard I didn't bump that coyote who, turns out, was a man, who ran into that hot fence all by himself. And I got witnesses. They'll say, 'Don't lock up Bea on account of her bumping a coyote who don't know where he's going.' The trick is to tell the judge and tell him and keep telling him until he gets tired of hearing it and says forget it."

From: MotherOfBradley@aol.com
To: BCole@Bellissimo.com
Date: May 17, 3:22:45 p.m.
Subject: Mother is Miffed
Sent from the Internet

It is three in the afternoon. Do you know where your mother is?

Let me begin by saying the poet who penned "The influence of a mother is beyond calculation" was certainly no mathematician, because having spent two long days and nights in your gambling hotel home, I didn't find an ounce of my influence, young man. The twins, without the structure of the well-oiled machine that is MY home, behaved like little hoodlums. Your nanny is expecting. OUT OF WEDLOCK. The supposed father of the child, the young man known as Baylor, who apparently has permission to bound through your front door at will, is belligerent and disrespectful. Your sister-in-law, Meredith, who operates as if your gambling hotel home were her gambling hotel home as well, was unwelcoming to me and downright discourteous to LeeAnn. And the only word I can find to describe the larger of your two indoor pets is *atrocious*. As you must surely know in your heart of hearts, I will always love you, regardless of your questionable life choices, so keep that in mind as you return to the pandemonium that is your household and find yourself motherless.

It was upon learning that your wife, like a cat, seemingly has more than one life, LeeAnn and I made the heartbreaking decision to return to Texas having barely laid eyes on you during our stay. How would you imagine we traveled, Bradley, as today is The

Lord's Day and Pastor Landry was busy doing His work and thus unable to retrieve us? By public transportation? No. We returned to Texas via a fortuitously timed chime of your doorbell. Expecting more mayhem as I opened the door, I was surprised to find a young man seeking asylum. After assuring me he was all but a member of your chaotic household, which didn't surprise me in the least considering all I'd witnessed with my own two eyes, I granted him refuge. Through inquisitive conversation over coffee and almond pound cake I learned his name was Edward Crawford. Further inquiry revealed him to be the poor soul whose life has been all but ruined by your current wife, as he is the man who was previously married to her.

Twice.

Two times, Son.

Did you know Edward is completely devoted to his mother? He's an only son like you, Bradley, although unlike you, as an adult, he chooses to live but a mile from his childhood home where his mother continues to reside. He dines with her thrice daily. He seeks her counsel. He respects and admires her. It is obvious to me that he worships and adores her. He has crowned her His Best Friend, interchangeable with The Best Woman He Knows. Bradley, have you spoken to Edward at length? Have you heard his side of the tragic story that is his heartbreaking history with your wife? I would advise you to sit down with him at your earliest convenience.

After hearing LeeAnn's and my predicament, and innately sensing that I, a virtual stranger, was at my wits' end, Edward, like a knight in shining armor, volunteered to drive us home in your foreign car, as his vehicle was indisposed. He assured me you wouldn't mind. And it is with no qualms I share with you that Edward and LeeAnn got along fabulously. They appear to be far more than fond of each other. Opportunities must be seized, Bradley, lest they slip from your grasp.

As we gathered our things to depart, upon realizing LeeAnn's luggage was quite substantial as she had prepared for a much longer stay <u>to aid and assist you</u>, Edward deftly (as he was unable to find an apparatus on your foreign car to assist) accessed your trunk with a large power tool so that he might load LeeAnn's belongings. Can you imagine our collective shock when we found the trunk of your car laden with the Jubilee corn from Maynard Turbin's garden? Corn I sent home with you more than a week ago? Edward carefully unloaded the Jubilee corn and delivered it to your kitchen, then waited patiently as I prepared it.

You will find the Jubilee corn in your Frigidaire.

LeeAnn has agreed to never speak of the incident to Maynard Turbin.

I trust you will survive until we meet again, and that won't be anytime soon, as I will be on holiday. And I will not be alone. I will be vacationing with Herbert Turner. You know Herbert. Our widowed neighbor four doors down and across the street who has asked me repeatedly to accompany him to his <u>one-bedroom</u> beachfront condominium in Galveston so that I might ride the Ferris wheel with him at Galveston's Historic Pleasure Pier. Upon arriving home and freshening up, I marched straight to Herbert's front door, knocked, and said, "It would be my pleasure to ride the Ferris wheel with you, Herbert."

How do you like that, young man?

Should you need me, I'll be vacationing.

Sincerely,

The Woman Who Grew You in Her Body

MEDIA EXPERTS JOSÉ RUIZ AND TIFFANEE JONES NAMED VICE PRESIDENTS OF BELLISSIMO CORPORATE COMMUNICATIONS

NEWS PROVIDED FOR IMMEDIATE RELEASE BY
BELLISSIMO ENTERTAINMENT, INC
BILOXI/Sunday, May 17, 3:00 p.m./PRNewswire

As part of our Community Skill and Development Career Program, Bellissimo Entertainment, Inc, is pleased to welcome **José Ruiz** and **Tiffanee Jones** to our Communications team. José and Tiffanee will eventually oversee digital, internal, and corporate communications. The Bellissimo looks forward to José and Tiffanee developing communication strategies, overseeing copywriting for sales and marketing initiatives, and building brand recognition. For additional information, contact our new Director of Corporate Communications, **Nelson Miller**.

From: baylor@bellissimo.com
To: davis@bellissimo.com
Day: Sunday
Subject: Hey

Hey, Davis. It's me. Baylor. I know you're busy being not dehydrated and going back and forth to the hospital to see Fantasy, but I have big news that can't wait. I'm going to be a dad. Do you know if there's any way to tell if it will be a girl or a boy? Did you get my emails?

    Peace out.

DOUBLE WEDDING KICKS OFF
REOPENING OF BELLISSIMO

BY NELSON MILLER
WEBMASTER @ BiloxiTruth.org
Former Staff Investigative Reporter with Gulf Coast Herald
Sunday, May 17, 3:30 p.m.

Greetings to my 12,522,730 followers, and sadly, or gloriously—I'll let you know—this will be my last post. To properly thank you for your invaluable support and assistance, I'd like you all to join me and my mother at the event of the season, a double wedding at the Bellissimo Resort and Casino where I have recently accepted the position of Director of Communications. I feel certain those of you in Australia won't be able to attend the nuptials on such short notice, so to those of you who are close enough to join us, please know casino capacity is fifteen thousand souls. First come, first served wedding cake. And congratulations to the happy couples, Mr. Old English Sheepdog Cotton to Miss Goldendoodle Candy, and Mr. José Ruiz to Miss Tiffanee Jones.

A Note from Davis

Dear Bradley,

I didn't want to wake you. I barely wanted to wake myself but couldn't wait to snuggle with Bex and Quinn and drink COFFEE! The girls and I are on our way to the hospital to take Fantasy a pepperoni and sausage pizza. The hospital's cafeteria is serving breakfast, not pizza, and none of the pizza deliveries are open at nine in the morning. I called Bellissimo room service and talked them into a pepperoni and sausage pizza. As soon as it arrives, the girls and I are off. It will be this way with Fantasy until she's back on her feet—both feet, thank goodness—and honestly, I don't mind at all. I wonder, having come so close to losing everything, if I'll ever mind anything again. (Don't hold me to that.) (No Hair's already texting to see if I'll be at my desk tomorrow, because WE HAVE WORK TO DO. I texted back to say I needed a few days with you and our daughters, I need a little rest, and I need to be there for Fantasy when she's released from the hospital, none of which No Hair was very sympathetic to, and I found myself minding.) (Then I figured it out.) (He just wants things like they used to be.) (We all do.)

Listen, about last night. I wasn't trying to be rude to Christina Aguilera. The offer of her two-story tour bus for us to get away for a few days, the incredible master suite upstairs and crystal chandeliers downstairs notwithstanding, was a chance-of-a-lifetime, but I'll be honest with you, Bradley, I might not ever be ready to set foot in another doublewide. I didn't mean to overreact. Somehow I made it through being adultnabbed, Hell Island, The Conductor, and almost losing Fantasy without falling apart, and I certainly didn't mean to start sobbing uncontrollably just because Christina Aguilera offered us her tour bus. I'm sure I scared her. Do you think I should send her flowers? I've already been on the phone ordering flowers for your mother to thank her for helping with the girls. I don't know where they picked up that Grandwitch business, television probably, but I apologized anyway. This new pup-the-size-of-a-car, Bradley, Cotton. How much does he eat? His bowl is the size of our kitchen sink. I filled it; he ate it. I filled it again; he emptied it again. I filled it a third time, turned my head for two seconds, and the kibble was GONE. One more thing. Our refrigerator is full of corn. Where did all this corn come from? Oh, and my laptop. I can't find it anywhere. Do you know where my laptop is?

I love you so very much,
Davis

Gretchen Archer

Gretchen Archer is a Tennessee housewife who began writing when her children, seeking higher educations, ran off and left her. She lives on Lookout Mountain with her husband and a misbehaving sheepadoodle named Kevin. *Double Wide* is the tenth Davis Way Crime Caper. You can visit her at www.gretchenarcher.com.

In Case You Missed the 1st Book in the Series

DOUBLE WHAMMY

Gretchen Archer

A Davis Way Crime Caper (#1)

Davis Way thinks she's hit the jackpot when she lands a job as the fifth wheel on an elite security team at the fabulous Bellissimo Resort and Casino in Biloxi, Mississippi. But once there, she runs straight into her ex-ex-husband, a rigged slot machine, her evil twin, and a trail of dead bodies. Davis learns the truth and it does not set her free—in fact, it lands her in the pokey.

Buried under a mistaken identity, unable to seek help from her family, her hot streak runs cold until her landlord, Bradley Cole, steps in. Make that her landlord, lawyer, and love interest. With his help, Davis must win this high-stakes game before her luck runs out.

Manufactured by Amazon.ca
Bolton, ON

20286374R00149

5\24